# *We Are Eternal*

**Bianca Orellana**

**A Wings ePress, Inc.**
**Young Adult Romance Novel**

## *Wings ePress, Inc.*

Edited by: April Bennett
Copy Edited by: Jeanne Smith
Executive Editor: Jeanne Smith
Cover Artist: Richard Stroud



Wings ePress Books
www.wingsepress.com

Copyright © 2018 by Bianca Orellana
ISBN-13:  978-1-61309-650-5
ISBN-10: 1-61309-650-x

Published In the United States Of America

Wings ePress Inc.
3000 N. Rock Road
Newton, KS  67114

## *Dedication*

To my rock, Ricardo, a hero to me and the rest of the world
in every way possible.
Thanks for enduring all the insanity
that led to this point.
And to Ricardo Jr., my living, breathing heartbeat.
You two keep me going.

* * *

***One***

## SENSES

On the Big Day, I awoke to desperate, childlike sobbing.

The time on my cell said 11 a.m., so I dismissed my alarm instead of snoozing it again. The crying carried on through the house, so resonant I felt the sorrow like it was my own, and I was afraid of how normal it was all becoming.

Instead of getting up right away, I lay still as death, allowing the numbness to work through my body and coat every bone, muscle, and organ; I wouldn't be able to drag myself out of bed until the process was over. I'd taken to picturing that *Wolverine* movie scene where the crooked military guys inject Logan with adamantium. The fictional metal alloy worked its way through his body, too, coating his bones and making him unbreakable, unkillable, practically untouchable.

This, I figured out, was a symptom of Stage Four: Depression.

I considered how I'd handled the other stages. I became dependent on my little numbing routine during the Stage One days, a.k.a. the Denial days. Denial and depression ended up feeling pretty similar. The key difference was *recognition*. When I was in denial, I wouldn't recognize what had happened; when the depression set in, I was so aware of what had happened it overtook my entire being. Both resulted in numbness.

I worried I hadn't spent enough time in Stage Two, because I was never one to get properly angry about anything. Didn't anger parallel passion and feeling? If Dad's death didn't infuriate me, did I not care enough?

The duration of his funeral I spent in Stage Three, bargaining with God like I hadn't since my thirteenth Christmas. When I approached his open casket for the final viewing, I couldn't wrap my head around seeing such a wide and easygoing man stuffed into such a narrow, silk-lined space, gussied up in a suit and tie.

Dad's favorite piece of advice for my sister and me (and incidentally our least favorite): *You can't control anyone or anything but yourself.* I watched his broad, solid, empty chest and begged God to let me control something else, just one thing other than myself. A couple of my relatives started singing "In the Sweet By and By;" their voices sounded deflated at first, then a few more joined in, ballooned and carried the song to the rafters. I willed Dad's chest to move, the internal pleas becoming screams to block the noise around me. I strained so hard my jaw locked and my face grew hot and my eyes teared. But he wasn't breathing, and his heart wasn't beating. I thought it never would again.

I continued numbing, lifting my heavy eyelids and observing the clouds through the slats of my yellowed vinyl blinds. They were the kind of clouds that threatened snow but rarely delivered in North Carolina, which meant another frigid yet fruitless February day.

When I was able, I rose and got dressed. I still didn't feel much like the Wolverine, but the imagery had jazzed up the waiting process.

I headed to the hallway bathroom I shared with Selma, pausing at her closed door to hear her pad around her room. We weren't sneaking out, but we still wanted to be quiet—dulling the sting of betrayal, I suppose.

Five minutes later, she joined me in the bathroom. We analyzed each other in the mirror from our respective ends of the double-sink counter. We both had our dad's rich chocolate skin and our mom's round, brown eyes. We both had petite frames, just different versions of it. I had two years and seven months on her, but she couldn't breathe without shooting up another inch, and she'd left me in the dust years back. She inherited all of Mom's genes, so she'd be a skinny, leggy, model-type. My lack of length had resulted in curvier hips and thighs.

"Things I'd rather do than acknowledge some other dude has Dad's most vital organ," said Selma. She balled her index fingers and gave our mirror a quick a *rat-a-tat*. "Go."

I inhaled, the sound sharp in my nose. "Give a feral cat a bubble bath. Then shave it. Go."

"Chop off all my hair and hot-glue it to my torso. Go."

We'd loved playing *Things I'd Rather* since we were little. Today, though, our answers didn't feel entirely facetious. "Bathe with the alligators in the Pasquotank. Go."

"*Ooh*. Develop a rare condition that makes me talk like Gilbert Gottfried. Go."

"Um. Accidentally step in a puddle with socks on. Go."

"*Ack*, Olive, that's weak," she lamented. "You didn't even try."

I leaned forward and pressed the heels of my hands into the counter's edge. We had a twenty-five-minute drive to Collins Court, time enough to decide how to approach Mom once we returned, explain how sorry—and not sorry—we were.

"I guess it's time," she said when I didn't speak again.

Mom had been awake for hours, and my sister and I found her in her usual spot in the living room when we came downstairs. Her gaunt cheeks bore the tear-stained evidence of the sounds that had yanked me from sleep. Her velvet robe and thick wool socks swallowed her rail-like frame, transforming her into another lump on the couch among the throw pillows.

I suppose she wanted to disappear. We each had our way of dealing. I preferred numbness. Stage One, her most valued companion even outside grief, still had her in its grasp. We expected that. She'd always taken herself away from us.

The past few months had been different, though. The longer she sat in that spot on the couch, and the more she became part of the room, the more the room became her. Her presence, and everything that came with it, enveloped me whenever I walked in.

Grief overwhelmed the senses. My parents taught me that. Grief spawned ear-piercing howling fits with tears and gasping and sweat that made the air feel heavy and sticky as a summer night. Grief smelled like sleep and un-brushed teeth and days upon days in pajamas. For some families—for mine—grief also smelled of beer's tell-tale yeastiness, liquor's bite, and wine's sweet-sour.

Whatever she could get her hands on.

Mom's grief was so predominant, Selma and I often avoided the living room, her space. Today, we were not going to deny her a goodbye. We couldn't, no matter how she felt.

When we hugged her—Selma first, then me—we wrapped our arms around a sullen stone statue. I knew she'd never forgive us for meeting the people who had benefited from taking the most beautiful part of her husband.

## LEGACY

The moment an organ is harvested from a registered donor, a timer starts counting down. Each timer has a particular limit, depending on the organ. Kidneys are viable for about seventy-two hours after death. Corneas get fourteen days. A liver lasts twenty-four hours.

But a heart is viable for a mere four to six hours after death. This meant someone—or a group of someones—made the crucial decision regarding my father's heart in less than a quarter day.

Several factors determine organ donor and recipient compatibility: a patient's weight, size, severity of illness, blood type, and locality, to name a few. Based on these factors, a network of doctors proclaimed York Lively the ideal recipient for Dad's heart in the early morning hours of November 19.

I've heard time is precious, but I disagree. Time is omnipresent and impassive and cannot accept our love. We can't put a value on time, but we do anyway, which focuses on the wrong thing. The *people* we spend time with are precious, whether we get a second with them, a minute, or—as I got with Dad—seventeen years, seven months, and three days. My *father* was precious. I miss the man, not the time.

## SECOND IMPRESSION

I turned right at the stone entrance sign and slowed the car to a crawl. I did so, in part, because of the 25 mph speed limit, and because you just don't speed through a neighborhood like Collins Court. Another part of me, motivated by the heavy knot in my gut, wanted to stall a little longer. I didn't know if I'd erupt in a fit of rage or disintegrate into a puddle of tears when the time came—either way, I was subjecting myself to certain humiliation.

Yet another part of me—the only part I'd openly admit to—let the car coast for Selma. The moment we arrived, she suctioned herself to the passenger window like a snail and marveled at the immaculately manicured lawns, the cream and gray stone and red brick facades, the freaking window boxes overflowing with pansies and violas and Lenten roses.

As I drove my twenty-year-old Honda up to the Livelys' Château-esque home, I imagined smearing a stain up the length of their cobblestone driveway. Inside, the car was no prettier, the disorder and clutter a visual representation of grief's downward spiral in my life. Before Selma and I left the house, I moved stuff around so she could get in and discovered I'd inadvertently collected twenty-six empty plastic water bottles; I grimaced every time I adjusted the driver seat and heard them crunch. Medical and legal papers and fluorescent Post-Its littered my floor and seats, because if I filed them away I knew I'd forget to handle them, forget appointments, forget all the important notes I'd made.

We approached the intricate wooden and glass double doors, and Selma let my frame eclipse hers while I rang the doorbell. It chimed, musical and elaborate, throughout the house. I sighed. A simple *ding-dong* does the job in my neighborhood. Not in Collins Court.

A bright-eyed woman in casual jeans with a high, dark ponytail answered the door. Jennifer Lively. New Life Network

Communications, an organization in the business of connecting donor and recipient families, required at least two months of regular correspondence before two parties could meet, so I'd spent the past eight weeks sending her emails. The one time we did speak on the phone, her voice was as comforting as her words had been in her electronic letters. Even so, I expected someone more stiff and formal in person. Someone in a ball gown, maybe.

"Olive and Selma Grant?" she said.

"Yes?" I stammered.

She enveloped me in a hug so tight and abrupt, I almost fell backward and took her with me.

"I'm so glad to meet you," she said, wrapping her arms around my sister, too. "Both of you. It's so good to finally have you here."

"Good to meet you, too," I told her.

I was being honest, I promise. Discovering Dad's life had saved another had filled me with bittersweet satisfaction. My qualms about meeting her son, York, came only from the fact that I already knew him.

Well, I didn't know him. I knew *of* him, knew his image. Everyone at our high school did. It seemed everyone knew what he'd done to land himself in the hospital the same night my father was killed.

And everyone still called the match a silver lining.

"Did you find the house okay?" asked Mrs. Lively, taking our coats as we followed her into the bright, high-ceiling foyer.

"You gave great directions," I said. "GPS handled the rest."

"Right." Her smile took the bite out of my anxiety. "I can hardly remember a time before technology told us everything. Our cars practically turn themselves on for us, tell us where to go, show us what's at our back bumper when we shift into reverse. Who needs a brain anymore?"

She laughed, and I think I smiled, but she could tell she had lost us.

While she hung our coats, my eyes followed the winding staircase upward, studying the cherry wood and treble clef-shaped wrought iron accents. Overhead hung a simple, spherical chandelier, the light in the center bouncing off its dozens of clear crystals.

I frowned. How did they change the lightbulb in that thing? How did they dust it?

"We're overjoyed you all accepted our request," said our hostess, leading us down a long hallway. "We weren't sure if it was too soon, or if we were being pushy, or if you thought we were lunatics." A short laugh burst from her mouth like a cry of alarm. "It's just when we realized how close our saviors lived to us—"

The words seemed to convolute in her throat. We hooked a right at a narrow wall where an obscure, delicate watercolor painting hung in a gilded frame.

The huge kitchen came right out of a high-end magazine, all stainless steel appliances, lily white crown molding, and soft-colored tile backsplash that shone like jewels. Muted wintertime light poured through the windows. A pot of something warm and savory bubbled on the stove.

And, I realized as my eyes stopped roaming in wonder, York Lively was standing at the sink. He tossed his head back once, then placed a fat orange pill bottle on a tray to his left.

I stared at his broad back and soft curls longer than a sane person would, awash in the conflicting sensations I once felt sitting behind him in ninth grade U.S. History, where our teacher was constantly plucking his slouched figure from the twenty or so eager, raised hands and forcing his participation. In eleventh grade we had biology together, a class he regularly skipped. I didn't sit behind him then. In fact, when he did show up, he hid in a corner with his friends and ignored the lessons. His grades must have been phenomenal, though, because he wound up "exempt" from the final exam. My best friend, Stefanie, and I joked his parents must have written some higher-up a big fat check, unconvinced he had really earned that "A."

I found Mrs. Lively staring at her son, too. She was smiling, the pink edges of her eyes barely containing her tears. The restraint made her unseasonably tanned face glow reddish brown like desert sand at sunset.

"Honey," she said. "Come say hello."

His upper body rose and fell with a deep breath, then he turned and smiled. His mom waved him over, and when he strode toward us I could remember him schmoozing his way up and down Fleet High's halls. The difference was now he didn't—or couldn't—hold himself as tall or strong, and his gait didn't flow as easily. The weight of his innate confidence encumbered his shoulders instead of floating on them.

"This is York," said Mrs. Lively as he stopped at her side.

"Nice to meet you," I said. I slapped a limp hand on my sister's arm. "This is Selma. I'm Olive."

He shook my hand, and one side of his full mouth curved up. "I think I knew that."

His voice, deep as always, never sounded so husky. Had it? Maybe I never noticed because he hadn't actually spoken to me before. Or maybe the effects of his condition—the discernable exhaustion, for example—had altered his voice. Maybe the medication he just swallowed hit him that hard, that fast.

Whatever the reason, it was distracting.

"Yeah," I said, "we're in the same grade, right?" I blinked. "We... *were* in the same grade?"

"Right," he said, like he'd been forced to confess something embarrassing.

"Please, ladies, have a seat," said Mrs. Lively, and we complied, taking two stools at the island in the middle of the kitchen. "It's so cold out," she said. "Coldest February in...eight years, I heard?"

"I prefer the cold," I said.

"Oh, not me." Mrs. Lively wrinkled her freckled nose. "Give me a beach in the Caribbean any day."

Again, we fell silent. I caught York rolling his eyes.

"Either way," she said on a *whoosh* of air, "I'm sure you wouldn't mind warming your bones. I don't suppose you ladies drink coffee?"

I did, in fact, enjoy an occasional cup of coffee. (Actually, I enjoyed an occasional cup of cream and sugar with a splash of coffee-flavored water. My tastes were still maturing.) However, I followed Selma's lead and shook my head.

"I figured as much," she said. "And we don't buy hot chocolate, I'm afraid. Would either of you like a cup of tea?"

"Sure," we said together.

She got a shining stainless steel kettle going, then instructed York to set a tray of sandwiches in front of us. She grabbed bowls and ladled a hearty portion of vegetable soup into each one.

"This is wonderful," I said. "You didn't have to."

"Of course I did."

A clock ticked somewhere nearby. Selma and I looked at one another, then at York. He slumped against the counter, and not in a cool, casual way—in a defeated way. I wondered if his mom had come up with the idea to contact New Life, or his dad, or both. I wondered when, or if, his dad would show up.

"Will you... be able to graduate on time?" I asked York.

"I won't be well enough to go back to school for another two months, if I'm lucky. Even then, I'll have to go to summer school if I want my diploma in time to start college in the fall."

"We got him into a crash course home-school program," explained Mrs. Lively. "He'll finish at relatively the same time as everyone else."

"But that means no prom," said York, "no more friends, no graduation walk. My senior year is officially over."

"That's rough," said Selma, the social butterfly, no doubt imagining having her entire senior year disrupted.

"I've learned a lot about perspective over the past couple months," he said. "I'd much rather finish school from rehab than not at all."

I stared at him.

"I mean—" His eyes grew wide. His mother looked down. "Sorry."

The kettle began to shriek, and Mrs. Lively yanked it off the eye and poured water over bags in identical china cups. York dipped his head into the refrigerator and served himself the biggest glass of sweet tea I'd ever seen.

"Water," said his mom, her eyes fixed on the tea bag she was mercilessly dunking in and out the cup.

His chin hit his chest. "I remember. This was for you."

"I'm sure it was."

He looked at me. "Transplant guidelines. I *need* to *keep hydrated.*" His mother heard all the air quotes around his words and shot him some serious side-eye. "I'm addicted to sweet tea, guys," he continued. "It's awful."

My dad loved sweet tea too. He had taken great care of himself throughout his life, but his ideal nightcap included a slab of red velvet cake with extra cream cheese frosting, and an extra tall glass of sweet tea.

York took water with him back to the sink, where he opened another pill bottle, this one thinner than the other.

"Impressive drug collection you've got there," I commented.

"You have no idea." He began to name them on his fingers. "A steroid, two immunosuppressants, a calcium supplement, and aspirin."

"Immunosuppressants?" asked Selma.

"Basically, my body knows your dad's heart is not my heart, so I need something to stop my immune system attacking it. I stay pretty healthy, thanks to my mom's constant, insistent, incessant, unending—"

Mrs. Lively cleared her throat.

"—loving way of staying on top of my diet and symptoms, but I'm more susceptible to infections and colds and whatnot. My doctor prescribed two of the medicines mainly to fend the effects of the other three."

"How do you keep up with it all?"

"Most I take once a day, though I used to stay hopped up on the steroids, pretty much the worst kind of drug. In the beginning, my face swelled up like a bean bag, and I had all these crazy mood swings. All my meds make me dizzy and give me headaches if I'm not careful."

"Sounds kind of miserable," I said.

"It is the cost of living."

After we ate, the conversation turned to how Selma and I were coping at home. Mrs. Lively said she couldn't imagine the months we'd had without Dad, our mom without her husband.

"Our mom is sick," Selma blurted, and my head jerked in her direction without my brain's permission. "That's why she's not here. She would have been here, but she's sick."

I cringed. Not exactly a lie, the excuse still exposed us, transparent as glass.

"That's all right," said Mrs. Lively, her light eyes studying first my sister before looking to me for...what? A clearer explanation? This situation needed another adult, and between Selma and me, I came the closest. My gut clenched, resenting my mother's absence anew.

"The bathroom," I enthused. At their startled reactions, I felt my face flame, and made my next words more normal. "May I use it?"

"Sure," said Mrs. Lively, pointing. "Just go back down the hall to the first door on the left."

I exited the kitchen too slowly to miss her whisper, "I think she's having a hard time. I'm so sorry for—"

I darted into the first room I saw: a living room of sorts. A tangle of dreamy curtains draped the one wall-sized window. The near-white carpet was undefiled as fresh snow. I felt fairly certain the array of plush furniture was not actually intended for sitting.

I no more belonged in this room than a discount store fixture, which is what I felt like in comparison. My heart pounded my ribcage, trying to break free, and I put a hand on my chest. Everything about my being here seemed wrong, and this whole situation was wrong, and I began to think maybe Mom had been right all along.

Whenever I searched my memories for things Dad used to say, I always held onto the warmth and bass of his voice, allowing it to wash over me in waves. Sometimes the waves came out of nowhere and knocked me over. Sometimes the blows were sharp, and sometimes they hurt, but I didn't want them to stop. I wanted them to wash over me. Sometimes I wanted them to take me under.

"My mom sent me in here to check on you," said York behind me. I heard him divvy each word so not to alarm me, but I couldn't tell if he did so for my benefit or his.

"I was coming right back," I assured him. "I just needed a minute."

He wrung his large hands, eyes darting about the room. "Look, I know this is weird."

"Not weird. Just—" I searched the grooves of my brain a moment. "Surreal."

We moved closer to one another, meeting in the center of the room.

"You think you'll ever be okay again?" he asked.

"Not really."

He inspected the floor. "Yeah."

"But I want you to be okay," I said, an effort at civility. "You're here for a purpose, you know? And I am glad my dad's life can continue through yours, cliché as it sounds. He was always giving. Overdid it sometimes. He might have offered you his heart while he was still alive if the moment was right."

"Jesus."

"I mean, obviously not. You know."

"Sure sure, hyperbole and all that. I just didn't realize I had such impressive shoes to fill. This is terrible."

I actually smiled. He did too, a benign smile, and my stomach somersaulted. He really was sort of beautiful; I always noticed, of course, his good looks as a whole, but I couldn't see the trees for the forest, to rearrange the old saying.

For example, I knew he had "pretty" eyes, but I didn't know a boy could possess such thick, dark eyelashes. I knew he was well-built because girls would gush about seeing him wet and shirtless at his legendary pool parties, but I never stood close enough to see how he towered over my five feet and five inches. I knew he had a jawline chiseled from stone, but I never appreciated it until now, observing how the anti-rejection drugs had puffed and smoothed the angles of his face.

I shook my head. There were people who'd have loved to be in my position, standing close enough to York Lively to pick apart his features. Now I had the opportunity, but his looks didn't matter, would never matter as much, because he had something I needed. Something no one else could give me.

"What?" he asked.

I'd dragged myself out of bed, defied Mom's wishes, and found it in me to shake this boy's hand. I couldn't let the pain I endured to come to this house be for nothing.

"Can I do something?" I asked. "Before I lose my nerve?"

"Yes," he said like a question.

I walked up to him. "Okay. Um. Don't move."

The top of my head just grazed his chin. I bent at the waist only, turned my head, and pressed my ear to his chest. My skin imbibed his warmth. His shirt material felt lush and fleecy—cashmere, I guessed. I didn't know anything about cashmere except it was expensive.

My ear devoured the steady *thump thump* inside his chest. Rolling, watery bleariness overtook my vision, and the tears spilled over. A viscous lump blocked my throat. My mouth fell open—*keep breathing, keep breathing*—to catch air around it.

Limp with anguish, I clutched the fabric of his shirt at his sides so I wouldn't collapse. He nestled his chin in my hair and let me listen as long as I wanted. His breathing was so deep and even you'd have thought he'd fallen asleep. He never protested, never made a sound.

Five minutes passed, and then I was coming up on ten, and York probably thought I was insane by now. In an abrupt motion, I righted myself and ran my hands across my eyes, imagining a honey bee darting away post-sting, leaving its stinger—and its guts—behind.

I muttered a short "thanks" and, forgetting myself, or too weary to care, plunked onto a nearby loveseat.

He and I studied each other and absorbed the quiet. Route 158 practically bordered my neighborhood, the faint drone of traffic and 18-wheelers constant and pervasive. Collins Court was different. The bucolic seclusion was so deep, you could hear the abrupt *crunch* and *snap* of the frost coating the lush grass and the naked tree limbs outside, a noise like cracking your knuckles.

He knelt at my feet and wiped my tears with his thumb. He didn't look embarrassed for me.

"You're not what I thought you'd be," I whispered suddenly, a thought that grew words too large to stay inside my head.

His eyes flickered, questioning. Then he blinked it away.

"Are you all right?" came a high, tight voice from the rounded entryway behind him.

I jolted, and he looked over his shoulder at his mother. Selma peeked round the corner beside her, one eyebrow raised.

"We're fine," said York, but Mrs. Lively was already gripping his arm to help him to his feet and swatting his dark curls off his forehead.

"Are you feeling okay, honey?" She cupped his face and stood on her tiptoes to examine him from hair to shoelaces. He just let her, his shoulders sagging, the corners of his mouth curving downward.

Eighty-five days had passed since his operation. Does one ever fully recover from something as intense as a heart transplant?

I stood and squeezed past them, nodding at my sister and wiping my face again. "I'm sorry I disappeared, Mrs. Lively," I said.

"I understand. If you need more time, you can stay here as long as you like."

"Actually, I think we should go. To see how Mom's doing. Since she's sick, you know. Plus, I think we've bothered you long enough and... York, you look tired."

"Oh, it's no bother," Mrs. Lively assured us. "Please believe me, it's no bother. We, my family, owe your family so much more than a hot lunch on a cold afternoon."

"You've made us feel very welcome," I told her. "Thank you. Again."

She led us back to the foyer, and York grabbed our coats. When he helped me shrug into mine, he tucked my hair over my shoulder, grasping it as one would a newborn kitten.

"I hope our families can stay connected," said his mom, "so we can let you know how the transplant is taking, so we can know how you're coping."

"We'd like that."

Well wishes and final hugs exchanged, Selma and I stepped outside. I breathed in cool, crisp air, expelling Lively house's warm, cinnamon-nut smell.

My sister and I loaded into the car once again, and my engine roared to life, shattering the Collins Court quietude. As I shifted gears and reversed, I observed the mother and son standing in the doorway. Mrs. Lively looked like an airborne bird with an injured wing, frantically flapping the good one to avoid plummeting. York looked like a wilted plant sagging under some invisible weight.

"You think she's still mad?" Selma asked when we were back on 158.

I calculated the amount Mom already had to drink when we left the house and the amount of time we spent at the Livelys'.

Though it was more a hope than a surety, I didn't mind telling her:

"I think she's already down and out for the day."

# *Two*

## PIECEMEAL

On the last real cold day of the season, our local meteorologist predicted snow. The whole town—the whole state—drained the grocery stores' milk and bread supplies, and schools promptly closed, all per the Southern custom. Spill a cup of ice on the ground, and the region shuts down.

That day, I pulled on my knit hat, shoved my hands into my fingerless flap mittens, and stepped outside, my Nikon adorning my neck. I clutched the camera in both hands, bliss surging through my fingertips, up my arms, and right to my mouth, pulling it up in a wide and surely maniacal grin. It just felt so good to hold...so right, secure and sturdy in my hands. One online review I'd read called this brand an "ergonomic delight."

I shuffled through my front yard, kicking up tiny balls of snow. The finest layer of white tinged the Evergreens and swirled when caught by a gust.

I took a few shots, wondering idly when I'd get the chance to develop them; my school's art department had an ancient, preserved, fully functioning darkroom, and I could lose all track of time in there if left alone.

When my cheeks and nose grew numb, I ambled back inside. I set my camera next to my seventies-era Polaroid OneStep on my nightstand, which had turned into something of a pedestal. One of my few childhood remnants, the piece of furniture stood a hair taller than a milk crate, delicate and babydoll. Its ceramic button knobs had a yellow gold rim and hand-painted dusty rose flowers, and the white paint had begun brittling off the top some time back.

My bed and dresser had grown up with me, got wider and taller; for some reason, none of us ever deemed the nightstand important enough. Funny how priorities change.

I made a floppy burrito of myself in my old polyester blanket and opened my laptop. Several minutes of mindless scrolling on Facebook passed before I even noticed the message.

**York Lively** - 2/21, 1:47pm
So I guess I seemed standoffish when you visited the other week. Truth is, being upright for any extended period still kicks my ass regularly. As such, I never told you how cool it was meeting you and your sister. My mom went on and on about the whole thing. She really wanted to make you guys as happy as you made her.

Thanks for, you know, for trying. You didn't have to. If you ever need someone to talk to, I'm here.

What.
He was an even nicer person than I thought.
I had no idea what the Universe was trying to tell me, but I was far too old and bullheaded to accept I might have misjudged someone's character.
I responded.

**Olive Grant** - 2/21, 3:14pm
It was a tough time for us all, for different reasons. Sel and I had a lovely time. And I can't fathom how you even managed "upright" in

the first place, so I'm impressed with the way you handled yourself.

Thank you, too. Thank you so much. For… you know.


I didn't hear back right away, so I browsed the Internet. I researched every expensive Nikon F6 lens—equipment I could never afford.

But I kept checking that damned Messages tab, re-reading his words, making sure I hadn't missed his reply.

That evening Selma and I found some marked-down stir-fry beef in our freezer and concocted a decent dinner with some rice from the pantry. Afterward, we took Mom to her room and helped her undress for bed. Then we retreated to our own rooms, and the house grew silent again.

~ * ~

York messaged back at ten to midnight. In the end, the rising sun was what forced us to bookmark the conversation and say goodbye. He wished me a good day at school, and I beelined to my closet to get dressed.

## WHAT YOU LEFT

We talked every day after that. The poor guy was bored daffy at home, and I kept him in the loop with goings on at school—as much as I could, anyway. I wasn't at the center of many Fleet High social circles, and we both knew it. But he was desperate for any glimpse of the outside world apart from a doctor's office or a rehab center, and I had top-notch investigative reporting skills.

Texting him kept matters the least complicated, the phone screens typifying a protective shield. He could know the "me" I preferred and never realize the true state of my life.

*So*


he texted by way of initiating conversation one day.

*So* I responded.

*Is your name REALLY Olive?*
...
*Yes*
...
*Like olive?*
...
*As in Kalamata*

People always reacted this way, as if I were messing with them. Why would I joke about being named after a pizza topping?

I texted:
*Not sure where it came from. Both Selma and I have odd names.*
...
*I like it, if it means anything.*
*Also cool: it's an anagram for i lOve.*
...
*What? Hahaha. Funny I never realized it myself. I don't think dear ol' Mom and Dad considered word play possibilities when they named me.*
...
*What DO you think they were thinking?*
...
*I haven't a clue. They never struck me as exceptionally creative people otherwise. They always stayed inside the lines.*

Several minutes later, he texted:
*Peace*
...
*Are you telling me goodbye or...?*
...
*You and Selma have names that mean peace.*

Had my parents done this intentionally? It seemed too coincidental, and my sister and I *had* endured more chaos than peace during our short lives.

*Wow* I texted.

He texted:
*You think some people spend their lives kind of knowing the impact they'll make on their loved ones?*

*Even if they don't know, consciously? Something stirs them up inside and suddenly they're planting all these positive bits in the world?*

This was such an accurate description of my father that I let myself wonder what else doctors might have transplanted to this boy's body.

## HONESTY

*I get to ask you one question, and you have to answer it honestly. In return, you can ask me a question and I'll answer honestly.*
*...*
*You sure?*
*...*
*Yes*
*But I'll go first*
*...*
*Shoot. I'm an open book.*
*...*
*How did you pass Mr. Morgan's bio class last year?*
*...*
*LMFAO*
*That's your question???*
*...*
*I have a bet going, so be honest*

*You won't believe me*

*...*

*I trust you*

*...*

*Okay*
*Ready?*

*...*

*Ready*

*...*

**drumroll**

*...*

*DUDE. EDGE OF MY SEAT.*

*...*

*I like biology*

*...*

*And?*

*...*

*That's how I passed*

*...*

*York*

*...*

*I told you you wouldn't believe me*

*...*

*But you were never in class*

*...*

*I studied and passed all the tests*
*Science is my best subject*

*...*

*Well. How anticlimactic. I think I wasted my question.*

*...*

*My turn now, right?*

*...*

*Yes*

*...*

*Anything? You won't mind?*

...

*I promise*

...

*Was it sudden?*


I last saw my dad alive on a late Friday evening, moments before he headed out the door to his second job as a warehouse machinist. He liked the fact he had an excuse to drink more coffee (he hated Selma and me forcing him to drink decaf after eleven a.m.). He also liked the no uniform bit, so if he had to work at night, he could at least be comfortable in his knockaround jeans and his favorite steel-toe boots.

I'd just finished making his coffee, and I was complaining about Mom. In the grand scheme, the problem wasn't critical. I think Mom tapped my car with hers in the driveway after she'd knocked back a few and decided to drive to the store for more.

Or maybe that was the day she stole money from me again. Come to think of it, considering it was November, I bet she stole Selma's birthday money.

Dad and I were standing in the kitchen in front of a sink piled high with dishes—my night to wash. This, on top of everything else, had put me in a mood so prickly, I made a cactus look downright cuddly.

He waited as I mouthed off, even though we both knew he was running late. The corners of his eyes had gone crinkly, and the one side of his mouth was quirked.

Then he said: "You know what I'm going to say."

And I said: "*Ugh*, yes, I do."

And we both spouted the old adage: "You can't control anyone or anything but yourself."

I rolled my eyes and thrust his coffee at him. He pulled me to his chest and kissed my bangs. I wrapped one arm around his waist and sent him off, my eyes already on the sink. I hunched against the cold air he let in when he walked out, and the patio door bounced shut with the familiar rattle of loose window panes.

*You there?*

*I'm sorry. You said anything.*
*I just asked because*
*I just had to know*

*...*

*It's okay*
*He was on his way home from work when a distracted driver crossed into his lane. He swerved and rolled his car down an embankment.*

*...*

*You get another question*

*...*

*Anything?*

*...*

*Open book*

*...*

*We're, like, eighteen. How did your heart fail?*

*...*

*I'm sure you've heard the theories*

*...*

*Everyone in Fleet has their opinions about the fine residents of Collins Court*

*...*

*Do tell. I've heard it all*

*...*

*You left your house late that night and talked your way into a bar with a fake ID. Alcohol poisoning.*

*...*

*That has the most truth I've heard yet.*
*Well done.*

*...*

*So how much deviates?*

*...*

*One small detail*
*It wasn't alcohol poisoning. My heart just kind of sucked.*

# SINK (OR SWIM)

In early April, I was brushing my teeth in the hallway bathroom when I heard the doorbell. A second later, Mom welcomed in Uncle Joe.

Of her nine brothers and sisters, he was the only one not estranged. He'd immediately assumed the role of "male figure" for my sister and me, probably because he had two daughters himself.

Selma emerged from her room with a towel slung around her neck. She reached between my shoulder blades to yank my hair in a wordless greeting.

I heard her turn on the shower behind me, then she grabbed her moisturizer from its designated spot at her end of the counter. She kept every perfume bottle, every tube of mascara, and every rainbow-colored hair bow she owned arranged with attention to detail that verged on obsessive-compulsive. She had always been this way. Sometimes I lapsed into the childhood habit of choosing an inconspicuous item to move one or two spaces over, one row forward or back. Not only did she always notice, she had a conniption. This wasn't necessarily because I'd moved her stuff, but because she knew I knew she didn't want anyone moving her stuff.

Our uncle's usually mild tone pulled a swift one-eighty, catching our attention. I flicked my head toward the stairs, and we lay on our stomachs at the top step.

"The church will pay Hewitt Power," he said.

"Good," said Mom, sounding excited. "All taken care of, then."

"They won't do it every month, Pam," he admonished. "They can't afford it. Plus, you can't exploit their charity."

She sighed. "All right. What about May?"

"You have options," he said. Paused. "None are as secure as you finding a job. Steady, reliable income."

"Joe—"

"And you've got to stop this."

"Stop what?"

"This! This." I jumped when he spat the word, then looked at my sister when he calmed himself in the next breath. She sighed and pushed herself to her feet.

"You should start considering your daughters' welfare," Uncle Joe said. The bathroom door slammed shut behind me.

"I am," Mom said. "That's why I—"

Mom liked to pretend we didn't know she was drinking all the time. Or maybe she really though she had everyone fooled. I constantly struggled to crack the mind of someone so deep in denial, someone who couldn't even decipher her own truth.

I made a show of walking downstairs, so not to sneak up and embarrass them. My uncle and I embraced. He towered over me—most of Mom's family did. (Most people did.) He was round, not stick-shaped like the rest of my aunts and uncles. A good squeeze around his soft middle expressed the faint scent of aftershave.

"How are you feeling?" he asked, as he did every time.

"I'm all right today," I responded, as I did every time.

His dark, round eyes flipped through me, noted all the dog-eared pages. Why did adults do that? Why were they allowed the luxury of denial while people my age were forced open?

"Less than two months, and then it's graduation time. Are you excited?"

"Almost there."

"You can let yourself be happy," he said. "You're going to college, you got a scholarship, you'll study an exciting field, and you'll meet new people. It'll be a fresh start."

"Right. I know." I smiled, because he was right, and I'd seem ungrateful if I didn't smile. "But sometimes it doesn't seem to matter."

*Without Dad.* We knew the last part.

"Please make yourself a good life," my uncle said. "Please live, despite this. Live, Olive, understand? It's not easy, but it's crucial."

I glanced at Mom. A slack, haggard face stared back. She wallowed in her pity pool, unwilling to try moving forward. Dad's death hadn't created the pool, just plugged it for good.

And anyway, I *was* living. I was holding it together when Mom wasn't. I was my little sister's rock. I was surviving. I was living.

# *Three*

## PASSING

Three weeks before graduation, I polled the senior class for the final newspaper article of my high school career. I titled the piece "Fleet High Seniors Disclose Graduation Anxieties" and posted the results I gathered.

The most common answers: tripping in front of the audience, flubbing a speech, and forgetting a cap or honor cords. I envied my classmates their normal, uncomplicated fears.

My mom often drank before major events. I still cringed whenever I remembered her dropping my cake on the kitchen floor in front of all my friends at my twelfth birthday party. Her siblings still refused to talk about the liquor-fueled comments she made at my grandfather's funeral. She downed a six-pack of beer every holiday and toasted away a bottle of wine at every wedding. A high school graduation was a big deal, and Dad wasn't there to see me walk, which only reminded her he wouldn't see Selma walk either.

I was already leaving Fleet High School as the girl whose father was killed, not the girl who took great pictures or edited the yearbook well or wrote fantastic newspaper articles. I didn't need "mom showed up to graduation drunk" added to the list. I couldn't let my personal life overshadow all I'd worked for. I couldn't let my sister continue at our school with that legacy.

On Graduation Eve, York invited me to the huge party he was throwing the following night. Though he acknowledged partying might be the last thing on my mind with the senior year I'd had, he also pointed out celebrating the milestone didn't make me a bad person.

I hesitated answering him, unsure of how to feel. I always assumed I'd remain an outsider looking in on his circle of friends. Naturally, I wondered how The Other Side lived, but I never really wanted to be one of them; I wasn't a partier, and large gatherings drained my life force.

But I liked him. Contrary to everything I believed to be true about myself, I liked York Lively, and I liked talking to him. I'd enjoyed discovering his pond had a deep end beyond the shallows. I thought maybe we could get along, become good friends.

In the end, I declined his invitation with some wiggle room. I admitted it'd be great to see him again too, and we didn't have timing on our side, and I wished I felt more confident about putting myself back out there, and family stuff would probably keep me busy all day anyway.

We said goodnight, and I fell asleep wishing we could have kept talking so I wouldn't have to think about why we couldn't keep talking.

## FAILING

At breakfast the next morning, I guessed Mom had already put away half a six-pack. However, she stood straight and tall wearing an iris-colored blazer, an eyelet lace blouse, and white slacks. I gladly accepted the compromise.

At graduation I collected my diploma, then cheered as Stefanie nabbed hers. We had become best friends in fifth grade, though we shared few personality traits. In fact, her bubbliness used to overwhelm me, but eventually we discovered our similar interests. And she often did antisocial non-activities with me out of love.

Graduation day, however, she wouldn't let me off the hook.

"Imagine, if you will, telling Everett Grant about this party," she said at the celebratory dinner her father had reserved at Kahlo's, our favorite restaurant.

My ears quirked; it wasn't every day I heard my father's name. "I'm imagining."

"If you asked him for permission to go, what do you think he would say?"

I used my fork to rake the sour cream slathered atop my humongous and delicious *enchiladas rojas*. "He would say, 'Get the hell out this house and don't come back until you've partied your face off.'" I raised one eyebrow. "Paraphrasing."

"*Exactly*," she barked. "You've had a rough year, and I don't think you'll feel any better if you spend graduation night sitting around your house."

"You underestimate how much I love sitting around the house." I took a swig from my bottle of Mexican Coke and winked at her.

"Stop that. Stop joking. This is serious business."

"It's a party. It's the complete opposite of that."

"It's serious because loneliness is becoming your hobby, and your dad wouldn't want that."

I searched desperately for our server, Juan Luis, who had great hair and a thick accent. I'd request more of whatever if it meant derailing this conversation. Frustration and grief welled in my chest and belly and throat.

"I don't want to see that happen," she said, her voice quieter and less demanding now. "That's all."

I exhaled. She trifled with her food. We ate a few chips and salsa. The salsa's spices and herbs and cold, fresh tomato masked the so-soness of the chips.

"I just don't think I have the energy to tolerate all the noise," I said, "and all the activity. I don't have it in me to see all those people— those people who know me as 'that girl'—and fake a brave face."

Stefanie sat back and furrowed her brow. "Fair enough. But look: God willing, this will be the last time you'll ever see them. Anyway, the only person that matters is the guy who has your dad's heart. I think seeing him again will be therapeutic."

Juan-Luis-with-the-Great-Hair shuffled by and asked if we were okay. Stefanie requested more chips. We grew quiet again, and I eyeballed our parents. Every time Mr. Velez's lips met his beer, Mom's head followed the drinking motion.

"I would only be there fifteen minutes," I said.

"What?" Stefanie mumbled around the rice she'd just shoveled into her mouth.

"How can I say I've 'partied' if I don't spend any time actually partying?"

"That's how it goes," she said. "Anyone who stays at a party the whole time has no life. You would know this if you went to parties more."

I scowled. "You're coming too."

She laughed, a confident and hearty sound. "Are you kidding me? That was the goal!"

~ * ~

I picked a gray button-down shirt dress, then I wrestled my hair for ten minutes before conceding and swooping it all into a high bun.

Stefanie arrived wearing a crop top and shorts. She decorated her face in my bathroom before we left, scraping some mascara and eyeliner onto her brown, doe eyes.

Closer to York's neighborhood, Stefanie rolled down her window and hung both arms out, letting the wind whip and tousle her thick, black hair. Summertime air flooded the car, a distinct smell I only associated with North Carolina. At night, the day's fading heat mixed with cooler air, a spicy and tepid and inexplicable combination.

Once again, I coasted through Collins Court, motivated by the same mix of nervousness, obligation, and courtesy—this time, for Stefanie. As she admired the half-million-dollar homes, I listened to the night sounds. Frogs belched, crickets and cicadas trilled, the fireflies outnumbered the stars, and the night smelled quintessentially, enchantingly summer.

Cars lined York's street. As we passed the house, we heard the music within. People crowded his driveway in front of the three garage bays. Some used the front lawn as their dance floor. I coiled with a frenzied feeling.

I parked a block away. As we walked, I crossed my arms over my chest and angled myself forward. Stefanie pulled my dress, slowing me, and her lips spread into a smirk. I grimaced.

I noticed practically every person I saw held a red Solo cup. A few held Heinekens and Coronas. We passed four giggly, slinky girls, their voices syrupy and their smiles easy.

We were almost across the street when I heard a deep voice say: "Kalamata!"

I tripped to a stop. "What?"

Strong, healthy, filled-out and face angular once again, full-fledged pre-February York began sauntering toward me. I almost didn't recognize him in the crowd. He'd thrown a plain gray t-shirt over his broad frame, and his dark, curly hair spilled from underneath a beanie the color of a bloomed magnolia leaf.

"Holy shit, you're here," he said. His soft hazel eyes pierced mine, unashamed. He grinned, practically vibrating with excitement. A car swerved around us.

I threw a quick glance Stefanie's way. Someone who didn't know her might think her amused, but I saw the worried edge to her cocked eyebrow.

"Here I am," I croaked and attempted a bright smile.

"Thank God," he said. "I was totally depressed earlier today. But now you're here, and you may not believe this, but you've seriously made my whole party. I couldn't care less if everyone else left."

He spoke like a four-year-old tying a shoe—*Bunny ears, Bunny ears, playing by a tree*—one wrong loop threatening to tangle his entire sentence.

"Oh," I said. "Cool."

I jumped when another person blared their horn, but York didn't. His smile remained as his eyes scanned me.

"Can we move out of the street?" I asked.

"Yeah," he said on a laugh. I liked him laughing.

Back in his driveway, he tapped the shoulder of a friend he called Nick. Nick might have been biracial. Black squares framed his dark eyes. Other than a cursory nod and tight smile in our direction, his phone dominated his attention, the glow coloring his face blue-white.

"This is Stefanie," I said. York shook her hand.

"Do you ladies want a drink?" he asked.

"Sure. I'll take —" Stefanie started, then cut her eyes at me. "Cheerwine?"

"How random. I like your taste. But I'll have to check my 'fridge. Olive?"

"Water, please."

My now-former classmates crowded the foyer and greeted York as if he'd just arrived. People sat and stood on the tall, winding staircase, and I could see their fingers poking through the wrought-iron accents I so loved. Elegant light from the spherical chandelier flooded the area, illuminating all the rowdiness below. Kids lined the walls and filled the large rooms off the hallway. The gorgeous watercolor painting hung in the same spot.

Wealth had its benefits, I supposed. Barring a pesky spot of heart failure, consistency greeted you every time you walked through your front door.

In the kitchen, two kegs marked the counter's ends. Several buckets filled with ice and beer studded the floor. A huge crystal bowl full of questionable blue punch teetered over the sink. I flattened my arms as two people bumped me while we passed the island. There was a body for every square inch of the huge space.

York dipped his head into his refrigerator, and Stefanie and I flattened ourselves against the counter beside him. "Where are your mom and dad?" I asked.

"What's that?" I heard him shoot back as things clanked around in the 'fridge.

"Your parents?" I shouted over the music. "Where are they?"

He stood with a Dr. Pepper—similar enough to Cheerwine, in a pinch—in one hand and a water in the other, then he shut the door with his hip. "Oh. My technical 'graduation' isn't until mid-July, so they went out of town for the weekend."

"That's... convenient."

"As convenient as I could manage." He smiled and handed us our drinks.

I wasn't familiar with sneaking around behind my parents' backs, and Mom and Dad never went away unless it was for their anniversary, which hadn't happened in years. I didn't know what York had said or done to convince them to leave, but he must have been quite persuasive. How often did he use that persuasion in other areas of his life?

I looked around to stop the possibilities spiraling in my head. "You must have invited the entire senior class," I said, only half-joking.

"It's one of the better turnouts for a Lively shindig," he said. "It's the perfect goodbye, don't you think?"

My smile must have given away my dissension, or he had the gift of perception, because he chuckled. "Parties aren't for everyone."

"They are most certainly not for me."

"You'd think after all those months talking I'd have gathered that."

"We always got sidetracked when discussing our social lives and hobbies."

"That we did." He leaned his butt against counter. "I know your favorite subject is English. I know you take good pictures."

"She's a *photographer*," Stefanie said. "She took pretty much every EC picture in your precious senior yearbook."

"That serious, huh?"

"And she's got the fanciest, most expensive camera you've ever seen in your whole life."

"Stefanie, you're exaggerating," I said.

"Tell me all about it," said York, to my surprise.

"It's nothing."

"Anything you're passionate about isn't nothing," he insisted. "Plus, I'm a junkie for high-tech equipment."

"Actually, it's really not that high-tech," I said, feeling the word vomit bubbling into my throat. "For the type of camera it is, anyway. It's an F6 35mm, so it uses film."

"Like real film?"

"Yeah. I chose it because it works well with all types of flashes, especially when you stick with traditional film. It has a standard intervalometer, so you can leave it unattended to take shots at intervals all on its own. And it has this infallible color Matrix Meter that gives you brilliant and clear exposures, no matter the lighting in the shot. Plus, with its internal memory I can log at least thirty film rolls at once, which is pretty impressive."

I asked for it four years prior—*Product Number 1799* I remembered saying, breathless, in my thirteen-year-old voice—after some extensive research. The thing cost an arm and a leg new; used, it cost a hand and a foot.

Since Dad died a month before Christmas, the holiday skipped our house almost entirely. But when I opened my bedroom door on Christmas morning, I saw the medium-sized, plain brown box. The removable lid bore the words *To Olive* in Mom's tidy script. I figured the months and months Dad must have saved just to buy it secondhand, and I cried and hugged the box for hours, imagining his excitement to see my reaction. He'd left me a capturer of moments I could never capture him with. I saw a beautiful sadness in that.

Music seeped into my head and flushed out the memory, bringing me back to the party. I found Stefanie staring at me, her lips quirked in amusement. York was staring too. Heat flooded my cheeks and burned my neck and ears. Could I be a bigger nerd? Could I have advertised it more thoroughly? Thank God for chocolate skin—it hides embarrassment so well.

"You were totally a member of The Photogs, weren't you," York said.

"I was vice-president," I admitted, surprised his status hadn't prevented him knowing about our school's photography club.

"That's so cool."

"You think?"

"Sure. Photography is an art, which makes you an artist. The world is all at once too technical and too pretty, and it desperately needs people like you."

His words, despite the way he slurred them, made me happier than I would ever admit. I was actually going to thank him when an imposing boy approached the counter and slammed his shoulder into York. The boy fiddled with his back to us all, and then, as if by magic, produced two filled shot glasses. He handed York one, who wordlessly downed it. York's cheeks turned pink, and he shook his head a couple times. Otherwise the moment passed as if it hadn't even occurred.

He might as well have taken a hit of cocaine. All sounds muted as I registered York's—Dad's—heart beating as his face flushed, his veins pumping poisoned blood through his body.

"Excuse me?" I said when I realized he asked me another question.

"You sure you only want water?" he repeated, presenting a dark beer bottle. Stefanie stiffened and eyed me.

"I'll take that," said a yellow-haired girl who slinked between York and me and slipped her fingers around the frosty bottle neck. "Unless your friend here wants it," she said, examining me.

"Oh, no," I said. "Have at it. I don't partake."

Her expression suggested she thought I might be mentally handicapped. "Oh."

When she walked away, York lifted an eyebrow. "Aw, you're rejecting me. And I went to so much trouble."

He was being funny, I knew, but I sighed, weary of this topic already. "I don't prefer being impaired, cognitively or otherwise."

"I didn't know..." His smile faded and he widened his eyes as much as a cognitively or otherwise impaired person could.

I didn't understand people's unadulterated aghast whenever I mentioned I didn't drink. Personal life aside, I was underage. We all were, and we shouldn't have been drinking anyway. Getting wasted and waxing nostalgic about all the other times you got wasted seemed to be the only thing being a teenager was about anymore. I knew I'd have to endure the same nonsense in college, and I'd already prepared myself.

I was silent so long I appeared to worry York, so I said: "You're fine."

"I mean, I figured you... after the shitty year we've had, both of us, I thought... you were like... everyone else, you know?"

He squeezed his face and clamped his eyes shut. "That's—that's not what I—"

"I know," I snapped, because I did know. I knew first-hand alcohol made you do and say stupid, stupid things, and I knew why I wasn't like everyone else. And I knew York Lively *was* like everyone else, even though I'd convinced myself otherwise.

I knew I didn't belong here, allowing my classmates to not-so-subtly gawk at me, no matter the number of verifiable reasons they had. I knew I couldn't continue watching York destroy the best part about my father.

"I was wrong about you," I said. I ignored his bewildered expression and made my smile quick and tight. "You are exactly what I thought you were."

I didn't consider anyone's personal space anymore as I stalked through the crowd. I needed the fresh air outside, because if I didn't leave that kitchen, my lungs would collapse.

I heard my name. His voice. I walked faster, past all the loose, sloppy, happy people whose conversation skills had degenerated to random chortles and strings of words.

No one followed me right out, which didn't bother me. My presence at this house embarrassed me now. How did I ever think I had any chance at a friendship with York? He was hardly my type. His dark hair and dreamy eyes and his jokes and his quick wit had lured me. He lured people.

Someone gripped my shoulder, and I knew Stefanie had caught up to me. We scrambled into my car, and I was surprised my tires didn't squeal as I pulled away.

She waited until Route 158's darkness enveloped us, which took exactly fourteen minutes. Then she muttered: "This is what happens when you're pushy, Stef. It all goes to hell. Why are you so pushy?"

This earned her one slight smile. "I'm curious myself. Could it be you were jealous and wanted to eliminate any possible threat to our exclusive friendship?"

"That must have been it."

I sat back and relaxed my arms. "Well, worry no longer. That guy is no Stefanie Velez. He does not have what I want in a friend."

That fact sat like a bitter pill in my gut all the way back home.

**York Lively** - 6/29, 5:03pm
I know the exact reason why you haven't answered my texts or my phone calls, and I don't blame you. I couldn't process what your friend told me at the party, but once the shots wore off, I wanted to punch myself for being so clueless. I didn't consider what it would do to you, watching that, making the connection to your dad. I guess I liked being the old me. It's been a long time. I could tell you I got caught up in the moment, or I was pressured, whatever, but I don't want you calling me a liar too. I'm just stupid.

I know an apology isn't enough, but I am sorry. I'm angry at myself for screwing this up. You're one of the few people I've ever really wanted to get it right with. If I could have done the night differently, I wouldn't have even started drinking, whether I thought you'd show up or not.

**York Lively** - 6/30, 8:39pm
And if you ever stop being mad, I want to make it right. If I have no chance, I understand. But I'd like to try.

## *Four*

## FLYING THE COOP

I moved into my dorm at Northeastern Carolina University almost two months to the day after York's last message to me. I couldn't get out of Fleet fast enough. A short drive across the river to the neighboring Pasquotank County got you to the university in fifteen minutes max, but I didn't care.

NECU had top credentials, but if I had a different life, I never would have chosen a state school. The plan had always been to abandon North Carolina all together as soon as I got the chance. I planned to travel, study abroad, go somewhere totally different. But losing Dad annihilated the possibility of ever leaving my mom and sister.

My Journalism major (concentration in Photojournalism) complemented the English minor I chose. Neither field was especially pragmatic or easy to get into without a lot of hard work, but I followed my heart. I decided to hit the ground running my first semester and enrolled in the first half of an Introduction to Journalism course. I was happy... for about two weeks.

On the first day, I swaggered into Professor Spaulding's journalism class, performed the exercises, and took on the article assignments with total confidence.

And then I failed my first test, a test on concision. I failed spectacularly. I couldn't seem to grasp the concept of shoving every important idea into one or two sentences. This shook me, but when I got my first assignment back—an argumentative article—I knew for sure I was in over my head.

I wrote about whether or not the designated smoking areas around campus should be extended another ten feet from buildings. I wanted to see them extended. With my F6, I captured a high-quality picture of the bench in front of my dorm with thirty or so cigarette butts strewn around.

Professor Spaulding asked each student to stay after class so she could return our articles and consult with us on them. She didn't intimidate me, not only because I felt confident in the work I had done, but because she was insane. Her waist-length brown hair had a mind of its own, smelled like nutmeg, and flowed wild and free behind her. She always looked like she was rooting for you; she kicked off the first day like a cheerleader, all *rah-rah* and *sis-boom-bah* and assuring us we would all *kill it* in her class.

And she had a story for everything—I especially got a kick out of her explanation for her awful chicken scratch:

*When I was a kid—now remember, this was in the late sixties... I know that paints me as Methuselah's mother in some of your eyes— anyway, when I was a kid, it looked like I was going to turn out left-handed. Back in those days, lefties were practically pariahs in society! Okay, they weren't pariahs, but left-handedness was highly discouraged. Can you imagine? People treated the natural lateralization of a person's brain function like chewing gum in church or wearing a white belt with red shoes: they discouraged it. Anywho, when it looked like I'd be a leftie, my parents began the complicated and totally unnecessary process of training me to use my right hand instead. It took some time, but I'm a righty now, like the majority of the other decent, upstanding members of society. Only problem is*

*I'm still left-handed in the brain, so my hand doesn't know what to do! So that's the story of how my parents ruined my handwriting for life. If at any time y'all have trouble reading my notes up here, I'm happy to translate.*

Professor Spaulding quickly earned a place in my heart, and I wanted to do well for her. And as I approached her desk for feedback on my article, her face held nothing but smiles and sunshine, convincing me I had nailed this one. Then I saw the "C-" at the top of my paper.

"Your writing is technically correct, Olive, and I can tell you have passion," she commented. "What your articles lack, I'm afraid, is substance."

Substance. That's it. She called me shallower than the water around a hippo in a kiddie pool.

"You write to complete assignments, and often they don't tell me what I know you want to convey. You had a problem with subjectivity, as you were supposed to present both sides of your argument equally. Aside from that, you didn't give your subject a point."

"A...point?"

"You didn't make it matter to us. You didn't give it a soul. Do you see what I'm saying?"

High school is a cocoon, a warm, cushy state suspended in a time outside the real world. Everyone tells you that life will be different once you hit higher education, but no one tells you the same classes you took in high school are ten times more intense in college. No one tells you the A's you got in high school will probably become C's in the same subjects. I had a hard time recovering from such a blow to the ego.

## PAST LIVES

I once favored the holidays over all other times of the year, even when my family was struggling to make ends meet. Dad's death demolished the cozy, happy season like a wrecking ball, and I hated it. I didn't hate Dad, of course, and I didn't blame him, though I guilted myself all the time.

Still, I hated it.

I went home for Thanksgiving, not to eat or visit with family, but to help Mom get through the week. On the anniversary of my father's funeral, which fell on Thanksgiving eve, she screamed and cried half the day, then drank and slept the other half. You might as well have wiped the holiday off the calendar for the second year in a row at the Grant home.

That Sunday I have to admit I practically sprinted back to school. I finished all my exams and dragged myself back home when the semester ended.

Uncle Joe worked with Mom and every resource he knew of to keep the bills and mortgage paid. I wanted to do my part as well, so over Thanksgiving break I applied for and accepted a job as a part time library assistant at the library in my hometown.

I always loved libraries; Stefanie seemed more than a little convinced I'd get used to the work, graduate to full time, never use my degree, and never leave Fleet. I would just have to be careful, because every little bit of income helped at this point.

College-level winter break came earlier and lasted longer than high school-level. My mother, engulfed now more than ever in her alcoholism, apparently attempted to get into the mood to make dinner on Christmas Eve. But when I came back home from work that afternoon after the library closed early, I found a pot of water practically reduced to vapor on the hot stove and my mom passed out on her stomach on the couch. Selma and I ate turkey sandwiches that night.

I went back to work the day after New Year's Day to get some additional hours in before my second semester started and forced me to cut back.

The deep golden-orange glow of the setting winter sun bathed the whole of downtown. The streets bustled—as they tended to this time of day—with people headed home. I pulled up to Fleet Public Library at five until five and sat in the warmth as my car hummed around me. I worked a mere four hours a day, but I could accept that. For four blissful hours here, I could forget the gloom at home and perform my uncomplicated job.

On Tuesday nights I worked with a page I liked. She had a terse yet oddly hilarious way about her and a sense of humor so dry you needed a glass of water to get it down. Her sensible short haircut, black-rimmed glasses, and functional cardigans made her look older than her twenty-two years.

"Is this not the thickest book you've ever seen in your life?" she asked as we emptied the book drop together.

I glanced over and acknowledged the behemoth in her hands. "Someone's an overachiever."

"For God's sake, it's called *The Infantry Hero*," she moaned.

"War?" I asked.

"World War One," she affirmed.

"Older gentleman patron," I predicted.

"Someone from each generation of his family fought in every major war of the last two centuries."

"Including him."

" 'Nam."

"Nah," I shook my head. "Korea."

"And he loves reading about war because his family's military legacy is his biggest source of pride."

"And he left trash in the book."

She guffawed. "You're good." She handed me a thin, worn piece of paper someone had folded into thirds like a brochure.

I opened it up to deem its importance and discovered a handwritten list with no title or any other indication of its purpose. Someone had scrawled seven items down:

Eat a chocolate bar, one of those giant ones they sell at The Candy Shoppe in the mall

Change my quote

Time capsule!

Climb the stump at Whittmire Gardens

Streak

Chase the sun

Get a tattoo

I smiled at the random little collection of words on the to-do list. "You know," I said, "we should not get this much joy out of judging people based on their book choices. We really should be ashamed."

"Then say we're collecting statistical data about human personalities and call it science," she said, scanning the last book and choosing a cart to shelve. "There. Feel less guilty?"

I shook my head at her and tossed the paper into the trash.

~ * ~

Two nights later, I stood at the front desk, lost in the task of placing some books on reserve for an elderly woman who had called in earlier. A finger tapped the side of my monitor and a glottal voice said, "You got *Game of Thrones*?"

"I'll be happy to look that up for you in one second," I said brightly.

The man was rather large and appeared generally displeased to be standing. He shifted his weight from one foot to the other and said, "If you could point me in the right direction..."

I stepped over and rested my forearms on the counter. "Well, first I need to know what version of *GoT* you want. The books? The graphic novels? Season One, Part Three on DVD? Or I could send you in all the directions if you like."

"There's books?"

I chewed a piece of skin off my lower lip. "Audiovisual section, TV shows, under 'G'."

"Thanks."

The man moved away and revealed York Lively. He was standing in the spot directly behind, as if the two had planned it.

"Hi, Olive."

"Hello," I stammered.

He glanced over his shoulder. "Is this what the library is for, now? Directing people to the DVD collection?"

I shrugged. "Of course. Books are old news."

"Funny. I hadn't heard about that." He ran his fingers through his dark hair. "How have you been?"

"Good."

He nodded. I could tell he wanted to ask me. He was dying to ask me. *Where have you been? Are you still angry with me?* Was I?

Surely I had too much negativity in my life to be angry with another person.

"How have you been?" I returned the question.

"Pretty good. I started at Northeastern in the fall, so I've kept busy with school."

A short hacking sound escaped my throat. "Are you kidding? I go there too."

"The world gets smaller when we're around one another."

Sometimes it felt too small.

"Wonder why I've never seen you around," I said.

"I live at home. Also, I'm pretty sure our majors keep us on two totally opposite sides of campus."

"How are you so sure?"

"Well, I'm either sure you majored in photography, or disappointed that you didn't." A smile slipped over his lips, slow and easy. "Which one is it?"

Where had he learned his conversation skills? A butter factory? "You're sure," I admitted. "Kind of. Photojournalism."

"Fitting."

"Thanks. I thought so." What little cool I possessed began to seep through every pore in my body, and I urged myself to pull it together. "What brings you in here?"

"I have left an item of grave importance in a book at this library. I'd like to know if anyone has found it."

"Let me check the Lost and Found," I said and opened the long drawer behind the desk. "You're not alone. People leave all kinds of things in books: old family photos, bills, car registrations, check stubs, credit card statements, voter registration cards—you name it. We once discovered a lock of perfectly preserved strawberry blonde hair tucked inside a donated Agatha Christie."

"Gross."

"The library has seen worse, I'm afraid. So, what did you lose?"

"A piece of folded notebook paper."

I eyed him over my shoulder with a raised brow. "Any other distinguishing characteristics?"

"Not really, sorry. It was a list, if that helps. Written in blue pen."

"What kind of list?"

His expression turned sheepish. "Kind of a personal one."

I shot straight up. "You left it in a book called *The Infantry Hero*?"

"One-thousand eighteen pages of destruction and valor."

"The list said something about chocolate bars and tattoos?"

"You read it?"

I leapt to the trash can and started digging—fruitlessly, I already knew—through a day's worth of holds lists and paper coffee cups.

York strained to peek over and down at me, and when I could hide from him no more, I met his gaze with an apologetic one.

"Everything cool?"

"I threw that list away the other day," I told him as I stood. "I'm really sorry. I had no idea how important it might have been."

He smiled. "Olive, it's fine."

"Really?"

"I don't need it—I have it memorized. The hard copy helped me stay on track, I guess."

"What did all of that stuff mean?" I asked the question before I could stop myself. I always had this incredible amount of curiosity, especially when it came to people. It put journalism right up my alley. "If you don't mind the question."

"They were goals." His eyes never met mine. "I wrote them forever ago. It's my bucket list."

"Cool. You done any of it?"

"Nope."

"Why not?" I blurted again.

The small smile on his lips told me he was crafting as partial an answer as he could manage; I could see the tip of that iceberg and the huge chunk of remainder that hung right below the surface. "I've had other distractions. Mainly, the book you found the list in."

My shoulders fell. "Right. You must really be interested in World War One."

"Oh no, God no."

"So you love to read, then."

"I hate reading."

"You *hate* reading?" Had his rose-red lips really put those two words beside one another like that?

"With the white hot fire of a thousand suns, I do," he said merrily.

I *oof*ed. "God, that hurts." Our differences were piling up—I wondered how we ever got along as well as we had. "Then what in the world possessed you to pick up that thousand-page monster?"

"Oh, it's the awesomest coincidence. The author is my dopplenym."

I'm a logophile by nature, and even though I'd never heard the term, I deduced its meaning immediately.

"Hold on," I said and ran to adult fiction. There, in the "L" section, sat *The Infantry Hero* by York Oliver Lively-Bingham.

I brought it back to the desk and set it on the counter. "Okay, that's pretty damn cool."

"Isn't it?" He placed his hand on the leather cover. "I couldn't believe it. I figured I must have been this writer guy in a past life and forgot what I wrote, so I'd better brush up."

"Whatever your reason, anyone who finds a dopplenym in an author should definitely read their books. Same goes for actors and movies, musicians and music. It is indeed the awesomest."

"Will you write a newspaper article about it?" he asked. "The phenomena? My very cool discovery?"

"That might be a good idea for a piece. But better let someone else do it. I'm not a very good writer."

"I'll bet you're better than you think." It was one of those responses nice people give when you're being self-deprecating, but it sounded sincere in his mouth.

"So, will you add reading the dopplenym titles to your bucket list? Because I'd definitely want to do that before I kicked it, if I had the chance. Or is the list a done deal? Surely there's more you want to try to do before you die."

His expression changed then, and I couldn't make it out: surprise, chagrin, or wonder. I imagined he hadn't detected this area of my personality back when we first started talking, hadn't realized how eager I could be.

"You're really interested in my list, aren't you?" he asked.

I couldn't tell if he wanted me to back off, so I pursed my lips, embarrassed.

"Tell you what," he said and placed his elbows down. With his height, he would have made the perfect impression in my position behind the tall counter. "I would be glad to tell you all about it. Over dinner. Tonight."

I blinked. What just happened?

"It's a long story," he said. "One you don't want to hear at work between customers."

I knew his game, and I didn't know if I wanted to play. He had wanted back into my good graces for months. Silently, I commended him for seeing the opportunity and seizing it.

Did I really care that much about his list? Probably not. Probably, part of me *wanted* to strike up a friendship again. I had enjoyed getting to know him, the him I knew existed somewhere in there along with the other stuff. We all had our shortcomings. He'd just seen my rude, prying side, and he still wanted to talk to me. It balanced out.

"Um. Sure," I said.

He straightened up. "I will meet you at Paco's Fish Tacos at nine-twenty."

Before I could even ask who in hell Paco was, the door had already swung back into place behind him.

## RISKY BUSINESS

Paco's Fish Tacos was exactly what it sounded like.

I drove ten minutes deeper into Fleet before I happened upon the small, almost shack-like restaurant. The slate gray paint was chipping off all over, which was charming in a rough kind of way, and outside on the patio sat four old, wooden picnic tables.

York pulled into the parking lot shortly after I did, and we entered together. You could hear cooks hollering at one another in the kitchen over the sizzle on the grills. Almost every chair had a butt in it, a good turnout for night time in the dead of winter.

Since I had never even considered the possibility of a fish taco, I allowed him to order the same mysterious dish—Wahoo with Paco's signature honey horseradish sauce—for both of us. The server brought us our sweet teas.

"I don't think anyone ever said that fish works with everything," I said.

"Trust me. This works."

"You're quite the risk-taker."

"Trying a taco with fish in it is your idea of a risk?"

"Honestly, going out with you is the first risk I've taken in…" I rubbed my forehead, feeling around for the one raised bit of scar tissue left from the time I bumped my head at age six. "Ugh. Wow."

"Why?"

"I've got enough uncertainty in my life. There are too many what-ifs when you stray outside your comfort zone."

"But you came out with me tonight anyway." He took a long drag on his straw and never once broke eye contact with me.

"I… guess I followed my gut on this one."

After he put his cup down, he asked, "What does your gut tell you about me?"

I didn't know if he really wanted my answer or just wanted to flirt, so I tried to answer carefully. "I get this niggling feeling to be around you, not so much an itch, more like a tiny cavity. It kind of hurts, but it kind of doesn't, so you push at it with your tongue until it's right at the edge of irritated."

His eyes twinkled with amusement. "Did you just compare me to a dirty hole in a tooth?"

"Rotted away by a little too much indulgence."

Our server stopped in front of our table. "Two orders of Tavi tacos?" She set our plates down in front of us, and I stared at three soft flour tortillas packed with cubes of fish, lettuce, tomato, tiny bits of mango, and cilantro.

"Do they scare you that badly?" York joked.

They did smell good. I gathered one up and took a wary bite. Flavor bursts punched every taste bud on my tongue, warm and cool and a little sweet and spicy in my nose only.

"Told you," he said.

"No, no you didn't," I said. "You called this 'good.' 'Good' isn't adequate enough. I want to live on this plate."

"Glad you like it." He took a big bite and smiled as lettuce and sauce plopped onto his plate from the other end of his taco.

"Um. So what is your major anyway?" I asked. When he raised his eyebrows in question, I clarified: "You said we never see each other because we're always on opposite sides of campus."

"Right. I'm majoring in Biology. With a minor in Marine Bio." He puffed out his cheeks.

"Don't sound so overjoyed. You're creating a scene."

"I like biology, remember?"

"But you don't want to major in it."

"I'd like to major in life, in travel, in getting lost and finding my way back. Makes me sound like a hippy, doesn't it? At any rate, my parents would never allow that. They want me to have practical aspirations, ergo: biology." He presented the word with palms to the ceiling. "Bio keeps my options wide open. It's kind of difficult to get a job in the marine bio field, but at least this way if I don't get to do what I really like, I have a back-up plan."

"If you can't be passionate about your career choice, why even put any effort into your classes?"

"You do what you can until you can make your own rules."

I had already spent several years looking forward to the day when all my uncompensated journalistic work would pay off, the day I would be hired somewhere to report on news topics of my choice. In the meantime, all I had were Professor Spaulding's well-intentioned but painfully blunt appraisals, meant to cut into the heart and soul of my work but which instead cut into me. Cut deep. Before college, I saw myself as superior. Now I felt like a hack.

Our server came back and we ordered a piece of vanilla bean angel food cake to share. "I've never had it," I told him.

"Angel food? My God," he said, even though it was just cake. "You need a bucket list."

"I could cross off a good four goals after these two hours with you."

"That's why I'm good at bucket lists." His expression turned thoughtful. "You don't realize what little things in your life are actually big things until you think all of it will be gone soon."

I swallowed hard. "How close were you?"

"According to my parents, one doctor suggested they think about funeral arrangements."

"Oh."

He beamed. "Anyway, I decided to write the list while in recovery. For the very first time, I thought about what would make me feel alive. I never wanted to skydive or swim with dolphins or whatever. Before my heart gave out, I was planning to half-ass the rest of my days here on this earth, and everyone was going to let me. Then, suddenly, I wasn't going to be around anymore, and I wasn't going to get to change the way people thought about me. It felt terrible. Almost as bad as dying, if you can believe it. Perspective is weird when you're dying."

I stared at him. "Your brain is an astounding clockwork."

Our server brought the dessert and two forks. I took a light, spongy bite and melted into my chair.

"Why did you do it, then?" I asked after a minute. "Why did you throw that graduation party?"

He seemed taken aback, and then his face became startlingly blank.

"You said you liked feeling like the old you," I said after a few moments. "Why did you go back?"

He shrugged. "It was easy."

I nodded. The body flowed with habitual actions, and it resisted change just as instinctively.

"And... I guess... people expected it," he said.

"You care a lot about what other people think, don't you?"

"I don't think I do as much anymore."

"But you gave up on your list."

"I never planned to do it, Olive."

"*Why not?*" My nerves sparked with an urgency I hadn't expected. "Why even take that much care to think about your goals and write them down?"

"I think we all have this innate desire to finish what we've started, you know? So if I never start, I'll never fail. It took facing death to bring out all I really wanted in life, and I'm glad I know."

"It just seems like a waste."

York Lively had eyes like a scalpel with a dull blade – every cut dug deep to break through, and it felt as agonizing as it sounds. I finished the last of the cake and smashed the tiny crumbs with the back of my fork. Activity in the restaurant had wound down. I wondered idly about Mom and Selma at home.

"All right," he said.

"What?"

"I'll work on my bucket list."

"You will?" For some reason I felt relieved. Maybe because I felt it somehow redeemed me for throwing the original, beloved list away, or maybe because I had actually successfully persuaded someone. Argumentative article be damned—maybe I simply didn't translate well onto paper. *Not every journalist is the same, Professor Spaulding.*

"You're right. It does seem like a waste, doesn't it? Why call it a bucket list if I let it sit there?" He sat back. "Plus, I'm young, and I'm kind of bored, to be honest, and I'm...I'm here. I remember bargaining with God in the hospital, saying dumb stuff like, *If I'm still here next week, I'm going to really* live, *you know?* That's where the list came from, partially. So it'd be, like, blasphemy if I didn't do it."

"I don't think blasphemy is the word you want."

"Heresy?" I shook my head. "Whatever, it isn't important. You get my drift."

"This is really cool. I'm happy for you."

"But I have one request."

"What's that?"

A smile tugged up one corner of his mouth. "Help me do it."

"Huh?" My voice cracked.

"Do my list with me. Help me finish it."

"How am I supposed to help you?"

"You're apparently a great motivator. You can keep me on track. And...I don't know. It'll be more fun with a friend instead of by myself?"

I shook my head. He was reaching now.

"I kept this whole list a secret because I didn't think it mattered to anyone else," he said. "It mattered enough to you. That's all I needed to get started."

"I don't think—" This time I couldn't come up with the right words.

"What?"

He sparked with earnestness like a live wire, and I fizzled like a limp cut cord, unraveling from top to bottom.

"I have to be honest with you..." I started, then stopped again.

"If this is about the party—"

"It's not that. It's not...only that." I sighed. "To be honest, you... scare me."

He blinked. "I scare you?"

"Surely you understand that."

"I—" He pursed his lips and shook his head. "Yeah, I do. I understand."

Then I felt bad in that moment, because he really did think he fully understood, and I never intended to tell him the truth.

"We're not very much alike," he continued. "You're kind of quiet and smart and nice, and I'm..." He laughed. I remembered how much I liked his laugh. "I'm a mess. But I scare you?"

"I want you to do amazing things. I want that for anyone. I want you to do amazing things with my dad's heart. But I...I have a lot on my plate. My life is still kind of a wreck. You're in a different place than I am, and you've got...different priorities."

I could tell he wanted to protest, but he knew whatever he said would only prove my case.

"So I don't think I'm the right person to do your bucket list with you," I said, injecting finality in my voice. "But I think you should do it, and I think you should start right away."

He hung his head a little and rubbed one of his index fingers with the other on the table between us. "Well. I can't start right away."

"Why not?"

"I've got this school project."

"But we're still on winter break."

"Lame, right?" He grinned. "Actually, next semester I'm in part two of this course. The professor planned to assign this project when we got back, but he's so cool, he gave us the opportunity to bank one guaranteed 'A' on our lowest scoring test next semester if we finish early and present as soon as we get back. I'm taking advantage of his generosity."

"You're quite the self-starter."

"I may be crazy, but I've never passed up a free 'A', and I never will."

I laughed, which appeared to please him. The same look fell across his face whenever he managed to make me laugh, and I couldn't figure out what motivated it: Was he really that desperate to redeem himself to me? Did he just like making girls laugh? Did he like my laugh?

"So anyway," he continued, "I'll be at Kill Devil Hills this weekend. For the project."

"Kill Devil Hills?" I asked, and he nodded. "Outer Banks?"

"Have you never been to the Outer Banks?"

"No."

"And you've lived in Fleet your whole life?"

"Born and raised twenty-five minutes from this very spot."

"That is criminal." He did genuinely seem pained by my words.

We left at close to eleven o'clock, having loitered for longer than the acceptable amount of time. The temperature outside had dropped, and the night felt very dark. Not a single car passed by on the lonely road in front of Paco's Fish Tacos.

York rested against his passenger side door and crossed one ankle over the other. His dark curls unraveled and recoiled around his head in the cold breeze.

"Thanks for inviting me out," I said. "Once again, you've broken right through my comfort zone."

"You are...welcome?"

"I mean it. I'm glad we cleared the air. And I'm glad you're doing well." I gazed at him for longer than I'd ever let myself before, and he stared right back. "How...how do you feel?"

He knew what I meant and didn't falter for a second when he said, "I've been perfect."

I scrunched my face to muddle the emotion welling in me. "Good, good. I'm glad it's doing you some...good."

He nodded somberly. "You should really see the Outer Banks some time."

"I know."

Call me bat-shit looney, but I wanted to like him. I wanted to feel exhilarated like most girls did when they hung out with a cute guy. I knew I had no time for it, and I still wanted it.

I could tell he wanted it with me, too. That's what sealed it.

"You need some help with your project?" I asked. "I'm not a science person by any means, but I could help you hold your stuff, maybe. And then I could see Kill Devil Hills, too."

He beamed behind pursed lips. "Sure, thanks. I'll call you Saturday morning."

"Okay."

He waited until I started my car, and then he got into his. He came out of the parking lot behind me and followed for a few minutes before he turned left down the long road that would eventually take him back to big, beautiful Collins Court.

# *Five*

**REALITY**

I felt the wrongness the moment I got home. After you've suffered tragedy, you come to recognize the subtle warnings. That's why it's such a shock when the bottom drops out from under people who have never had any bad luck: they had no bearings to begin with.

"Selma?" I called out. "Mom?"

I rounded the corner at the end of the hallway that led to my parents' room. The blood started centimeters beyond the edge of the wall—a thick, dark red puddle the size of a tea saucer—and trailed right through my parents' open door.

I stopped cold in the middle of the hallway. "Mom?"

"In here," my sister snapped.

It took a moment for my feet to move before I shuffled the rest of the way to my mom's room. She sat on her bed, hunched over with her back to me. Her shoulders quivered like she was laughing, or crying. Selma stood in front of her with her arms crossed over her small chest.

"What's wrong?" I asked, my stomach heavy with dread and discomfort and—

"Don't you get off work at nine o'clock?" my sister answered with another question. "Nine-fifteen is when you said you'd be back, right? Nine-fifteen on the nose?"

—and defensiveness. My little sister pelleted me with questions as if she were a responsible adult and I were the one barely out of adolescence. It's why I bristled with it immediately.

"I—" I looked at my mother's back again. "Are you guys all right?"

"I texted you. I texted you, like, a thousand times. And I called you. Why didn't you come home when you said you would?"

"I grabbed dinner. With someone."

Selma huffed and stalked past the bed. She bumped my shoulder as she made her way through the door. "Hope you had fun."

"What happened?"

"Ask her!"

I went over to Mom. "Oh, God," I said when I saw her face. "Did you fall?"

My sister had fixed her up with an ice pack, which she held over her mouth. "Tripped," she garbled.

Her wet, bloodshot eyes and the way her head bobbed—like a buoy in a vacant pool—told me the word "tripped" was her edit to the story.

I hugged her, told her I was sorry. Then I tucked her into bed with a gallon jug of water on her nightstand.

I spent the next thirty minutes or so on my hands and knees, scrubbing at the carpet with a brush and a tube of foam cleaner. I lost myself in the sound of bristles running back and forth, a sound broken only every so often by a small sob from Mom's room. I did not go back in there again.

When I was done, I stopped at Selma's bedroom door, knocked, and entered one millisecond later.

"I hate it when you do that," she said from her bed. Dad's ancient laptop sat on her lap, and she was listening to one of his favorite music playlists: Sounds of the Seventies.

I flopped down beside her and she bounced too. "You still mad at me?" I asked.

"Immeasurably."

"I'm sorry."

"You sure are."

I sighed. "I apologize for not following through."

"I needed you." She closed the laptop and the music cut off with a snap. "You're all I've got, okay? You're away at school, and you're finally out of here, and I get that, but I'm still here. I'm stuck here. You're all I've got until I can get out, too."

"I know that." I wrapped my arms around her and she squirmed. "I promise I'll make sure you're taken care of from now on. No more distractions."

"I get it, I get it. You love me." She flipped open the laptop again and began browsing the Internet. "What distracted you so much, anyway? Who'd you go out to eat with?"

"This guy."

Her eyes slid to mine, followed by her head. "A guy. You went on a date instead of answering my phone calls?"

"I went out with York Lively."

"What? I thought you hated him." Selma's features fell back into place. She wasn't annoyed now. Now I had her questioning my rationale. "Didn't you say he wasn't as nice as we thought he was?"

"He showed up at the library tonight by chance, so I had no control over the situation." I glued my eyes to the computer screen. "Anyway, we talked, and it turns out he's good people. He's taking care of Dad's heart. He's taking care of himself."

She studied me for a few moments. "Well then. I guess he's not any old guy, so you didn't pull a complete dick move tonight."

I began scooting off the bed. "Good talk, Sel."

"Is he, you know, okay?" I heard when I reached the door.

I turned to look at her, but she wouldn't look at me.

"He says he feels perfect," I said.

She nodded. I cracked the door behind me when I left.

## THE DEEP END

My first year in college so far wasn't going as well as I'd expected. My dorm mates were best friends and were always out at dinner and parties and clubs, and even though we got along fine, I could tell they wished they had gotten placed with a more extroverted person. As far as my performance in the classroom, I'd come out of my first semester a solid "B" student. So, for my second semester I planned to register for more classes within my major—classes I wanted to take—hoping the change would bring up my GPA.

I got back to campus before my roommates did, before most people, I imagined. I arranged the textbooks I'd already purchased on my desk and unpacked all the clothes I'd washed at home. My stomach groaned, and I went to the kitchen for a bowl of cereal.

York called before the milk hit the corn flakes. When he said Saturday "morning," he meant it.

"You'll need rain boots," he told me. "And maybe a rain jacket. Warm socks, for sure. And your camera."

Ever so slightly alarmed, I thought about reneging on the offer for a second. "Y-yeah. Okay."

"Be there in fifteen," he promised.

~ * ~

OBX was in the thick of the off-season, so most of the shops and eateries had closed nearly two months before.

"This place has a lot of history, right?" I asked York, looking out the window as he drove us down the length of Highway 12.

"It does. Also has a lot of fish."

"It's dead out here," I pointed out. "This is your idea of a fishing trip?"

He brought one rod, which he called a surf rod, and a small tackle box. He also wore a long-sleeved shirt and cargo shorts, which made me feel silly in my rain gear, especially on such a decent morning. Did he plan to throw me into the ocean?

"Actually, it is," he said, "but I'm not here to fish for pleasure, *per se*. My project is for a biological oceanography class, and my professor told us all to take pictures of fish, any kind of fish, and when we present he'll help the class identify all the different species."

He turned off the main road and down a very narrow street that led right to the ocean. The time showed right before ten o'clock, and the sun shone behind an abundance of fluffy, white clouds, making the sky bright but not too much so.

"Clearly, Internet pictures aren't allowed," he continued. "Aquariums are fine, since it's winter and always stays cold out here until pretty much May. But my professor wants pictures of marine life we can't readily identify."

We drove right onto the sand and parked against a grassy dune. "I didn't know you could drive on the beach," I said.

"Only during the off-season, but yeah, you can here. Makes beach fishing quite convenient."

Save the wind whipping our clothes—the rustle from the hood of my jacket constant in my ears—it felt like a lone, quiet world loaned to us for the day.

"This is my favorite spot," said York. "Kind of secluded, away from the hotels and inns." He pointed to the left. "Drive a mile that way and it's a different place."

It was the emptiest beach I'd ever been to, the kind of scene you saw advertised on websites: sand and sun and ocean and no people. I always wondered how photographers got those kinds of pictures.

While I daydreamed about all the shots I could get out here, I happened to glance at York. He watched me shyly.

"'Bring your camera'," I repeated his words, nodding.

"Is it...do you like it?" he asked.

"I couldn't have thought of a better way to spend a Saturday morning myself," I said.

It took him very little time to bait his hook. While he set up, I took pictures with my Nikon. The vast ocean had too many potential focal points, so I let all the pictures I took capture only a small piece of it in the corner, above, or below. In photography, it's called the rule of thirds. You divide your scene into three equal parts and put the main subject off-center to make it stand out.

The marbled white and cloudy gray gulls circled the air above us, squawking dissonantly like glorified vultures—illustrious symbols of pure and serene beach life fighting for the putrefied remains of washed-up sea creatures.

I stuffed my pants good and tight inside my socks and my boots, which were mint green with fuchsia and coral polka dots all over them. York wore these totally unattractive tall, rubbery black things.

We got close enough to the water for it to cover our boots to the tops of our feet. He cast his line, keeping within a certain perimeter. Before Selma was born, Mom, Dad, and I would visit my paternal grandparents' mountain house every summer. My grandfather would always take me out to the lake and try to teach me how to fish. I never got into it, found all the effort and waiting beyond tedious and too unsatisfying for such infrequent rewards.

York waited in absolute silence for less than ten minutes before his patience and skill with a rod and reel earned him a fish.

"Not bad," he said. He measured it with the palm of his hand and gave it about eight inches, but size didn't matter. I snapped several shots with his phone for him, then he tossed it back. "You having fun yet?"

"Loads," I said. "I assumed we'd be out here all day. Turns out I've underestimated you."

The water and wind roared all around us, and I wrapped my hood tighter around my head. After he cast his line again, I stepped back and took pictures of him with both of my cameras. I got shots of the gulls as they loomed around his line and plotted to steal the anticipated catch, then I zoomed in on his face, his focused eyes, and his full, parted lips.

He caught four more fish within the hour, two more types. He brought some excitement to the activity, mostly because I didn't have to wonder if his efforts would produce any spoils.

We leaned in to review the pictures I'd taken for him. "You think I'll get an 'A'?" he asked.

"Is it even a question?" I gazed at him. "This is a side of you I haven't seen yet."

"Which one is that? Responsible? Assiduous?"

"Focused," I said as a synonym. "I guess marine biology really is for you. Must be nice to be that secure in your career path." I tried not to say this bitterly, knowing the career I wanted eluded me for such a small, frustrating reason.

"My dad is the one who got me interested in the ocean," he told me. "He taught me how to fish. Taught me about the different species, too. When I was a little kid, we came out to this very spot almost every weekend." He chewed on the inside of his cheek and his eyes flickered over the water. "Maybe that's why I'm so reluctant to get into a career that focuses on the ocean, you know? Because I learned to love it through him."

I stared at him. "What the hell happened, York?"

He must have noted my alarm because he smiled an almost-smile, the kind that made his mouth twist at the corners only. The guy couldn't not smile if his life depended on it.

"I'm a financial burden," he told me almost nonchalantly. And I would have believed he really didn't care, but the look on his face, however brief, was so clearly troubled it changed all the dimensions of his features.

"How?"

"I made life harder for us when my heart gave out."

"You...made...? What do you mean?"

"He blames me for it all. He's never said it, but he makes these passive-aggressive comments, looks at me like I owe him."

"That's insane," I said. "You didn't ask for a bum heart."

"Yeah, but organ transplants aren't cheap. Then there's the time I spent out of school in recovery, the time he had to take off work, the time my mom had to take off. All he sees are the medical bills, the inconvenience this caused, the dent it put in their income. All he knows is for the first time in...ever...we're struggling to make ends meet."

His forehead creased as his dark eyebrows pulled together, and his hazel eyes looked weary, but the almost-smile didn't budge. I still didn't know how well I could trust his words, but I recognized that face. I'd seen it before as it stared back at me in the mirror.

"Listen," he said. "All that stuff I said and did at the graduation party...I'm really, really sorry."

"You weren't thinking. And what you said wasn't too horrible."

"But I was being insensitive. The way you feel about drinking is none of my business. I just..." He shook his head. "I've never, ever met anyone like you. I mean, kids our age like to do the same stuff. I just fell in line. And, I guess, it's easy to get so drunk that you feel good and forget." He seemed to reach some revelation then.

"I suppose I understand."

York gathered his tackle box and rod and we strolled north on the beach in the direction of this long pier. The dull wood structure extended about two-hundred feet into the ocean, skeletal and vacant, stretched out as if trying to grab at the sun for warmth. He told me he'd fished off its outermost point plenty of times, said the intensity of the wind up there didn't compare to the shore, but you caught much bigger fish that far out.

"Pretty cool," I said.

"Pretty cold." Though the sun shone bright as it could, the water at the beach in North Carolina would always be freezing in January, and it sent an icy spray into the air whenever a wave broke.

We didn't talk a whole lot, and we discovered all at once that we could be together without having to fill the dead air. He told me facts about the Outer Banks and historic Kitty Hawk, Kill Devil Hills, and Nags Head.

"Look," he said, practically skidding to a stop. My eyes followed his, coming to rest on a long, shimmering stream.

"I love these," he said, moving closer. "You should check this out."

"It's a ditch."

"It's a tide pool," he informed me.

"Really?"

"Well, it's a pool of water created by the tide." His lips quirked. "We're a flat coast, so you won't really ever see a true tide pool here, which sucks, because they're some of the most incredible habitats."

I stood beside him and bent over to place my hands on my knees when he did. Overnight the surf had chipped away the dark sand and created a shallow ditch that now sat untouched by the ocean and surrounded by frozen sea foam.

"It's low tide," he told me, "and we've happened upon a littoral series."

"How can you tell?"

"Excellent question. We're in the surf zone, and these long lines of water that zig-zag all over the beach are called runnels, and the raised bits here are sandbars. Certain organisms can live in certain kinds of pools based on how often the tide comes in. There's seaweed floating in the runnels but no actual vegetation is growing. You can see hermit crabs digging around in the sand, too, but that's about all you'll find around this particular beach."

"You can tell all this just by looking around?"

"Crazy how much you can learn in a few short months," he said. "And this is just one type of zone. The west coast is a whole different environment. I'd love to see the pools over there. Much more diverse."

His wide eyes scanned the sandbar, his dark curls hung over his forehead, and he bit his lip in absorbed concentration. It made him look so young and...good. A thing this small brought him so much joy, fascinated him so immensely. He was impulsive and young and prone to self-ruin. And he was good.

"I'll do it," I said.

He raised his eyes to my face and smiled. Maybe hadn't heard me, or maybe he hadn't understood.

"I'll do your bucket list with you."

His smile grew bigger. "Yeah?"

I nodded.

He gazed at me for so long I should have grown uncomfortable, but I didn't. I stared back, wondering what I had gotten myself into.

"Good," he said, "because I was *this close* to inventing a cockamamie excuse to keep coming to the library."

"Oh?"

"Yep. Something about having to research more books written by my dopplenym. I hadn't worked all the kinks out."

"What would have happened when you read all the books?" I asked.

"I would have had to find a new author."

"You hate to read."

"I can learn to love it."

My heart became an apiary, feelings buzzing and bumping into one another like mad, and I tried so hard not to go all dumb and melting in his presence. The muscles in my face woke up at once like I'd never smiled a day in my life, which felt odd and invigorating but mostly really painful.

"All right, then," he said on a grunt as he hoisted himself up. "We've got some work to do. Come on—let's go to the mall."

## *Six*

## SUGAR HIGH

York drove us into the heart of Pasquotank County. I'd visited the mall dozens of times in my life, of course, but somehow I didn't remember ever having given The Candy Shoppe a second glance. An Orange Julius and a Build-a-Bear flanked the loudly-colored store, and the trio made up a one-stop shop of every kid's dream and every parent's nightmare.

He made a beeline for the back and stopped in front of the display of gift and novelty chocolate, some non-commercial brand wrapped in blue paper and gold foil. One even had a bow wrapped around it.

"These are the biggest chocolate bars I have ever seen," he said.

"Ditto." I cocked an eyebrow at him. "Did your mom bring you here once and refuse to buy you one of these or something?"

"Or something."

"Well, let me just say I am so happy I changed my mind. There are worse tasks than eating chocolate."

"Bet you can't eat a whole pound of chocolate, though."

"You have this crazy talent for putting words that don't belong together into the same sentence. 'Hate' and 'read.' 'Can't' and 'eat' and 'chocolate'...."

He laughed and dragged the candy off the wall. It cost nearly thirty dollars with tax.

"Let me give you some of the cost of that," I said as we exited the mall.

"You're here for moral support," he reminded me. "You don't have to worry about helping fund any of my shenanigans."

Back in the parking lot, he stood smack in the middle of the lane, so I joined him. I glanced around sheepishly as people drove around, but he only seemed to notice me. This was his thing, apparently. At least when it came to me.

"So where should we eat this?" I asked.

"Good question. My mom wouldn't be happy if she saw me with it." He tested the bag's weight again and grinned.

"Want to come back to my dorm?" I suggested. "I've got a pink hammer."

"How appropriate."

~ * ~

York examined my campus home and raised his eyebrows in either surprise or approval. My roommates and I hadn't yet taken down the Christmas decorations—including the tiny white and pink tree—in the living area and hallway.

My dorm had a kitchenette, a common room, one and a half bathrooms, and three private rooms. Yancy, who hailed from Baltimore, and Morgan, from Greenville, had provided most of the decor, the reason for the pink curtains, pink coffee table, pink kitchen towels, and pink decals on the walls. I contributed a lot of the more practical necessities: pots and pans, a toaster, a shower curtain, bathroom mats. Trash bags. The room would have been far less rosy hued if I lived by myself.

"What's your favorite color?" York asked, both randomly and on-cue.

"Not pink."

"Lies."

"Actually, I think my favorite color is taupe. I've got this cushion headboard at home that's taupe, and a lot of my bedroom furniture at home is a variation of the same hue."

"I would love to say that's awesome, but I have no idea what taupe is."

"It's the color of sand."

"Oh, so like, tannish?"

"More like grayish brown."

"Why didn't you just say that?"

I sighed. "I forgot boys don't have as wide a color spectrum as girls do."

He sat in my desk chair, and I sat cross-legged on my bed.

"There's one question I have before I support you in this," I said.

"And I assume it's 'why?'"

"There's no point in me helping you make a statement if I don't understand the language. Get it?"

He put a hand over his heart. "You're a wordsmith. Okay. You're going to learn a lot of tidbits about me during our time together, and I think this a good place to start." He reached over to dig the candy out of its bag. "It so happens that I have a number of food allergies and sensitivities, and chocolate is one of them."

"Oh, that's unfortunate," I said, without a hint of irony.

"I know! We live in a world that gives a two-year-old the delicious magic of chocolate and then snatches it away. It's sick."

"But what will happen to you if you eat it?"

"Small amounts are fine. However, I specifically searched for the biggest slab of chocolate this side of the Tar Heel State because I'm tired of little bites here, little bites there. I want to enjoy chocolate like I did the day I discovered I shouldn't have it. I broke out, threw up, and nearly scratched my skin off, but I was *happy*. If that's a way to die, I pick that one."

"Aren't you being a bit drastic?" I'd considered, before, how awful it would be to have a food allergy. I loved food way too much, and what an inconvenience on top of it.

"Drastic times, my friend," he responded. We unwrapped the colossal treat and broke it in half with the hammer, and he picked up his piece.

"Wait," I said. "Is gorging on inordinate amounts of chocolate in one sitting bad for your health?"

"Um. No."

"York." I put my piece back down.

"No, it'll be fine. I have this diet from my doctor and my mom makes sure I follow it. Anyway, I'm mostly told to stay away from salt, not sugar."

"Are you sure?"

For one of probably very few brief seconds in his life, the reckless abandon left his face. "Hey. My old heart was the faulty one, remember? I've got a new one, a stronger one, and I plan to keep it safe now. Promise."

I nodded and tried not to get emotional, because I didn't want to mess up his moment, especially since I had pushed him to do the list in the first place. I picked my hunk of chocolate back up and touched it to his, and then we dug in.

"Oh man," he said. He closed his eyes and took another bite, then another. He shook his head in disbelief. I think he forgot my presence for a moment.

"Is it good?" I'd tasted better, but I suspected his grunts of ecstasy came more from years of deprivation than quality.

"I cannot adequately describe to you how happy I am right now. We deny ourselves so much in this life, you know? And for what?"

I didn't have an answer for him. I had probably deprived myself of way more than a girl my age would. My family had gone without so much for so long, it didn't even feel like deprivation anymore. With my home life, it felt like necessity, like the most basic and obvious survival skill.

We chatted while we munched and consumed our portions in a ridiculously short amount of time, enjoying the sugary buzz and the pleasure of one another's company well into the evening. Back at school and separated from the realities of home, I felt normal again. York didn't want to leave. And I didn't want him to.

I had never eaten that much sugar at one time, not even as a kid. A pound of chocolate and two hours into the night, I began to clean. I whisked around, harping on the repulsive state of my dorm.

"It's filthy!" I announced. "I could clean this place forever. I could literally stay up all night and clean this place. I found leftover spaghetti in my refrigerator from before winter break! We are barnyard animals!"

I scrubbed every white line of dried toothpaste out of the bathroom sinks, swept every bare floor, and cleaned the scuff marks off the bottoms of all three bedroom doors.

At one point I bounced back into my room but didn't see York. Instead, he was standing at the bathroom mirror. The bright red blotches on his cheeks, neck, arms, and hands didn't startle me as much as his maniacal grin. He writhed with the urge to itch.

"Dear God," I spat. "Are you okay?"

"I've never been better," he said. "Got any more Benadryl?"

I helped him into my room, where he collapsed onto my bed and placed his hands on his stomach.

"Wait!" I said. "Documentation!" I grabbed my OneStep and took a picture of the red and green and clammy boy sprawled on my bed.

"Every time we take on one of your goals, I'm going to take a picture," I declared. "That'll be my job. I'll make sure we remember this forever and ever and ever."

"Good idea," he said. "Speaking of which, by your judgment, would you say we've successfully completed goal number one?"

"I would."

"Good. Then if you would be so kind as to help me to your bathroom."

I did. Then I took several more pictures as he tossed his cookies into my freshly cleaned toilet.

## GROWN UPS

I began my second semester two days later. My new class schedule kept me out of my dorm longer during the day and, for the most part, got me back in time for dinner almost every night.

On Wednesdays I had a break between Journalism and Public Speaking, so I texted York, who urged me to meet him at his job in the education department.

The brick and sandstone building matched pretty much every other building on campus and housed a number of departments. I found him on the second floor, back behind a row of classrooms, conference rooms, and a work lab.

"You look very important," I said when I saw him behind the administrative desk, the first face you saw when you walked in. What a sight.

"You look very pretty," he said.

"Thanks. So do you." I grimaced at myself.

"This old thing?" He took my comment in stride and gestured to his plain white and blue baseball shirt. The skin on his neck and the tops of his hands still sported the faintest hint of the blotches that had erupted from his chocolate overdose.

"What do you do here?" I asked.

"My official job title is Office Slave, but mostly I file student records and answer the phone. 'Department of Education NECU. How may I direct your call?'"

"You have a very good telephone voice."

"Countless people have mistaken this number for a phone sex line." He sat back and smiled. "How's your day going?"

"Pretty great, even though I'm in a class I love with a teacher who can't seem to find my potential."

"The journalism class? I still refuse to believe that."

"I hate that the truth upsets you so much. I trust your day is going well, too?"

"I had Spanish this morning, which was *muy complicado*. That means very confusing."

"I grasped that."

"Glad someone in this room has. I haven't taken a Spanish class in years. Anyway, I have Calc later, which will be awesome."

"Ew. Have fun with that." I never had the brain for math, in any form. Just the thought of sitting in a math class gave me anxiety.

"I'd have more fun with you, anagram I Love," he said.

"More fun than throwing up a pound of chocolate?"

The corners of his mouth danced. "Have I thanked you for how well you took care of me that night?"

"Profusely."

"Thank you."

"No problem. I mean, this whole list has gone so well already."

"Stay positive. Lucky for us, the other six goals don't involve food." He sat up as if stricken suddenly by a thought. "When is your last class over?"

"Three-fifteen. Why?"

"My last class ends at four-forty-five, then I'm headed home. You want to come with?"

"To your house?" I said, like the idea of being in his house was laughable, as if I hadn't already visited more than once.

"Sure. I figure since we're going to embark on this deeply spiritual journey of The Bucket List together, my dad should probably meet you."

I stood there a moment too long as panic swelled in me. I felt this way every time an opportunity came up for us to get closer. If I made a point to meet his whole family, wouldn't he want to meet my whole family? I knew if we kept hanging out, at some point he'd expect to meet my mom. He'd expect a situation that would eventually, randomly, culminate in an invitation to my house, and he'd expect an involved parent who would, at some point, try to hover subtly by offering us cookies or something. I wasn't too familiar with what normal mothers did.

"I feel like every excursion you randomly come up with for us has dual intentions," I said.

He put a hand on his chest. "Oh, Olive, what you must think of me." He didn't deny it.

"Um. I don't want to go over unannounced," I said lamely.

"You know my mom won't care." He smiled in a confused way. "Unless you don't—if you're still not comfortable or—"

"No," I said. I started to feel like I might want to tell him, to explain away all my strange behavior. "No, I'll come over if you want."

He leaned forward. "I want."

At my side, below the line of the desk where he couldn't see, my hand trembled. "What else do you want?"

He raised his eyes to the ceiling and appeared to seriously consider his answer. "It'd be cool to get an 'A' in Spanish," he said finally.

I lasted eight seconds more before I lost it.

~ * ~

York didn't stop talking the whole way to his house, but I didn't mind. I usually preferred silence over small talk, but today it helped distract me from my nervousness.

I had previously I met two boys' parents as a "friend" or something similar. I really liked one of the guys, but our relationship never got serious. The other guy I dated for a little over a year. After that chunk of time in my young life, I knew what I felt for him didn't run deep enough. I certainly wasn't in love with him. He didn't love me, either. We broke up right before my dad died, which made for an all-around miserable time.

I didn't feel as nervous to meet those other sets of parents as I did now. The fact that I didn't know what York's dad thought of me because I hadn't stuck around to meet him the first time seemed most plausible. I even toyed with the idea I liked York more than I realized and really wanted to make a good impression.

I decided that wasn't it.

When we parked in his driveway and began walking to the front door, his mouth stopped for a moment and he took what seemed like his first real breath since we got in the car. Only then did I see the way he rubbed his wet palms together, the way he took several deep breaths before we walked in.

My memories of his house hadn't done it justice. I didn't understand how a family of three could manage to have any sort of communication in a space this big.

As we made our way through the hallway that drunk kids from my high school had lined nearly a year ago, a squat, beefy English bulldog trotted up to us and sniffed my shins. I squawked, delighted. York hadn't mentioned pets.

"This is Porkchop. He's such a beast," he said with pride. "Say 'hey' to Olive, Porkchop."

The dog directed his round, watery brown eyes up at me, and I let him sniff my hand before I patted his head. He grunted—in approval I hope—and turned back down the hall.

"And over there is FancyFace," he said. I noticed a very round domestic longhaired cat on the first landing of the staircase.

"She does have a fancy face," I said.

"I'm pretty sure she knows it, too." FancyFace yawned and otherwise didn't acknowledge our presence.

In the kitchen, we saw the lower half of Mrs. Lively wiggling as she rummaged deep inside the refrigerator.

"Hey," York said, sliding his keys across the counter. "Look who I brought."

She righted herself with a jerk, her pretty, tanned face flushed. You'd have thought she hadn't heard the sound of his voice in a long time. Her eyes widened when she saw him, then practically popped out of her skull when she saw me.

"Olive!" she said and scurried over, leaving the refrigerator wide open. She gave me another nearly-knocks-me-down hug.

"How have you been, honey? How has your family been? It's been so long, and we wondered if everything was all right. York told me he saw you working at the library the other week and I couldn't believe it. I haven't stopped thinking about your family since! Well, really, I never stop thinking about your family—how could I?"

"Mom," York said.

Mrs. Lively laughed, noting my expression and my parted lips, frozen open in an effort to respond to her one-thousand questions.

"I'm sorry," she said. "I've just let almost year's-worth of stuff tumble out of my head. Do you wonder why I've been afraid we ran you off after your last visit?"

"It's okay, Mrs. Lively," I assured her. "I'm sorry we haven't kept in touch better. It's still a difficult time for us, my family."

"I understand. We thought about you all day on the anniversary in November."

"Thanks again for the flowers." I had been the only one to sign the thank you card I mailed, but even that had been a monumental effort with everything going on at home.

"It was the absolute least we could do. We didn't want to visit, didn't want to intrude." She walked over to York and smoothed the crease that had formed on his forehead. "I'm so glad you and York have reconnected after all this time! What a great thing you're both attending NECU."

I remembered then his mom didn't know about the graduation party he'd thrown last summer. How he managed to keep her in the dark I would never know. Maybe she kept herself in the dark.

Even so, she didn't know how close York and I were—or used to be—and didn't know I'd seen him more recently than a year ago.

"Yeah," I said. Then, a little more hesitantly, "Life keeps bringing us back to one another, I suppose."

I wound up accepting an invitation for dinner. I felt like a newborn without a mother—instinct compelled me to snuggle up to any amount of motherliness offered to me.

York and I talked about our majors, how different they were, and how differently our brains worked. Mrs. Lively, as it turned out, was science-minded just like York, and had majored in anthropology in college. She worked with several non-profit organizations and used to travel a lot before she was hired at the corporation where York's dad worked. After Mr. and Mrs. Lively married, she took on a less demanding role within the company so she could have time to freelance and be a more involved mom.

When she asked if I planned to stay at the library and pursue English further, I told her journalism was my passion, one-hundred percent. But I did admit I enjoyed my work as a library assistant, especially helping people do research, an area I obviously thrived in. I told her I was glad to help York find more books written by his dopplenym.

"He shocked me when he came home with these books," said Mrs. Lively as she seared some rosemary-covered chicken breasts in a pan. She said 'these books' like she didn't read much herself. "When he gets his eye on a target, it does you no good to question or try to deter him. I suppose I admire his uninhibited nature." She glanced to the side. "To an extent."

"I wouldn't call myself uninhibited," he protested.

"You're right. It's too tidy a word. You are wild." To me, she said, "He used to do backflips in my belly. He once jumped off the roof of our garage onto a trampoline to see how much 'air' he could get."

"Turns out the answer is a lot," he told me. "Unfortunately, what follows is a lot of hard, hard ground."

"He's always taken life by the horns," she continued, "which, you understand, is not good for my nerves."

"I love you, Mom."

"You have to admit, though, life is never dull around this kid," she said.

"Doesn't take long to figure that out," I agreed.

We ate chicken and asparagus and delicious, creamy mashed potatoes off real plates. I'm not a huge fan of asparagus, but I ate them anyway. Their kitchen felt much warmer and homier without all the drunken teenagers in it, just like that first time nearly a year ago.

I helped clear the table, and York and I loaded the dishwasher together while his mom packed away the leftovers and swept the floor. I noticed her making little piles of swept-up stuff and pushing them into the baseboards underneath the cabinets and dishwasher. She touched a button with her toe and I heard a vacuum sound.

"What in the name of George Jetson—?" I hissed.

"It's a hidden vacuum cleaner," he explained. "They're all over the house—already built-in. They're totally easy to install, though, even if a house doesn't come with them."

Every once in a while I would forget he had money, only to be reminded in the most ridiculous ways.

He took me upstairs, past FancyFace, who hadn't moved, and then down a long, curved hallway. I had never seen carpet so dangerously light beige, and they had it all over the house. Why hadn't they just picked white?

He stopped at a wooden door that hung ajar and stared for a few seconds in apparent incredulity. "My dad is home," he said like he forgot the whole reason he had invited me over in the first place. "Do you want to meet him now?"

"Sure."

The room beyond the wooden door had one wall of windows, a very large L-shaped desk, and several tall, inundated bookshelves. At the desk sat a man with his back to us.

"Whatever it is will have to wait," Mr. Lively sang.

York looked at me, cleared his throat. "Um... Dad?"

The man managed to visibly sigh. "We talked about this."

"We have company."

He swiveled in his chair. York got his eye color from his dad, that was for sure, but where York's melted like caramel, his were cold like gemstones.

"Hello," he said to me.

"Hello."

"This is Olive Grant," said York. "She's a member of the family mom and I met last year. You remember?"

"Sure, sure." To me he said, "I'm so sorry about your father."

"Thank you. We're getting back to good, for the most part."

"Glad to hear it." His eyes bounced to his son and back to me like tennis balls. "Watch yourself with this guy here. He's always gotten a thrill from testing the fates, and I think you've probably been through enough."

I blinked. York bristled.

His father winked.

"I don't mean to be rude," he said, "but I've got a few bills to pay before I can eat dinner." He turned back towards the windows. "Nice to have met you, Olive."

"You too," I said.

York practically dragged me down the hallway. "I appreciated the condolences," I said.

"Yep. He sure seems sorry about a lot of stuff," he muttered. We stopped at a door at the hallway's dead end. "This is where I hibernate at the end of every day."

He had a navy blue comforter on the bed, one wall dominated by electronics, the variety of which I knew as much about as he knew the difference between taupe and grayish brown, and a pile of dirty or clean clothes kicked into one corner of the room. A book called *Nature in Action*, another title by the dopplenym, lay on his nightstand.

"I'm almost done with it," he told me as I fingered the cover.

"And how do you like it?" We sat down on the floor, the bed too intimate a place. Mrs. Lively told us to keep the door to his room open twice before we even made it to the stairs.

"You can imagine my excitement when I found out the guy had written more nonfiction. That said, I don't despise it. I'm not sure I get it, but it's making me think, at least."

"What's it about?"

"It's basically a philosophy and self-discovery semi-autobiographical hybrid. There's some stuff in there about the rationality of being connected in body and spirit, but it's weird because he makes it seem like science and creationism are interchangeable. Most people believe in one or the other, you know? Apparently, he got the idea from some Dutch philosopher named Baruch Spinoza."

"That is kind of odd. What was this other York Lively about, anyway?"

"That's just it: I can't get a clear answer. He was born in England in the late nineteenth century and only published three books. The first one I read, *An Introduction to Rationality*, came out in 1915 and didn't do well at all because people didn't get it. He had basically formed his own religion from the idea that if every person made themselves happy and focused on bettering themselves, they could ultimately create a better world, which made self-interest the most moral trait."

"That's ass backward," I said. "It also makes sense."

"My thoughts exactly! Not many others of his time shared the sentiment. I don't know if he needed to be heard, or needed to be famous, or both, but about six years later, he banked on the World War One epic and churned out *The Infantry Hero*."

*The Infantry Hero*, as it turned out, told the story of a sensitive and artistic young man named Henry Georges who became one of the 2.8 million men drafted into the war as a part of the Selective Service Act. He arrived in France in July of 1918, made several friends in his regiment, and watched some of them die as he fought in four unspecified and gruesomely detailed battles. In his final battle, he decided to run back to danger with a ragtag group that he somehow ended up leading, in order to rescue one man, Eric Bober. During the course of the story, Henry realized he was becoming someone unlike himself in battle—bloodthirsty and vengeful—and began to regret joining the military. He wondered how he would come to define himself as a person when he got back home—*if* he got back home.

"It's the most basic, bloody, formulaic hero's journey trope of a story I've ever read, not remotely similar to the cerebral work he put out before," said York. "And people ate it up."

"That kills me," I moaned. "I see it all the time at the library. The big-name authors with the predictable storylines are guaranteed checkouts. People just want to be entertained."

"It must have sucked for the guy. Some years later, he published *Nature in Action*. Took him five years or so to write it, and he used his fame from *The Infantry Hero* to get readers. Turns out *Nature in Action* got worse reviews than his first book, probably because more people read it. The other York Lively didn't write another book and died in 1954, broke, I think."

I frowned. "That's where it ends?"

"That's all I got. He seems pretty deep, more like an idea rather than a person... like Walt Whitman, Ayn Rand, and Kafka all rolled into one."

"You sure know a lot about a lot of different writers for someone who doesn't read," I said in my most casual voice while my insides melted. I was impressed. More than impressed.

"I didn't say I don't read. I said I hate to read." That made me wince. "This guy is probably one of the biggest thinkers of our time, and no one cared to figure it out. He put his heart and his philosophy out there just for people to crap all over it."

"That's depressing. He sells out with *The Infantry Hero* and it doesn't even work out in his favor."

"Hey, formulaic doesn't equal awful. If it were made into a movie, it would be a little like *Saving Private Ryan*."

"I liked that movie."

"Really? Me too," he said. "What genres are you into?"

"Most entertain me well enough. I'm not big on nonstop action though. Not a huge fan of sci-fi, either."

"And I can stomach everything except sappy romances. A little regular romance is bearable. Sappy romance, shoot me."

"I guess there's only one type of flick we can agree on."

"Horror."

"Chainsaws and demons and phantoms, oh my!"

"That's it," he said, slapping his knee, "we've got to see a movie together. How's Friday night?"

"Uh," I said on an exhale. "Hold on there, guy. A movie is different from Paco's Fish Tacos. I just met your dad. Your mom still doesn't know me that well."

"She likes you."

"Obviously."

"No, aside from the obvious reasons. She really likes you, you."

"How do you know?"

"I can just tell. She and I are on the same wavelength. We're pretty close." His expression turned introspective. "My dad's not around as often, as you can see. Well, he's around Fleet a lot, but not around me."

"Oh."

"He's kind of obsessed with work. My mom always said that, then I started saying it, so I guess it's true now. After this whole heart debacle, the dynamic in my family got really weird. My dad doesn't like when the rug is pulled out from under him."

"That doesn't give him the right to treat you differently because you got sick. To blame you for it." My expression must have been rather nasty, which appeared to both amuse and unnerve York.

"No, it doesn't," he said.

I reached forward and touched his hand. His skin warmed mine. He stared down at our connection for a moment.

"Our parents aren't supposed to be perfect," I said. "As kids, we think they are, but once we let go of the idea they've got this being human thing all figured out, we can stop holding ourselves to such ridiculous standards."

His eyes hinted he knew I was speaking to myself as well as him, but he didn't ask.

"Plus, you're totally likeable," I continued, sitting up and taking my hand away. The warmth remained. "And, honestly, some of the stuff your dad says to you seems remarkably dicktastic. You don't need that negativity in your life."

His dark eyebrows shot to his hairline. Then laughter burst from him, so abrupt I jumped.

"Dicktastic," he repeated. "I'll have to use that sometime. 'What a dicktastic comment, Dad, thank you for your input.'" He laughed again, a sonorous, vibrant sound.

# *Seven*

## METAMORPHOSIS

While I had a break between my classes one Tuesday, York came to my dorm to pick me up. My roommates and I were in the kitchen when he arrived with his backpack still slung over his shoulders, and I noticed right away the change in the atmosphere of the room.

"This is my friend, York," I introduced him as casually as possible.

My roommates introduced themselves one after the other, Morgan speaking the moment Yancy finished so that it sounded like one name, so that they sounded as joined at the hip as they really were.

"Nice to meet you," York said. "Yancy, huh? Awesome name." She laughed and shook her head. Morgan exhaled a couple times but never appeared to inhale.

"Yeah. 'Bye, guys," I said and grabbed my bag off the counter. I barely closed the door before the smile escaped me.

The text messages started as soon as we left:

*WHO is York again, now?*

*When did you meet him, EXACTLY?*

*Are you two dating?*

*How did you land such a babe oh my God not saying you lack the looks or personality to land a babe, but Jesus is he a BABE*

"What?" York asked.

"My roommates have forgotten how to human."

"What do you mean?"

I smirked. "I have not known you very long, Mr. Lively, but we both know you are far from dense."

"I'm honestly at a loss." The corners of his mouth fluttered. "However, I accept zero responsibility for what may or may not have occurred in that room."

We decided to go to Starbucks. I splurged on a cup of sweet, hot, high-calorie goodness, while York got a drink made with coconut milk. We settled down to discuss his next bucket list goal.

"So, I brought a thing," he said. He pulled a thin book from his bag, and I recognized the blue and silver cover, the dolphin mascot, and the word *Metamorphosis* displayed in intricate font on the cover.

"Oh my God," I said, "I haven't seen this in a good minute." I leaned in to flip through our senior yearbook. "I took that picture. And that one. These, too."

"I was so excited when I got it. I mean irrationally so," he said. "Like my entire high school life had led to that moment. Dumb."

"No it isn't. Everyone is always that excited. Made me feel kind of like a popular kid myself." I rolled my eyes, regretting the confession.

"You were popular, come on."

"No, York. A thousand times, no." I sat back, and all at once I became hyper-aware of his strong forearm draped across the back of my chair. "Not that it mattered to me. I did like being part of a tradition that always means so much to everyone. Every time I heard someone talk about how well that one important school event was covered, or how much they liked that one picture that would immortalize them for all time, I could imagine myself as part of each person's experience."

"That's a cool way to see it. You helped put together a kind of highlight reel of everyone's year." He flipped to his senior photo. "For seniors, that sums up the whole four years. It defines us. It shouldn't, but it does."

He stopped on the glossy, colored page. Larrimore. Lavely. Leetz. Little. Lively.

Yep. Just as I remembered him: the indifference in his eyes, the coiffed hair. I don't know if he looked different to me now because I knew him a little better, or if he had grown up that much since we graduated—

York's eyes flickered back and forth across the page in an almost frantic way. "Amazing how quickly it can all change," he said.

A brief search through my memory brought me back to senior photo day. Early September, the 4th. York's heart failure—the day my father died—November 19.

I dragged the book over to me and flipped one page back. Goins. Grady. Olive Grant.

I stared at myself.

My mother was so hungover that morning, she hadn't even dragged herself out of bed to help me with my hair. My dad, who had gotten home less than an hour earlier, should have been showering and then lying down to cop a quick snooze before reporting to work at ten. But he stood there, tall and dark, one shoulder against the doorjamb, a small grin on his lips as he watched me fuss over myself in my bathroom mirror.

"You look fine, you know," his deep voice billowed around me in the small space. Living in a house full of women had buffed away his edges and made him perceptive and gentle.

"Maybe."

"Back in my day, we'd roll out of bed, walk out the door, slap the ridiculous senior outfit on, and get the picture down in maybe four seconds."

"You're a guy," I stated the obvious. "I think across the eons women have worried over their appearance, especially in pictures. Plus, you wore that gigantic afro in your senior photo, so your judgment shan't be trusted."

He laughed then. The sound erased all but a tiny bit of my foul mood. He had that ability.

I felt better at school that day than I had anticipated I would when I first woke. I donned the black senior drape and my necklace with the small saltwater pearls—not one of them like the others, not one of them perfectly round—and I smiled a real smile, because my dad would be home for dinner that night, and I had aced an English test, and the day had turned out not terrible.

"Amazing," I agreed with York. He also seemed lost in his own memories of that day, no doubt an ordinary day for him, too.

Then he said, "My whole senior year—all of high school—up until this point right here," he turned back to his page and pointed at himself, "doesn't matter. Not just to me, but in the grand scheme."

He took out a badly crumpled piece of paper, on which, I discovered, he had rewritten his bucket list. He had crossed out "Eat a chocolate bar."

"This brings us to my second bucket list goal: Change the quote." He flipped toward the back of the yearbook and stopped when he got to the Senior Quotes section. "Look at this. Just look at it."

*"You miss 100% of the shots you don't take"* appeared above his name on the page.

"It's actually a good piece of advice," I permitted.

"I just wanted something that would sound kind of badass, like an action verb. I literally Googled 'cliché high school senior quotes' and saw this one on three top ten lists. Could I have tried any less?"

"Young people tend to shy away from any sort of depth. I'm not sure why. We aren't mature enough to handle it? We are, but we're afraid of what it might say about us?"

"How do you pick one set of words to sum up your entire academic life?" York asked. "I guess I picked a piece of shit quote to rebel against the ridiculousness of such a request. Now that I've been through some stuff..." He sat back and exhaled. "I really feel the need to define my life."

"You don't have to do that," I told him. "You don't have to have your whole life figured out just because you had a teensy brush with death." He smiled, which filled me with something indescribable. "You can accept who you were."

He nodded for a moment. "You're right."

"I am?"

"Absolutely. I won't change the quote I gave, but I'll add one. One that means more to me now I've done a bit more living. And a little dying."

I had a different brush with death than he had, but it had arguably defined my life by the same measure. Did I want to change my quote, too? What had my quote even been?

*This moment will just be another story someday.* We read it together.

"See? I didn't give such a clever quote, either," I said. "It was supposed to be a play on my becoming a journalist."

"It's not so bad."

"That settles it," I said. "I'll add a quote too."

"Perfect." He reached into his book bag. "Baruch Spinoza, that guy I told you about who influenced the other York Lively, wrote a book called *Ethics.*" He pulled the book out. "I'm reading it on the side. The religious people of Spinoza's day were…overzealous, for lack of a better term, and he broke away to develop his own concepts about the self and the universe. I researched him a little…he called himself a rationalist, someone who's all about reason and logic and intellect."

"The other York really did form his philosophy from Spinoza."

"Right? And now, I don't know, I think get it too. The other York said Spinoza's lifelong obsession with being the absolute truest to himself was highly admirable." He widened his eyes. "This has become some sort of crazy, philosophical journey for me, and I just wanted to get through a few books."

"But this is good, because now you're significantly influenced. So, what will your new quote be?"

"God, put me on the spot, will you?"

"You're telling me you haven't already thought about it? You?"

"Actually I have. Still, we can't choose all willy-nilly. That's how we attached to our immortally youthful images those terrible clichés in the first place, remember?"

"Fine." His hand brushed my upper arm slightly, but I felt the sensation throughout my entire body. "What do you want for the future, anyway? Where do you see yourself five, ten years down the line?"

"Ten years down the line, age twenty-eight." He sat back. "If it's truly up to me, I'll have finished up a bunch of travel by that point. I'll have seen most every place I want to see, and I say 'most' because sometimes I can be a rational guy, and, rationally, the list of places I want to visit is pretty long."

"Pretty much what I expected you to say. What about settling down? Could you do it?"

"You mean marriage and kids and stuff? Sure. I'll need to make sure I've gotten with the kind of girl that can stomach my reckless abandon and…what did my friend Nick call it one time? My maddening optimism."

"Yeah." I had been existing on a day-to-day basis for a long time by that point, even though my mom spent all her time whittling away at her health, her life. I sometimes forgot I was a healthy person with so much more life ahead of her. York awaited his future with bated freaking breath, even after his heart already failed him.

Practical, those little what-ifs, but they sure got in the way sometimes.

"You got your camera with you?" he asked.

I always carried around the OneStep; I didn't trust my expensive camera to not go off and get itself stolen. I handed him the Polaroid, and he raised it above our heads to angle it down at our faces. The camera sneezed, then stuck its tongue out at us.

"Explain this to me, if you would." He placed the picture in front of us on the table. "Why does it take an instant photo time to show up?"

"The image needs exposure to light."

"So the reason you haven't shown up in this shot yet is your image hasn't been exposed enough."

"Exactly."

"Keep this picture, will you? It probably sucks because I am by no means a photographer, and I'm used to my phone's auto-focus, and I don't have the magic eye that you do. Keep it anyway, though, and look at it from time to time for me. When you do, remember how blurry your image was before you got exposure, and take pride in how beautiful you are in the light."

I stared at him for a long time, unembarrassed to do so now. I had to squint, though I'm not sure why. It must have been all the light.

## *Eight*

## MEMORY

My first assignment for Intro to Journalism Two was a feature about an individual who inspired me, someone who had really conquered some odds. I took a very brief moment to exercise pure, unadulterated vanity and consider writing about myself. I also considered York, but I didn't know him well enough yet not to spin him in a superficial "Isn't it so great that I manage to be a happy guy even after my sudden, severe illness?" light. I had to put some real thought into this assignment.

I decided to go back to my roots. Even though being at home tended to stress me out, I had compartmentalized that part of my life into an orderly, clearly marked box. Granted, the box was huge and always seemed to be smack in the middle of the room, but I could skirt past it without any trouble now. Dad's death had unpacked the box, spilled its contents all about. Made it a little harder to navigate the room, but I rolled with the punches like a champion boxer. Muscle memory.

My uncle worked as a sous chef at a soul food/Creole fusion restaurant in Chowan County. On my first night home he brought over enough baked spaghetti to feed a couple of people for several days. I assumed Selma had made the request, since she hadn't had a home cooked meal in a long while.

The four of us sat in silence around the dining room table. Mom ached all over, weak and tired because she hadn't had a drink in a couple days. When she went without, withdrawal gripped her, made her writhe in pain and throw up any food or drink she tried to put on her stomach. She had headaches and the shakes and broke out in cold sweats. Once when I was eleven or twelve she had a seizure in the middle of the night. She'd been doing so well, regularly attending meetings and staying away from alcohol entirely. I went into my parents' room and saw my father hunched over her in bed, and I had to call an ambulance before I could console Selma.

If I abstained from some horrible addiction and felt like I might die as a result, I'd probably do whatever I could to take the pain away, too. I guess my anger for my mother came from the idea that she should want to do the hard stuff for her children no matter what.

I knew I told York our parents weren't supposed to be perfect, but I hadn't discredited the hurt he must have felt nonetheless.

## SOBER

My best friend Stefanie greeted me at her front door the next day and wrapped her arms around me.

"Fucking college," she said as she led me in. "We don't see each other as much as we thought we would." She was all the way across the state at Appalachian.

"Come home more often," I said. "Better yet, come to NECU to spend the weekend with me. We'll smoosh into my sumptuous twin bed and have us a sleepover."

"I'm sure every guy within a fifty-mile radius would line up at your window to catch a glimpse of that porno fantasy." She swung her dark hair as she turned to grin at me. "By the way, how is York Lively?"

We'd talked at great length about my reconnection with him, all except for the list, which seemed too personal. Because of my home life, the normal guys-centered "girl talk" that happened between most best friends usually remained pretty one-sided with us, so this new development had her practically salivating.

"He's nice to talk to," I said in such a way you heard the whisper of *and that's all.*

"You do more than talk. You went to his house again. You met his dad."

"Circumstantial. We had an important project to talk about."

"You went to dinner with him."

"It wasn't a date. At all."

"You went to the beach with him. You two hung out at your dorm a couple times."

I rubbed my face. "I mean—we didn't—"

She slapped my shoulder. "Olive, you suck at this. I say that with love."

"I feel it, the love."

I followed her into the kitchen, where her mom stood at the stove. Stefanie's parents emigrated to the U.S. in the eighties, her dad from El Salvador and her mom from Guatemala. They met in Texas, married, and moved to North Carolina after Stef's older brother was born.

When Mrs. Velez saw me, she yanked her hands out of a bowl of mush and wrapped her arms around me. "*Hola, Olivia. ¿Cómo estás?*"

"*Bien. ¿Y usted?*"

"*Bien, bien, gracias a Dios.* You look beautiful."

"Thank you." Mrs. Velez hardly spoke any English, and I hardly spoke any Spanish, so our conversations had gone this way since I met her.

"*¿Y papá?*" Stefanie asked.

"*Allí en la oficina,*" said her mom, pointing over my shoulder with her lips.

Mr. Velez sat at his desk in his office. He tapped his fingers to the Mariachi music drifting from this old style radio he'd had since before I met Stefanie. The man had the money to upgrade to any sleek, modern, name brand music machine he wanted at any time.

"Good to see you." He stood and gave me a hug. He smelled like pure tobacco and a hint of cologne, and he had russet-colored skin and luxurious black hair. His mustache commanded respect. My forehead came right to the bridge of his nose, but what he lacked in height he made up for in charisma. He owned a masonry company and had to communicate with contractors quite often, so he'd picked up the language of business.

"How is school?" he asked.

"I like it. Ended up with a three-point-four grade point average last semester."

"Very good!" He nudged his head at his daughter and stage-whispered, "You'll tell this one over here to buckle down and focus like you, eh?"

"*'Apa, ya no me regañes porque* I already told you I need a math tutor."

"In her defense, Mr. Velez, math is impossible. And stupid."

"When you are met with *imposible*, you have to work ten times harder to make it work," he said.

"My dad used to say stuff like that," I said on a sigh as Stefanie and I sat down across from him. He used to say 'If it's your weakest subject, you should focus on it even more.'"

"Brilliant man, your dad." He sat back in his chair, and I took out my pen, notebook, and tape recorder. Stefanie would translate for me, and I wanted to make sure I captured it all.

"Would you mind if I quoted you on that, Mr. Velez? What you said about impossible tasks?" I had to practice conducting an interview in a professional way.

"Sure," he said.

"Would you say you've lived your life by those words?"

"If I have, I did not realize it until this very moment." He laughed.

"Tell me a little about your early life, Mr. Velez."

Gilberto Velez was born in Uluazapa, El Salvador. He left school in the eighth grade and went to work soon after. His family had no car, and there were no paved roads where he lived, but he learned early on how to ride horses, tend livestock, and cultivate lush crops.

He lived in El Salvador through a great deal of the civil war, which lasted from 1979 to 1992. He arrived in Houston in his mid-twenties, whereupon he worked many different minimum wage jobs that fostered in him an even stronger work ethic and desire for the good life.

"When did you finally go into business for yourself?" I asked.

"I visited North Carolina in 1995 and...how do you say, Stefanie? *Unos primos me mostraron una tienda que estaba de venta.*"

"He had cousins up here who told him about a storefront for sale."

"Uh huh," Mr. Velez said. "So I bought it, and it, uh, it had much success for a long time."

A little while later he bought two properties, which he fixed up and then rented out to people. After he discovered how well he could do with brickwork, he started the masonry business and hired a few of his friends to first work with him, and then, eventually, for him.

"It's great that someone with an eighth grade education can come to the U.S. and be so successful. Do you feel like that's your biggest personal accomplishment in life so far?"

He wrinkled his brow at his daughter.

"*¿No sabes lo que te preguntó?*" she asked.

"*¿Me preguntó sobre la educación y el éxito?*"

"Yeah."

"I don't understand what you mean," said Mr. Velez, cluing me in. "Sir?"

"You mentioned my education in El Salvador."

"Yeah, well...here in the States, we tend to base success on one's level of education."

"Oh. Yes, I see that. That's why I pay so much for my children to go to college, right?" He smiled at me. "But I think I got taught all the best lessons in El Salvador. I learned how to work hard and how to take care of myself. I know math and how to write. I know how to... *mantener los negocios,* how to talk to people, eh?"

"How to do business," Stefanie explained.

"There are so many different types of minds out there," he said. "*Buen sentido* is what we say in Spanish. Some can afford to go to school for years and years, and some, like me, *solo podemos usar buen sentido.*"

"It means, like, common sense or whatever," Stefanie said.

"I'll make sure to quote you just like that," I told her, and we smirked at one another. "So, Mr. Velez, what you're saying is you picked up the basics of business from others and use what you learned to your advantage."

"Advantage," he said, digesting the word. "Yes. I told myself if they can do it, I can do it too. I don't think it's remarkable. I had to do it."

I nodded and turned off the tape recorder.

"My dad is so matter-of-fact," Stefanie said. "Guess you didn't get the fascinating interview you wanted?"

"Actually, your dad inspires me more now," I told her.

"I have no idea why," he said.

## FALLING

I got back to school after dark on Sunday and called York so we could chat while I transcribed the interview from my tape recorder.

"I remember this friend of yours," he said. "She's the one who chewed me out the night of my graduation party."

I slowed a little, taken aback by the memory. I had forgotten she spoke to him after I stormed off, and either she had forgotten, too, or hadn't felt the need to rehash it. "Oh? What'd she say?"

"To be honest, I don't remember much." I caught a whiff of embarrassment as he attempted to go into full detail, but he *had* been completely wasted, so I didn't rule out the possible memory problem. "The words that stick out to me the most are: *Don't you remember the reason why you invited her here in the first place? Why you know her at all?* And *Hasn't she been through enough?* Here's this girl standing on her toes to jab at my chest and chastise me in front of all my friends. Idiot me was seriously confused for longer than I care to admit. And then, as she's walking away, it all clicks."

I had stopped typing by this point. I loved Stefanie so much.

"Well," I said after a prolonged pause, "I think she's probably forgiven you, too." I stuck my pen back in my mouth and resumed my work.

"I wouldn't be surprised if she never wanted to see me again."

"I'll take you home with me one day," I slurred.

"You have no idea what I just heard."

I yanked the pen out of my mouth and jabbed it into my hair. "I meant so we could all hang out, maybe. You'll see she's way laid-back."

I felt a twinge of anxiety that verged on sadness when I thought about him hanging out with me and my friends, wondering why we never went to my house like we went to his. He'd give me all the time in the world to grieve over my father, but he would always wonder.

"But first, we have important work to get done," I said, my voice too bright. I typed at a frantic pace now, as if rocketed from a slingshot. "What's next on your list?"

"The time capsule."

"Right. What's that about?"

"It's a long story."

"I like stories."

I heard him shift around. "It's not particularly serious or deep. When I was a little kid, I had a best friend named Daniel. We played together every day, had sleepovers almost every weekend, went camping together, the whole bit. He liked to come to my house because he didn't live in the fanciest place, and it was just him and his mom. Not that any of that bothered me, but I guess it bothered him, so I went with it. One day when we were really bored, we got the bright idea that in years to come people would want to know how awesome we were. So we stole this old metal toolbox from his garage and put a bunch of stuff in it. It was decent timing, because he moved to Virginia Beach a year and a half later."

He paused, and the silence felt significant. I stopped my work again and looked up.

"Anyway," he continued, "I don't remember what we put in the box, and I kind of need to know."

I've heard time is cruel, but I disagree with that, too. Time is actually pretty conciliatory.

And why not? We plan our lives around the neat little measured units on our clocks and calendars. We're in a constant state of worship: praising time, cursing time—either way, it commands our attention. So why wouldn't time go along with our delusion of control, letting us believe it can be boxed into seconds, minutes, hours, days, weeks, months, and years?

"Does anyone live in the house now?" I asked.

"I drove by last year after I got out of the hospital. Only one car in the driveway."

"Ooh. Iffy. Do you remember where you buried the box?"

"I haven't the faintest recollection."

"How will you convince the new owners to let you dig around their backyard?"

"I'm not sure. I suppose that's where you come in."

"I think you're more persuasive than I am," I told him.

"Maybe you can help me figure out how to approach it, then."

"Sure." I paused a beat. "I think it's pretty cute you made a time capsule with your friend. I made one of those once, tried to bury it under the sand at my elementary school playground. A plastic pencil box. I put a note, a Canadian silver dollar my dad had given me, and my favorite book in it. Even then, I had these romantic ideals about how burying a piece of myself for someone else to dig up might immortalize me."

"I've never thought about it that way. The whole immortality part, I mean."

"And you don't have to start...I discovered my 'time capsule' the very next day. I think some kids kicked it up. They took the Canadian dollar."

"Aw."

"No one cared about my words, no one wondered about the book. That probably had to do with the fact it was a very popular book for my age group at the time. Still, it killed my ideas about immortality, I'll tell you that."

"I'm sorry."

"Such a kick in the ego, right? I chose the shiniest coin I had and I really liked it, and I think I wrote an insightful letter for my age, and even though the book—"

"I mean sorry it killed your ideas about immortality. Just because your note wasn't important to a bunch of snotty elementary school kids doesn't mean it wouldn't have been important to someone down the line. I'd read anything you wrote."

"You've never actually read my writing, have you?"

"I have not. Not intentionally, anyway, though I did technically read a newspaper article or two back in high school."

"Oh, yeah."

"But I could, though?" The shyness of the request, almost like he had asked for permission to read my diary, surprised me.

"Of course. I'll drum up a rough draft of this inspirational person article I'm writing for class and you can, um, take a look at it."

"If you write anything like you speak, I think I'll probably really like it."

"Oh, you're...you can be so nice." I shook my head. "Could you please tell my professor how great I am?"

"I'll tell anyone you want me to tell. I'll shout it from my rooftop."

"You promise? Tonight?"

"Getting the ladder now."

"Don't fall for me, please."

"Already have."

# *Nine*

## REPARATIONS

We left for Fleet on Tuesday afternoon. On the way there, we talked about how we would go about asking the new owners if we could, in essence, destroy their backyard.

"The idea is to be as straightforward as possible," I said. "If you beat around the bush, it'll make them suspicious. I know it seems like straightforward will overwhelm them, but really your request is pretty simple. You tell them about your medical history to evoke sympathy, and you immediately offer to clean up whatever mess we make."

"We?"

"I'll help you dig. I'd feel like a jerk if I sat around taking pictures while you sweated and grunted."

"How very gracious of you."

The small, plain, one-level ranch house sat on a small patch of land. A crooked Spanish oak tree with moss that hung to the ground like long gray hair on an old woman dominated the front yard.

York knocked on the screen in front of the door and waited. He shifted his weight back and forth, balancing on first the balls of his

96

feet, then his heels. This particular item on his bucket list made him more anxious than he let on, so I had to bite the inside of my cheek every time I wanted to pry.

A plump woman of average height with curly, strawberry blonde hair opened the door after about half a minute. "Hello," she said through the screen.

"Hi," said York.

"Hi," I echoed.

"How can I help you?" she asked.

"I apologize for showing up unannounced. My name is York. This is my friend, Olive."

"Nice to meet you." She opened the screen then, but stayed firmly inside her doorway.

"My best friend lived in this house about seven years ago," said York. "I used to spend a lot of time here with him. He moved away and—" He blinked a few times, then set his jaw. "A little over a year ago, I almost died. I came to the realization that I must still be here for a reason, so for the past few weeks I've been on a mission to tie up some loose ends before…you know…in case it happens again."

The woman's honey-colored eyes flickered back and forth between York and me. "Please come in." She pasted a belated smile on her lips as we slid by her.

Inside, the home reminded me a lot of my grandmother's house: two plush love seats upholstered in dark jacquard fabric on either side of the living room, family photos tacked onto nearly every inch of the walls, and numerous and varied brass knick-knacks. This woman couldn't have been older than forty-five, but everything about her home looked cozy and passed down.

I wondered how much of this place York remembered, whether it all flooded his brain or trickled in, whether he felt the way he thought he would about it all. His eyes scanned every inch of the room, but otherwise he wore that charm that made you want to give him whatever he wanted.

"I'm Agnes, by the way," said the woman as we sat down. "Would either of you like a drink?"

"I'm fine, thanks," I said.

"Me too," said York. "I don't want to put you out any more than I'm about to."

She blinked a few times before she disappeared around a corner. "Hey, Denny?" she called out. "Denny, we've got company."

We turned to one another. *Remember, dear, less is more*, my eyes said.

"My husband will be out in a minute," she said as she settled down across from us. "So. You two grew up in Fleet?"

"My house is actually about eight miles north of here," I told her.

"I'm a little farther out," York said vaguely.

"Well, you can't travel too far in any direction in Fleet," she said. "That's why we moved out here, Denny and I. We like it better this way."

York and I nodded. "So," York said, clearing his throat, "you moved in a while back?"

"Five years ago now. Long after your friend moved away, I suppose. I'm glad you have some nice memories of this place. We like it."

Her husband entered the room then. He was a thin man with kind eyes and more hair on his arms than on his head. "I'm Dennis Holt," he said, leaning down to shake first York's hand and then mine. "Nice to meet you two."

We told him our names and he sat down. "Did we offer you two a drink? We've got soda, bottled water, sweet tea, of course."

"Graciously declined, thank you," I said. It's practically a rule of the South to offer someone a drink when they enter your home, even if you don't know them from Adam, were not expecting them, and have no idea what they'll ask of you.

"What can we do for you?"

"Right," York said. "I—we—don't want to take up too much of your time. I told your wife that my best friend, Daniel, used to live here, and I used to spend a lot of time at this house. One day we decided to make a time capsule to...kind of seal a bond of friendship. Then he moved to Virginia, and we lost touch."

"That's too bad."

"And then fifteen months ago I suffered acute heart failure and needed a transplant. Olive's dad had recently passed away and his heart saved my life."

"Oh, how awful," blurted Agnes. "And…miraculous, I suppose."

"It was both awful and miraculous," he agreed. "I wrote up this bucket list while I was recovering. It's mostly a list of regrets, to be honest, and one of them involves finding the time capsule that we buried in Daniel's backyard. This backyard."

Dennis and Agnes eyed one another.

"So, what I'm asking is—if there's a way I could—" He appeared to be considering his words, like I told him to. "Mr. and Mrs. Holt, I would like to dig up your backyard."

Straightforward. Well. That was as straightforward as it got.

He smiled. I smiled too, although I'm positive it made me look like I was having some sort of stomach issue.

"You, um, need to search around for this time capsule?" asked Agnes.

"Yes ma'am. I don't remember where we buried it—I was ten, after all—so I'd need to hunt a bit."

"I'm not sure, son," said Dennis. "It's the time of year to seed my grass and—"

"Denny is very proud of his grass," said Agnes. Her tone suggested she couldn't have cared less about her lawn if it sprouted literal dollar bills. "He's gearing up for summer, you see, and —"

"This lawn got neglected for a long time," said her husband. "No one lived here, you know, and it needs a lot of babying. I need to nurse it back to health before I—"

"The seeds have had all winter to permeate," Agnes said, "but early spring is right around the corner—"

"Right around the corner," echoed Dennis. "And the lawn needs that second round of seed so it can grow lush and healthy."

"I'm offering my complete cooperation to help repair your lawn after I've messed it up," York said. "Tell me what to do, and I'll fix it."

"I'll help," I said. "My dad was nuts about our lawn, too. It's good you haven't seeded it already, you know, since if we got to stomping all around back there now, it'd hinder germination. At least after we dig a bit, the soil will be loose and in a perfect state to take in the seeds and whatnot. We can even dress the top with some good compost."

Everyone stared at me.

"That'll be...on us," I said.

"You two are serious about this mission of yours," said Mrs. Holt.

"Quite," said York.

"That's a yes from me, then." Mr. Holt looked betrayed, but she ignored him. "I think it's important this young man find his time capsule."

"I really appreciate this."

Mr. Holt sighed. "Do you at least have an idea of where it is?"

"I can think of maybe three places we might have buried it."

He seemed to weigh those odds and eyed his wife again. "You'll help seed, too?"

"We'll all help seed!" she said brightly. "When would you two like to come by?"

"Um. Saturday?"

"Perfect."

~ * ~

"What was that about?" he asked me on our way back to school.

"What?"

"Did your dad really teach you all that stuff?"

"He really did." I remembered all the late spring mornings I spent outside with him. "He always had me out there raking, showed me how to seed the grass a couple times. He's the only reason I have any sort of a green thumb. My mother, bless her, only keeps bamboo in the house because of its apparent inability to die." He laughed. "My dad took lawn care almost as seriously as Mr. Holt back there. Like, it's grass, guys."

"Well, you convinced them—another reason why I'm grateful to your dad. I don't think I would have gotten in the door without you."

"Don't sell yourself short." I eyed the bridge ahead that would take us over the Pasquotank River.

"You told me I would hear a long story about the time capsule," I said quietly, "but you didn't tell me a long story the other night."

He smiled. "Guess I wanted to spare you. All right. Wanna know the rest?"

"If you're comfortable."

"Daniel and I lost touch because I became a cool kid. He moved away, and I went to a new school, and puberty and hormones were wreaking havoc, as they tend to do, on our fragile, developing minds. All of a sudden, I was this popular boy from a well-to-do family, and I made a bunch of friends, different friends. He tried to keep in contact with me, but I forgot about him—on purpose or not, I couldn't tell you. All I know is at some point it became natural to forget my childhood entirely.

"I did think about him from time to time, mostly during junior and senior year, when I stayed out late at night with my friends or had to figure out how to make up bad grades in a class after I had slacked off. In the hospital, after I wrote the bucket list, I searched for him on Facebook. I had this idea that we'd reconnect, and maybe I could visit him, apologize, if he even cared."

I had asked, and now I couldn't stop him. We breezed through the stoplight on the drawbridge.

"Meningitis." He emphasized each syllable slowly in a voice hard and thick but resolute. "Junior year of high school. Old R.I.P.s plastered his Facebook page, now some sort of memorial page. Somehow I made it out alive and he didn't. What are the odds? Two guys grow up together and life whacks them both far before their time.

"I have a lot of regrets, Olive," he repeated. "I forgot my best friend, and now I can't even tell him I'm sorry. This is the least I can do for him now."

I nodded and sat back in my seat. "You know, a noble and earnest deed easily cancels out a bad one."

I heard the smile in his voice when he said, "This is why I need you."

## FALLING

In Photo Media class the next day, I turned in a roll of unprocessed black-and-white film I'd exposed the day before. I used the film from

York's and my day at the beach, and I let the memory of the mildly terrifying moments that started us on our bucket list journey envelop me.

He spent a lot of time at my dorm, and his presence drove Yancy and Morgan crazy, in the good way.

We would sit in my room—he in my computer chair and me cross-legged on my bed—and he would mostly talk. To be honest, I didn't always listen, just watched the way his lips curved around certain words and shaped certain syllables.

## PROSPECTS

Saturday rolled around and York picked me up again. At the house, Mrs. Holt offered us hot cocoa, and I accepted a small cup. You don't decline a beverage or food too many times in a Southern home. Her husband offered us his shovel, the reluctance as palpable as the snap in the February air around us.

I made York stay still for a picture with the Nikon, but he made a funny face. "This backyard is a little...longer than I remember," he said.

Certainly bigger than the front yard alluded to. The width of the yard spanned the house, but it stretched far back, fenced in on both sides and open at the end where a creek ran behind most of the houses on the street. On the other side of the creek, a small patch of woods separated the Holts' property from the next.

We started at the creek, since no one would really notice the damage back there. York dug several holes along the bank, then expanded a little further into the lawn.

"Don't overexert yourself," I told him. "Let me dig a few holes."

"You calling me weak, I Love?"

"You literally had one weak muscle in your entire body, and while it was the most important one, at least it wasn't irreplaceable."

He cut me a small smile. "Unfortunately."

I dug a few holes myself. It took more effort than I had expected it to. He took a couple of pictures of me, then he put my camera down and got behind me. He wrapped his arms around mine, placed a foot on the top of the shovel, and loaned me some elbow grease so I could jab deeper into the ground. His chest and stomach bumped my back a couple times, and I almost forgot why we were digging in the first place.

Two hours and fifteen small, deep holes later, we began to feel guilty. Every time we looked at the house, there stood Mr. Holt at the back door. Mrs. Holt came outside once to see if we were okay and told us not to mind her husband.

"I get it, though," York said. "We're pumping a dry well here. Might be best if I head back home and regroup, search my memory some more. Maybe I can figure it out and come back... next Saturday?"

"I think you should. You'll catch your death of cold out here. At any rate, I think Denny is about to have a stroke."

York and I made our way through the house and through the front door, shaking their hands as we departed.

"Don't worry," York said. "The next time we take a shovel to your yard, it'll be in the right spot." He patted Mr. Holt's shoulder and sauntered out the door, and you couldn't see the man's face for his eyes.

~ * ~

I got a B-plus on my article about Stefanie's dad. Professor Spaulding and I discussed it after class. She called it a unique story (read: "actually interesting") and a profound, fair report.

"You know and I know of Mr. Velez's staggering journey to success, but you didn't beat me over the head with that. You see? It gave the subject matter so much more depth."

"I think that had a lot to do with Mr. Velez himself," I admitted. "He's so frank."

"And you captured that. That's a skill. You let me make up my own mind about him, as he did for you."

"Thanks."

"You really are a good writer. You draw emotions from readers with your words, and not all people can do that. Now you've...focused your technique a bit." She winked at me.

I called York later on that day and told him the good news.

"Great job. I had no doubts."

"I think I'm finally getting the hang of this," I said. "Thank God, because I had zero backup plan for my future career."

"None whatsoever?"

"Didn't think I needed one."

"And you say you don't take risks."

## DIGGING

He went over the details of his childhood and his friendship with Daniel all week. Memory works in a curious way; one small recollection opens another, then another, until your mind is full, and all the warmth or the excitement or the anguish connected to those recollections follows suit.

I hadn't had a terrible childhood, just an unstable one. My family kept a lot of the bad things well-hidden from my sister and me—so well, in fact, that the few oddities I'd noticed about my mother did in fact just seem odd.

Both my parents had very good jobs. Both attended college—my mother in particular loved and excelled in school. She used to sit with me and practice my letters, crafted my childish scrawl into a particular loveliness. My parents listened patiently while I read them my short stories and really bad poems, and they let me take music lessons and dance classes simultaneously when I didn't know which one I loved more. I picked up a camera at age ten and didn't look back. My parents provided for each of my interests until they no longer could. When I had to drop my music lessons, it was as if a fresh bulb had replaced a dim one, illuminating every corner of our room, highlighting all the ugly.

York told me he used to drag Daniel around his backyard on geology expeditions. They would wade in the creek in Daniel's backyard in search of stones and amphibians, climb trees, and play in the ocean at Nags Head or wherever at the Outer Banks they so happened to visit on family outings.

"Danny liked to play video games," he told me. "A lot, all day long. I stayed inside a lot with him. He came outside a lot for me."

"Stefanie and I are total opposites in that way, too. We compromise."

"Exactly. Danny hated to sweat and get dirty and get mosquito bites. I loved all that stuff." He sat back. "That's what we had been doing outside that day, the day we decided to bury the box. I remember there was a bad ice storm that past winter, and this fat old tree had fallen in his backyard. Missed his house by inches. They got most of it sawed off and hauled away, but the bottom half still lay across the lawn, so we would climb on top of it and talk about nothing, come up with crazy ideas."

"Whose idea was it?"

"I can't remember. Probably mine. I know he's the one who got the tool box and the shovel. He's the one who decided what we should put in it."

"A kid walking around with a shovel probably looks pretty ominous to a parent."

"Oh yeah, for sure. That's why he snuck it outside. We had to be really quiet about it, and we had to pick a spot where his mom couldn't see us by glancing outside the glass door in back."

"His mom never mentioned a fresh mound of dirt...?" I prompted.

"No," he said, his tone turning pensive. "And she noticed everything."

"We checked the back of the yard. And the middle. But it wouldn't have been in the middle."

He bolted upright. "We went to the side, the right side. I forgot about it the other day because there used to be this crabapple tree by that spot. We ducked around the tree, he covered me, and we buried it vertically against the fence between his house and the neighbors'."

"Where? Close to the house? By the creek?"

"I want to say closer to the house. There was a blind spot and—" His eyes widened.

"Tell me where you want me to stand when we get there."

~ * ~

Our new development thrilled Mr. Holt. It meant fewer random holes.

York walked outside and to the right while I stood at the open glass door. "Come closer," I instructed. "I can still see you."

He inched along the fence. "Here?"

"Little closer."

When he moved out of sight, I said, "Start digging!"

Mrs. Holt wished me luck again as I slid open the glass all the way to step outside. I turned to her. "York said there used to be a crabapple tree there where he's at. Did you have one when you moved in?"

"Sure did. Such a pretty tree. We tried hard to keep it alive—it added such color to the yard. We told you no one bothered to take care of this property for a long time. The tree became overrun with pests and was on its way out when we bought the house."

"That's a shame."

"It is. I have so many landscaping ideas. Denny can have the grass. He puts all our spare money into it, and I...I'd just like a flower or two. A pretty tree." She patted my back. "Go on, dig. I'm sure you'll find the box in no time, now."

Still, we dug for a while. I started to wonder if we were off by a hair or two.

"I don't remember how deep into the ground we would have buried it," York said on a grunt. "With all the time and energy we had, we could have jammed it six feet under."

After five minutes, I took over. "How excited do you think he would have been to see this box again?"

"Ecstatic. The moment we stuck that box in the hole felt significant. I've had a hard time remembering much else, but I remember that. That was probably the whole point."

I stopped for a second. "You think it's like what you told me about my dad back last year? That somehow he knew all along? I mean, you said it yourself: what are the odds that both of you would meet death so young?"

"It messes with my head to think someone could inherently know all along that they're going to die young."

He took over again, and I wandered off for a second to get some shots of the holes we dug the weekend before.

"Wait," he said. He jabbed the tip of the shovel right in the center of the long hole, about three feet into the ground and maybe a foot out from the fence.

"You find it?"

He let the shovel drop and scraped around a little before dropping to his knees and moving away dirt with his hands. I got down to help him, my heart pounding when we began to tug on the red metal box.

"This is it," he said on a deep sigh. "God, finally."

He sat Indian-style on the cold ground for a moment, tapping it with his fingers, the underneaths of his nails black with dirt. I sat on my knees in front of him and let him remember. Then we took it inside, where, upon seeing it, Mr. and Mrs. Holt expressed relief that their yard hadn't been attacked for naught.

Old duct tape had the box practically mummified. We tried to pry it off, then resorted to a box cutter. The four of us peered inside.

We found a picture of two grinning, snaggle-toothed boys—one with dark, curly hair, and one with straight, sandy hair—taken at King's Dominion; a set of ticket stubs to a kids' movie (the boys had makeshift laminated them in clear packing tape, but the ink had faded almost beyond recognition); a blue and gold yo-yo; a folded note; a gold-plated compass, badly tarnished; and a set of leather bracelets, one with the purple Ninja Turtle on it, the other with the red one.

"I remember this trip," said York as he studied the picture. He touched the compass, then carefully he unfolded the note. "I can still read it!"

*"Dear us in the future, or whoever finds this box,*

*We are writing this note to* ~~comemeraite~~ *honor our awesome friendship. This is our very special time capsule where we have hidden all of our favorite things.*

*If it is a hundred years in the future and you're reading this, this is the way the world is right now: The U.S. is in a war. The best movie ever is called* Pups in Space. *And computers run the world. Maybe robots are in charge there in the future days. Maybe not.*

*The compass is York's and the yo-yo is Danny's, his favorite one. Please understand that they are important. We are the boys in the picture. York is on the right, Danny is on the left. We are best friends and we always will be.*

*Sincerely,*
*Daniel Joseph Strait and York Russell Lively, aged 10 & 10 and three-quarters."*

I snorted. "Russell."

"The imagination you two had," said Agnes.

"Why would we bury my compass?" York asked himself, fishing out the yo-yo. "I remember this, too. It glowed in the dark and lit up when you yo-ed it."

He wrapped it around his finger, balled it in his fist, and flicked his wrist. It flashed bright red and blue like the lights atop a police car as it skirted the ground and drew back up into his hand.

"Shut the hell up," he exclaimed.

"The damned thing still works," Mr. Holt echoed the sentiment, slapping a hand on York's shoulder.

York's face shone with wonder and gratitude. "Mr. and Mrs. Holt, you have no idea what this means to me. It may seem like a dumb box of junk—it may *be* a dumb box of junk—but it means so much more than you'll ever know."

"It was no problem," said Mr. Holt. "Obviously you miss your friend a lot. I hope you'll call him to let him know you found this. If you don't have his number, find it. Life is short, son." He dropped his arm. "I'm sure you have some idea of that now."

## QUANTUM LEAP

The outdoor deck behind York's mansion was ridiculous. It was a wood and brick area that covered about the same square footage as my freaking house. A pergola nearly taken over by white, sweet-smelling winter jasmine loomed overhead. A brick oven, a grill, and a brick fireplace sat on three of the four sides. Why did the Livelys ever even go inside?

We hung out for a couple hours back there, perched atop the cushy furniture with hot teas in hand, and then we migrated to his bedroom when the logs in the fireplace started to burn low. Mrs. Lively watched us the whole time, not only a warm presence, but ever-present. I could feel her eyes on me; more specifically, I could feel her eyes on my eyes on her son.

Part of it stemmed from his tendencies, and her instincts as a mom, I guess. But she mostly worried about his health, the apparent instability of it. What had gone so wrong so fast, and what would go wrong again?

My dad had a strong, healthy heart, but I wondered if Mrs. Lively worried it would fail, too. If it failed, I failed. She wouldn't mean to feel that way, but she would. I knew, because I would, too.

"Will you try to track down Daniel's mom?" I asked when York and I settled down on his bedroom floor.

"I think so. I have to figure out a way to do it so it's not too much for her all at once. She did lose her kid, after all."

"Strange how a bunch of random old toys and pictures could bring out so much emotion," I mused.

"Maybe we should bury a time capsule."

"What would we put in it?"

"I have no idea. You?"

"Nope. Maybe I...I'd like to know a bit more about York Lively before I bury myself with him."

"Fair enough. What do you want to know?" he asked as he sat against the bed.

"Whatever you want to tell me," I said, settling between his legs with my back to his chest. "There's got to be more to you than popularity and heart failure."

"Ha. Let's see: I'm a Gemini—"

I rolled my eyes, but I smiled.

"My favorite food is peanut butter," he continued. "And bacon. My biggest irrational fear is needles, which is why I want to get a tattoo."

"That was unexpected."

"I'm doing all the things I ever stopped myself doing because there's never been a good enough reason not to do them." His shoulders trembled.

"You don't actually see the tattoo needle, it's so small," I said. "It's just this buzzy pen-shaped tool, I think."

"Size is definitely an issue, but it's more about the pain it causes. One prick to draw blood is enough to make me cry out like a pansy. Thousands of pricks? Thank you, no. I went through enough of that when I was in the hospital, but at least then I was drugged up."

"I'll bet it's not that bad. I'll bet it's like acupuncture."

"I'll get through it somehow. That's why it's last on the list—I need to gear up. Anyway, I'm sweating already for thinking about it, so let's move on."

"All right. What else?"

"What else. I can juggle."

"*Really?*"

"It's funny the stuff you teach yourself when you're a bored only child in a big house."

"I demand you show me immediately."

I watched him toss around four hacky sack balls with little to no effort. He kept them suspended for as long as I cared to watch, so long that after some time, I admitted I was waiting for him to mess up and drop one. He let them fall, and they scattered around us.

I settled back in my spot against him. "More, please. I'm enjoying this."

"Well," he said. "I told you before I have a variety of issues with food. Full on food allergens are as follows: tree nuts, citrus, cinnamon, shellfish. Sensitivities: cocoa—of course—corn, milk, marshmallows."

"Marshmallows?" I practically screamed at him.

"Gelatin, really. It gives me hives. So many foods give me hives. Anyway, I've only ever had two marshmallows my entire life."

"So you've never had a s'more?"

"All that deliciousness I can't have sandwiched together and melting in my mouth," he lamented. "No, I've never had one." He buried his nose in my hair. "Um. That's all I can think of right now."

"It's a start," I said. I ran my palms over my knees and sank into his body as he repositioned himself against the bed.

"Now tell me about you, I Love."

"Me… I'm an Aries, which means I'm older than you, which is awesome." I felt his body hum with amusement. "Uh. Biggest irrational fear? Rollercoasters. I hate everything about them."

He didn't say he would ever try to persuade me to ride one, even though he probably would one day.

This was hard. I'd made my life exceedingly stark, all about my writing and my photo portfolio. Talking to him, I felt like I would burst. I wanted to tell him everything I'd forgotten about myself.

"I'm a pretty good baker," I said. "Before photography happened, I wanted to be a pastry chef. Also, I played the viola for five years."

"Really?"

"Started in first grade. I got pretty good at it, too. And I love food, new foods, contrary to what you might think after Paco's Fish Tacos. I'm with you on the bacon train, but chicken-and-gnocchi soup is my number one favorite dish. Uh. I like to pretend I can just hop in a car and drive to a new place, but actually I rely on my GPS when I go anywhere because I have the natural directional sense of an inanimate object."

He laughed. I swallowed. He accepted my every quirk, my cynical and wary nature, when he was this wide open field with no trees or clouds to cast shade. He wanted to be around me, still, and wanted to know more about me. Messy, broken me.

"My mother is an alcoholic," I said slowly. "A serious, career alcoholic—best in the business."

I chuckled nervously at my own sad joke. I felt him lift his head to listen.

"She has been an alcoholic for almost my entire life. She has been fired from four jobs, one of which let her go after twenty years. We almost lost our house twice because, for a long time, my dad was the only one able, or willing, to work; for almost a decade, up until the day he died, he worked multiple jobs to pay all the bills. My mother has stolen money from me and my sister. Her license has been suspended twice. She's been to rehab three times. She's been to the hospital three times, all for different alcohol-related injuries."

As if a black hole had swallowed up all the noise in the room, a sudden and enormous silence took over. He didn't speak for a long time.

Then he let out a huge breath I hadn't known he was holding. "Oh."

"Yeah."

I felt his head drop back again, but I didn't turn around, too mortified to look at him. "The dick you met at my graduation party becomes a bigger dick every time we talk about him," he said.

"He belongs in the past with the graduation party."

"Yeah, but—this thing with your mom, it's—"

"Pretty messed up. I know. I don't tell many people."

"You weren't going to tell me." He hadn't arranged his quiet words like a question, but they held all the weight of one.

"I...didn't think you'd stick around if you knew. It's not a normal home situation. It's complicated."

I let the silence hang there, wallowed in it. It's what I'd been most afraid of all along.

"You've lived in that negative environment for a long time," he said. "How do you *not* drink? What do you do?"

"No one has ever asked me that." I took a deep breath. "Probably...I guess I like to get away from it all whenever I can, in any way I can. I take pictures, obviously; getting lost behind the camera lens, imagining myself detached from the scene or the moment, it's like I'm in another room watching a surveillance camera. And I read, always a completely different book than the one I read before. And I daydream about all the places I'd like to be that are not...here." I tightened my grip around my knee.

"Like where?"

"Hmm. England. Kenya. Maine. China. California." I stopped, blissful at the thought. "California. Yeah, the west coast is pretty much the complete opposite of here."

His hand slid over mine on my knee, warm and smooth and completely enveloping. I stilled but let him leave it there. His fingers were wide and sturdy. Secure.

"I never learned how to process the negativity in my life," he said. "Maybe I need a new way to cope with all of my stuff, my dad, my health. Maybe you're my new way."

We met each other's eyes shyly. His mouth turned into a crooked smile, a question.

I smiled back.

# *Ten*

**FLUX**

We decided to wait until mid-March to tackle the stump at Whittmire Gardens, the next item on York's bucket list. We didn't very well want to climb a huge tree while dressed in multiple layers, so we chose a day we would only need jackets and regular shoes to protect us against the elements.

In the meanwhile, the resources we were using to keep the bills paid had begun to run dry. At the start of the month, we traipsed to the Salvation Army to request financial assistance. The government allotted Mom food stamps shortly after Dad died, which kept food in our 'fridge and pantry.

I didn't have too much pride to ask for financial assistance—I had to think about Selma—but every visit to York's house was a fresh smack of reality. He had said his family was struggling to make ends meet, but I think they defined "struggle" a little differently than we did. I envied the fact his parents had a backup, that, if all else failed, they'd at least be able to get by. We didn't have a backup. If we missed a couple of payments, we'd be out on the street. No house. There was struggling, and then there was drowning.

My mom's other siblings never offered help because they weren't there to be asked. Five weeks after Dad died, I stopped hearing from them, and I hadn't tried to make contact in a long time. Each one of them called Mom once a month, eight conversations that always ended at or around the two-minute mark like a timed test.

I managed to plow through every task that came up as mechanically as I could. At school I aced another journalism assignment, a short article about a splashy, flashy topic of interest from around the university. I decided to write about the Evangelistic preachers who often set up shop in the middle of campus and rattled off The Word for hours on end. These guys knew how to rile people up, and students always crowded around them, which meant I got plenty of opinions for my piece.

My writing delighted Professor Spaulding this semester. She asked if she could submit my preachers article to the student newspaper, and I even threw in some photos from the day's spectacle.

During all the highs and lows of this period, York and Lively seemed to punctuate the start and the end of every day. The absence of so many people I'd come to believe I could rely on made his presence all the more larger-than-life.

His lists. His determination. His maddening optimism. I didn't want any of it to end.

I knew all good things had to, but I chose not to think about that.


## SWELLS


Whittmire Gardens was located in a town called Edenton, a forty-minute drive from Fleet. York's seventh-grade class had once taken a field trip there to study the town's history. Basically this guy, Jonathan Whittmire, an affluent personality in Edenton at the turn of the century, developed the garden for his wife, Eleanor, and the town has maintained it since then.

"A couple people in my group dared one another to climb this massive stump," he told me that morning as I finished packing my bag.

"I was the only one who stayed on the ground. It intimidated me—not the height, or the dare, but the expectation. I had really started to care what people thought about me. I was too cool to climb it. I didn't take dares. They were being dumb. All the excuses I could come up with. My friends bought it, but I always knew I had chickened out."

When we settled into his car, I noticed a blanket and a mysterious Tupperware in the back seat.

"Might as well make a date of it," he said.

"Leave it to you to mix business with pleasure," I said.

"Dual intentions."

~ * ~

A long driveway connected the main road to the center of the park surrounding the garden. We paid five dollars for admission and then drove down another semi-long road before parking in a lot.

It did so happen to be a nice day: a clear, cool March afternoon, the sun shining, lots of people out. However, York took in the weather with passive aggressive amazement that put him as a true North Carolinian.

"This state is trying to woo me today," he said. His hand brushed mine in question before I let him take it as we strolled the outskirts of the garden. "I guess winter and summer have quelled their pissing contest for a minute to give spring its time to shine?"

"See, you blame the extreme seasons. I blame spring. I think spring is an attention whore. I think she doesn't know what she wants to be, so she takes from winter and summer at her will. I think spring has bipolar disorder."

"I Love," he complained.

"Oh my, was that not PC? A journalist can't afford to make mistakes like that. Should I have said multiple personality disorder? Doesn't seem as accurate a diagnosis—"

"I think you have a personal problem with spring."

"*Arg,* why do men always assume a woman's hostility is personal?"

"Because...it always is?"

"You want to know my real problem? My mindset is too black-and-white. Probably good for journalism, because I rarely let any gray feelings come between me and The Facts, but it limits me. I think life has to be one way or another. Pick one. Choose a side. Either you're spring, or you're one of the other seasons."

"That is problematic," he agreed. "There are more waves than there is dry land, after all."

"Cryptic. All right, you baited me—what exactly is that supposed to mean?"

"The earth is majority water, right? I don't know the numbers off the top of my head, so I'll guess seventy percent because the body is also seventy percent water, and it will be beneficial to my metaphor. So, since water covers most of the earth's surface, and water's waves are ceaseless, it's safe to assume that there are more waves than there are deserts or mountains or plains or valleys."

"I'm with you."

"You ever been stuck inside a wave?" he asked.

"Nope. Always stayed close to the shore."

"Smart. I've been stuck in a wave. For however long it takes, you don't have any control over your own body. It's hazy and gray and confusing, and you try to think clearly and make a decision that will lead you in the right direction, but the water is too strong. And you're subject to its pattern because it doesn't stop for you, no matter how much you want it to. Waves are a big force on this earth, Olive, and everyone will get caught in one at some point."

He studied the park for a spell. I let him think, mostly because his face became this ethereal thing when he was thinking.

"North Carolina is almost the same distance away from the technical North and the Deep South," he continued. "It has mountains on one side and the Atlantic on the other. Its position begs for spring to have an identity crisis. For weeks, winter and summer fight to be on top, like *animals*, until finally summer just kind of wins and takes its position. Like it earned it, instead of being born into it. Entitled bastard. And then there's poor spring, caught up in the wave."

"Did you say all that to make me feel sorry for spring?"

"Did it work?"

"I think I just learned a lot more about you than I did about earth science."

We ducked down a long path that led into a heavily wooded area marked by a sign that read: *Est. April 1921 by J. D. Whittmire, for Eleanor Stevens Whittmire.* The actual garden area sat twenty-five feet beyond the entrance to the woods, off the main path flanked with freshly planted coral- and lemon-colored tulips that tried so hard to come alive despite our current season's identity crisis.

Little placards indicating the plants and to what plant families they belonged studded the ground all around our feet. Larger placards warned us to keep our hands to ourselves.

The area boasted a few structures and sculptures with signs letting us know which organizations and school art programs had donated them over the years: There sat on a small hill a tall stack of cinder block-sized boulders arranged at impossible angles atop one another. A deeper trek into the garden revealed a beautiful gemstone mural of a sunflower nestled in a sea of turquoise and royal blue. A jewel-encrusted wrought iron bench sat in front of a miniature pond speckled with lily pads.

The pond sat at the end of a thin creek that trickled through a small region of the garden and underneath a square, red-roofed gazebo made of dark wood. The sounds of birds wrapped themselves around us.

I took out the Nikon—I always needed pictures for class—but I mostly admired the place. York and I didn't say much. Still didn't need to do that.

We found No Particular Direction and stuck with it for a long while. I took some shots without giving my lens the gift of an objective. The shutter sound bounced off the trees like the sunlight streaming through them. I took another photo, and another, hoping to go through them later and light upon some magic among the mayhem. I focused on my shutter's sound and nature's silent reply.

"Man," I heard York say. "Why is all this stuff bigger than I remember?"

My eyes settled on a bulky tree stump, lofty at nearly twenty feet tall by my guess. "This stump looked like this five years ago?"

"Yep. Who would do that? Chop it down?"

"Eh, don't be so quick to blame the person who did it. Maybe it assaulted him in some way: a big branch fell from the tree and struck the man's dear wife as they strolled this path hand-in-hand."

"On their anniversary after having just spent the evening caressing one another's faces and declaring their undying love for one another..." He closed his eyes and started to snore.

"Or maybe lightning struck the tree and fried the top portion to a blackened crisp."

"Damn. Baroque to brusque in seconds. You are black and white."

"I am as winter is to summer."

Parched bark the gray hue of a cadaver covered the stump, and stubs of limbs reached up and out, frozen in time, still desiring to grow leaves and have them turn colors and push them out like baby birds from a nest. Vines draped themselves across the stubs like scarves and latched onto the trunk and wound their way down to the garden floor. The trunk's roots gripped the ground like talons. It would have taken maybe five of me to loop around the bottom with outstretched arms.

"I like this stump," I said.

"Why?" It wasn't a question of incredulity.

"I don't really know," I admitted. "I can see its potential, what it could have been before someone chopped it down like that." I shot him a sideways glance. "And other such hipster bullshit reasons."

"I like the idea of it having a story."

"There's a lot it wants to say."

We watched it like we expected it to start talking. A small, chubby chickadee landed on one of its stumpy branches, lingered for a moment, twitched about, and then flew away. I took a few shots, moving around the circumference in a crescent shape to get more than one angle.

"You know what?" he said. "It's awesome that someone conquered this tree. It's so huge, but someone a fraction of its size took it down anyway."

"Kind of amazing."

"Kind of? You have a lofty view of 'amazing'." He walked over to the tree and stared up. His square shoulders rose and fell again. "Can I have your bag?"

"Sure." He stuffed the blanket and Tupperware inside it, then slung it across his body. He placed a foot on the base, gripped a root that ran down one side and pulled with all his body weight, didn't move far, gripped another.

"Does it seem easy?" I asked.

"Fairly so. Still, it's a long way up." He waggled his eyebrows at me over his shoulder. "Wish me luck."

"Um. Luck?"

He began to weave his way up the tree at a slow and deliberate pace. I watched the muscles in his arms and back contract as he made a conscious effort to keep himself steady. About halfway up, I heard his breaths begin to labor.

"Sounds like you're having a bit of trouble there. You scared?"

"Your words give me wings."

"I don't mean you can't still do it, but maybe stop for a second, take a moment, breathe. Actually, maybe you don't want to stop, not until you get to a really sturdy branch. Keep moving until then. But try to breathe."

"Olive, I love your voice, really. It's probably one of my favorite sounds. But right now, it's messing me up a little."

"Sorry," I said. "Sorry, I talked again." My head buzzed. He kept doing that, hitting me with these random revelations of feelings he had about me.

I gripped my camera as hard as I felt he should grip the holds on the trunk, kind of the way my dad would press his foot to the floor on an invisible brake pedal whenever I drove us anywhere. You wish, in moments like that, that instantaneous transference of strength or logic or skill were possible.

And so this climbing, which I tried desperately to supply with my own feet-firmly-on-the-ground assurance, went on for about two more minutes. I held my breath the whole time so I wouldn't take up one portion of the oxygen around us. I didn't want to mess with the flow of the atmosphere and send him crashing to the ground.

He stopped at the top, arms slung over the edge, then hoisted himself the rest of the way over. I exhaled.

"What's the view like up there?"

"I don't want to see it until you're up here too," he said on a wheeze.

"Right."

"I know you can do it. If I can, you definitely can."

I sighed and tested my weight against the same root he had first used to hoist himself upward. I'd observed the footholds he used and tried to follow the same path.

*Don't think about how far up you are*, I thought. *Don't think about the huge open space behind your back.* I really, really didn't like heights, one of the reasons rollercoasters bothered me so badly.

York lay on his stomach and held out his hand for me once I neared the top. He helped me drag myself over the side, then we got up together.

"Oh wow," I said. The diameter of the top of the stump itself exceeded York's height, maybe eight feet from one end to the other. Up here the wind felt stronger, the sun closer, and I could see the garden over a greater range.

York was hunched over, his hands on his knees, and concentrating very hard on his feet.

"Are you sure you're all right?" I asked. Mild panic blossomed in my gut.

"Mere, pure exhilaration," he said. He took a deep breath. "My chest...my heart is beating kind of fast. I need a second to..."

I couldn't take my eyes off him until his breaths became normal again. My dad's heart, beating too fast. I shot a quick prayer up for it not to fail him, asked Dad to give it a flick for that extra *oomf* it undoubtedly had once worked with to run his tall, strong body.

York squeezed his eyes shut and clenched his fists as if he were angry. Then he righted himself and observed the scene around us.

All the faces of all the people on the planet combined didn't equal how alive his face looked. I took a few steps back and snapped a picture of him with my Polaroid.

"*That's* amazing," I said.

I pointed the camera at our feet, both clad in hiking boots, touching the edge of the stump. His boots were well-made, holding up well despite their obvious age, and sported some brand name I'd never heard of. Meanwhile, the fabric on the toes of my obvious knock-offs had rubbed clean off, and the laces were ragged on the ends.

He laid out the blanket and we sat cross-legged in the center. He dropped his crumpled list between us and smoothed it out a little before he crossed out goal number four. He cocked one eyebrow at me, expression triumphant.

And I felt it, too, the simple glory of accomplishment. In the weeks after I told him about my mom, I came to realize he hadn't complicated my situation at all. He'd simplified it. He simplified every emotion I had, made each one clearer.

I leaned over and smashed my lips against his. Soft and warm, his mouth easily giving way to mine, he kissed like he was always prepared for it, like it came as second nature.

He let himself fall backward, and I landed on top of him. At some point I forgot to feel self-conscious and remembered how it felt to kiss someone I really wanted to kiss. He moved my hair back so it didn't hang around our faces. He didn't push, didn't touch me anywhere else, just traced his fingertips along the shells of my ears and nape of my neck.

I lifted my head and examined him. His lips had swelled a bit and his eyes had practically glazed over. And I wanted to kiss him again and again.

"My God," he whispered. "You are so beautiful."

I laughed, which startled the dazed look off his face. "What?" he asked.

"This is crazy."

"What's crazy?" Now he was smiling.

"This." I toyed with a couple dark curls on his forehead. "If someone sat me down in Mr. Morgan's bio class last year and told me you—York Lively—would one day call me—Olive Grant—beautiful, and right after giving me the best kiss of my whole life, I'd have driven that person to the nearest psych ward myself."

He laughed too. "You say things like this and I get the feeling you have no idea the way I saw you in school."

"You saw me?" I asked, smiling to honey the sourness in my tone.

"All the time. In the halls, your name on the newspaper. And we had classes together, you know. I couldn't not notice you." He ran his fingers through my hair. "And I used to think, 'This girl is really enigmatic and serious. And she's got a good head on her shoulders. And she probably knows exactly where she's going in life. She would never talk to me.'"

"And I thought the same thing about you," I said. "The talking bit."

"But now we have talked."

"We've done a little more than talk."

"Lucky, lucky me."

"*Shhhh.*"

His expression became defiant. "You, Olive...wait, what's your middle name?"

"Janelle."

"You, Olive Janelle Grant, are a beautiful, beautiful girl, and I am so lucky I get the chance to kiss you."

"And you, York Russell Lively, are..." I sighed. "You are...really something incredible."

Like any noble and good boy, he offered me the contents of the Tupperware he'd brought along. Inside sat two pieces of his grandmother's strawberry-rhubarb pie for us to enjoy, messily cut and slapped into the container, by him of course. I asked where his grandma had bought such sweet strawberries this time of year, whereupon he revealed she, like all grandmas, was a mystical connoisseur of desserts.

After we finished, I lay back on the blanket, and he lay on his elbow beside me. The sun streamed down through the trees and hit the back of his head so the shadows half-covered his face. We kissed again, the tart flavor of strawberry mingling between our mouths.

"Can we live up here? You and I?" I asked.

"I'm down for that."

"I'm not kidding."

"We have to eat, Olive. And finish college. And poop."

I grimaced. "Reality. Why does it have to exist?"

"'Those who choose not to live in the real world may journey wherever they like, but each one of us will end up inside solid ground.'"

"Nice. You come up with that yourself?"

"Actually, I got it from *An Introduction to Rationality*."

"You really took in what you read. You follow through on your promises, huh?"

"I like to think it's one of the things you love about me."

I touched his cheek. "I could fill all the pages in *The Infantry Hero* with things I love about you."

*Eleven*

## CHASING THE SUN

York first mentioned the trip in early April. He called me one day between classes and asked what I was doing later on. Since Morgan, Yancy, and I rarely hung out—as they were *always* out, and I just could not keep up—I had made a point to join them for dinner at the dining hall.

"Want me to meet you at your house?" I asked.

"Nah, I'll hang around campus until you call. I should probably study at the library." He had a pretty big chemistry exam in a week.

The bright dining hall teemed with students. At this point in the year, pretty much everyone, myself included, came out in public in pajama bottoms and t-shirts, no cares given. Morgan and Yancy, however, dressed up wherever they went.

"How are you and your friend?" Morgan asked after we sat down in a booth against a wall of windows overlooking a red brick bridge.

"We're great."

"How great is 'great'?" Yancy asked.

"Really great?"

"Gah, you always downplay it!" she pouted. "He's so hot, I mean. If you don't mind the compliment."

"I don't mind."

"Is he a good kisser?" Morgan asked in a dreamy twang.

"He is an unbelievable kisser," I said and smiled into my salad. I hadn't thought I'd ever be able to answer that question before three weeks ago. Now, I could think of little else.

When I noticed my roommates watching me expectantly, I added, "He doesn't use too much tongue. Um. His lips are nice." Morgan bubbled over with giggles.

"Does he have a great body?" Yancy asked.

"I don't know. Probably."

The girls eyed one another.

"You guys haven't had sex yet?" Morgan finally asked.

I felt a flame of embarrassment burn in my gut and rise into my chest, ignited both by the blunt question and the millisecond it forced me to actually consider sex with York.

"No," I eventually choked out.

Yancy picked up her breadstick and wielded it absentmindedly in her fist like a bat. "What? Girl, you've got mad will power, I must say."

"Thank you?"

"You'll let us know when it happens," Morgan said. "Won't you?

Some people meet their best friend in high school or younger, as I had, and because of the years of friendship, they can't see themselves without that person. Some people make their lifelong friends in college, because, by that age, they're wise enough to muddle through the shallow acquaintanceships youth can often produce and recognize a true-blue individual. The older you are, the better you know yourself.

I'd reached the point where I knew myself pretty well and, though I liked my roommates, we'd say goodbye to one another once May came around, promise to keep in touch, offer a few lukewarm greetings to one another over Facebook for the next six months or so, and spend the rest of our lives as an indistinct thumbnail picture in one another's "Friends" lists. The only people I'd talk to about my sex life would be enduring friends.

"You ladies will not be left in the dark," I lied.

~ * ~

York and I settled into my dorm room around 8:30. We laid on my bed and huddled close, because thank God for twin beds.

"I'm afraid I've started thinking about how to execute another goal that is a little further down the list," he told me, "which is bad, because I get pretty attention-deficit when I get ahead of myself."

He pulled out his list and held it above our faces.

"There," he said, *thwack*ing the paper with his index finger, "Number Six: Chase the Sun. What do you think that means?"

"Knowing you, it's probably something deeply personal and sure to have an enlightening result."

"Not deep, definitely personal, don't know if the result will be enlightening, but it's sure to bring us some perspective."

I settled deeper into my cozy little space between his body and the wall. "I assume you want to sunbathe all day. Or travel to outer space. One would be lost on me, since I'm quite tan enough, thank you. The other would be a little difficult to pull off, but I don't know all the connections you have."

"You're not taking me very seriously anymore, are you?"

"I am, actually. Vitamin D is perfect for lowering stress levels and stripping away depression. It's science."

"It's totally science. I'm in awe of you."

"I know some stuff. Anyway, outer space might have been far-fetched, but since you're so science-minded I thought you might have figured out a way to interpret it."

"I've spent time pondering the universe on a literal and figurative level. While space does fascinate me, it also makes me crazy. I can't think about the hugeness and all those undiscovered dimensions... that's for a different type of mind. I'm not that ambitious."

"Says the guy who for the past year has been on a constant quest for the meaning of his own life."

"See, that's an individual and subjective journey. I've simply happened to drag you along with me."

"You're not dragging very much anymore," I admitted. "I rather like chasing you around."

"You might change your mind after this one. My original idea for this goal: The North Pole."

I pursed my lips. "Okay, I may have been a bit too liberal with my encouragement when I said you could do *anything—*"

"Summertime around the Arctic Circle," he clarified. "You know, the time of year when the sun never really leaves the sky, just rises, dips down, rises again? I wanted to take a trip up there, because it's beautiful anyway, and because I wanted to follow the sun around all night. What's more amazing than a midnight sun?"

I thought about it, imagined all the photographic techniques I could use: a panoramic view, a multi-frame shot, a picture of York as he ran alongside every phase of the sun as it skimmed the horizon.

"Where do you come up with this stuff?" I asked.

"Apparently, on my deathbed," he said proudly. "However, I chose the Arctic Circle when I thought I'd work on this bucket list much, much later in life, if at all. For an eighteen-year-old with hardly any travel experience, no knowledge of the climate that far north, and a part-time job, a trip to the Arctic isn't likely."

"Only slightly more likely than space travel."

"Correct. But then you gave me an idea. A way to salvage this goal."

"Me?"

"You. The sun rises in the East and sets in the West. Us East coast folk have seen plenty of sunrises over the magnificent Atlantic Ocean. Am I right?"

"Sure."

"But when have we ever had the pleasure of watching the sun set over the Pacific? Have you?"

"Not once."

He took out his phone and began to mess around on the Internet. "So I figured we could follow the sun across the country. It's actually pretty easy to do, and even with all the stops most of those flights require, we could make it over in eleven hours or less."

"Wait. What?" I sat up a little. "Are you saying we should fly out West to watch the sun set?"

"We'll wake up ridiculously early one day.—I'm talking at the asscrack of dawn, here—watch the sun rise at the beach, then hop the next flight. Half a day, bam, we've chased the sun down."

I stared at him, my stomach clenched with excitement and nervousness.

"You said you've daydreamed about California," he reminded me. "So, go. Let's go."

"It's…an incredible idea. Still quite ambitious, of course, but who would you be if you didn't take risks?"

"But?"

"First of all, a trip like that will cost money I don't have."

He feigned offense. "You obviously don't have to worry about that. This is my bucket list, and you're along for the ride. I'll help you with whatever you need."

"I couldn't ask you to do that."

"Then don't." He grinned.

"What about your mom? I've seen the way she looks at me. I know she worries about you."

"You'd worry too if I was your kid. She likes you, I swear. My dad does, too. They know how big of a deal this list is to both of us. Their approval is a non-issue."

"Okay, the even bigger concern: my family. My uncle won't want me gone across the country for any extended length of time when my mom basically needs constant surveillance. Plus, they'll insist on meeting you first, and I'm pretty sure my uncle's Dad Instincts will go haywire if I say I want to go away somewhere with a boy."

I saw the wheels turning 'round in that brain of his. "Well, I planned to go in the summer anyway, a couple of months from now. By then we'll have a little more time under our belts."

"Then I guess you're meeting my family soon," I demurred.

"Don't sound so thrilled."

"I don't mean it like that. This is aimed toward them—really, my mom. I don't have the best memories of her interacting with people I bring around."

"Does it help you to know I'm ecstatic to meet her?"

"What on earth for?"

"Because it'll automatically bump me past 'special friend' and into a whole different category. Plus, look at how great you turned out. Your family must be great."

"Now *you're* not taking *me* seriously."

He sighed. "When will you realize how positively ruined I am by you?"

I didn't know what to say.

"I've got all the time in the world," he said. "I'll make them love me. I'll make them beg me to whisk you away on a random journey across the country."

"Oh, honey," I said. "There goes that maddening optimism again."

## LEGACY PT. 2

That month I got my final assignment for Intro to Journalism: a free article, no more than fifteen-hundred words in length.

I considered covering the annual Earth Day campus clean-up event, then shot down the idea straight away. I'd been impressing Professor Spaulding all semester, and I had to do this one bigger, more impactful.

Then, all at once, the perfect topic fell right into my lap.

## STICKING IT

York asked me what I wanted for my birthday. April 16 fell on a Wednesday that year, so I told him I wanted him to come home with me the weekend before and finally meet my mom.

I was sick with worry about being allowed to go to California. York wasn't on anyone's radar like he should have been for how much time we spent together. I should have told my mom earlier, should have brought him up once in a while so she'd at least be familiar with his name. But I was so dead set on keeping my home life physically separate from my relationship that I developed a mental block every time the opportunity came up. This encounter would have to be finessed down to the last detail.

On Saturday the twelfth I picked him up in the afternoon. He chose a crisp royal blue Polo shirt, and he looked so adorable when he was trying to make a good impression. On the way, I told him about some of the other times I'd brought close friends home. Most of those I'd entrusted with the secret of my family situation were understanding. At first. After meeting my mom, a lot of them backed out. People always thought they knew how to be empathetic, but you had a hard time getting them to stick by it. York was one of the sincerest people I knew, but he for damn sure didn't know what he had gotten himself into.

I had asked that my uncle be there, and he promised to come with cake. My anxiety lessened only when I saw his car in the driveway. York may not want to run now.

Then again...

"How many times have you met a girl's father?" I asked.

"Zero. Never been serious enough with a girl."

We stopped at the front door. I studied the familiar, tiny chips in the sapphire blue paint around the doorknob. "You think you got this?" I asked.

"Are you doubting me?"

"Just wanted to make sure you were okay."

"Is there a reason I wouldn't be?"

I kissed him on the cheek. "Nope."

I announced myself when we walked in, and my uncle came to the door to greet us. I stood to the side and said, "This is my mom's brother. Uncle Joe, York."

"Nice to meet you, sir," York said. They shook hands.

"Likewise. You're a lucky young man, for multiple reasons."

"More than you know," he agreed.

"And...how are you now?"

"Fantastic. Really. My doctors say the transplant took incredibly well, and there's no reason I can't go on to live a healthy life."

"I'm glad to hear that. Olive says you're studying biology at NECU?"

"Yes sir. I'm minoring in marine biology, which pretty much requires a master's degree, so I'll end up in grad school. I'd like to stay here on the coast and one day work at one of the marine life research facilities here in the state."

"Not bad. I'm impressed you plan to attend grad school."

I smiled, because if my uncle were almost anyone else, York would have very honestly retorted: "Only because I have to."

Mom emerged, dressed, coily hair combed, not teetering. This was all I had asked of her, and she had delivered.

"Hey, sweetie," she said and hugged me. I rested my head on her bony chest. I realized anew how tiny she had become; I could wrap my arms around her and almost touch both my hands together at the front of her ribcage between us.

Her tired eyes rested on York, and she stared. I introduced him the same way I had introduced him moments before, but this felt wary and experimental.

"Mom, this is the one who—" I turned to him too. "He's the one."

When she nodded, I noticed the glassiness in her eyes for the first time.

"Nice to meet you, Mrs. Grant," said York.

"Nice to meet you," she said. "I'm sorry we never got the chance to meet sooner. It's been a difficult time."

"I know. I'm sorry."

Everyone took to one another easily, and I relaxed a little. My uncle announced he was finishing up dinner and told us he would call us to the dining room soon. Mom urged York to make himself comfortable. Would this truly be a nice, normal experience? The day was still young, and I was staying on my guard, but Mom appeared relatively sober. She was a nice mom when she was sober.

I took York on a tour of the rest of the house. As we reached the top of the stairs, Selma came out of her room.

"Hey Olive," she said as we passed, "how's that rash of yours?"

"I'm afraid it's gotten worse. Now it looks just like your face," I snapped back.

Halfway to my room, we heard, "You." We turned and found her pointing at York. "Come here," she commanded.

He shot me an amused look, then obeyed, tucking his hands into his pockets as he approached.

"Remember me?" she asked.

"Of course I do, Selma. How have you been?"

"I've been all right. How have *you* been?" She emphasized the word "you" almost overdramatically.

"Good," he said on a sigh, seemingly relieved she was taking it easy on him. The poor, misguided fool. "Actually, I've been feeling great. My doctor visits are—"

"That's great," said Selma.

York hummed, his expression amused again. Only I could see it though, the way his eyes twinkled.

"I suppose my sister also has something to do with that?" asked Selma.

"Um." He looked at me, and I met his eyes with apologetic ones. "Yeah, I guess Olive has quite a lot to do with it."

She crossed her arms over her chest. "What are your intentions with her?"

"Oh, dear God almighty," I said.

"What do you mean?" he asked.

"Don't play dumb. Olive told me you're super smart."

He sighed again, and then he dropped to one knee before her. "Okay. It's painfully obvious you're the only one in this house no one can pull a fast one on. I can't tell you for sure what will happen between your sister and me, but I can assure you I've got a very, very good heart." He put a hand on his chest.

I watched Selma's brows knit in the middle of her forehead, then she stood straight as if jolted to life by electricity.

"Well," she said. "I think I can agree with that." She walked toward the stairs, widening her eyes at me as she passed.

I pulled York to his feet. "You shut my sister up."

"Is that a good thing?"

"It's an impossible thing."

We hung out in my room, and he got to browse my book collection, see pictures of a middle-school-aged me with Stefanie and my other friends, and thumb through my junior yearbook. He smiled at my National Honor Society picture.

My uncle had prepared pot roast with a medley of vegetables and roasted potatoes. A heavy, hearty meal usually reserved for the winter months, he knew how much Selma and I loved it, so it became my birthday dinner. Also, as I'd briefed him on York's number of food allergies, I think he wanted to make a meal he knew our guest would actually be able to eat.

Mom came in after we had all sat down, made a small plate, and sat at the head of the table.

"I usually serve cornbread with this meal, so I hope you don't mind if we eat some," my uncle said to York.

"Not at all," he said. "I'm one of few Southerners to never have had it. Makes me feel kind of special."

"How is that bucket list of yours going?"

"It's been so much fun to do with Olive. We've eaten way too much chocolate, dug up a time capsule, and climbed a gigantic tree stump."

"It's really more than a bucket list," I said. "York's fixing old regrets and taking chances. Life's for living, right? We all know that now. Good to find it out young, I guess."

My uncle sat back and studied me like he'd just met me. "I suppose that's true."

"So what's next on the list?" Selma asked.

We would not mention streaking, the next goal on the list. Not in a million years.

"With the stump conquered, we're almost at the end," said York. He lowered his head and took a bite of food.

"He's terrified of needles, so he wants to get a tattoo," I said.

"Oh yeah?" said my uncle. "I have a few myself. Don't worry about the needle—you don't even see it."

"So I've heard."

"You won't be getting one, will you?" Mom asked me.

Had her speech slurred a little on the words "getting one," or had I imagined it? Panic fluttered in my chest, and I sought Selma's eyes for confirmation. She sucked in her cheeks.

*Shit.*

"I don't know. I don't have any ideas for one," I said far too quickly, the punctuation getting lost.

"I can't see you with a tattoo," she said. "They're always so unattractive on girls, to me. You remember your father didn't like them too much either."

She chuckled a little, stood up, and muttered something about Dad under her breath.

"I'll be back in a moment," she announced. "Got to run to the restroom." She took even, concentrated steps toward the hallway and disappeared around the corner.

"What else is on the list?" Uncle Joe asked mercifully.

York eyed me.

"Oh yeah," I said. "York has this really cool idea that he calls chasing the sun."

"Okay. What does that mean?"

"The idea is to watch the sunrise here on the East coast and, in the same day, watch the sunset on the West coast."

Uncle Joe's hand, which had been bringing a loaded spoon to his mouth, froze. "You mean taking a trip?"

"Yep."

"Just you two?"

"Mm-hmm."

My uncle and sister looked at me, then at York, in unison. Family members have ways of showing they're related, reacting to certain situations the same way like their minds are synced. The intensity of their sudden, twofold curiosity made me want to crawl into a hole somewhere and hide.

"Oh, buddy," Selma said.

"Hey, listen, we aren't trying to go tomorrow," I said. "It was only an idea, anyway. It would be cool to do it, though."

"I'll be honest," Uncle Joe said. "You two don't know each other very well yet."

"Hence the reason why we're not trying to go tomorrow."

"And a trip like that would cost money," he said.

"I know that."

"And you two are mighty young."

"I'm nineteen. I wouldn't be gone for a long time, a long weekend at most. I'm gone for longer when I'm at school. Plus, you should trust your sister and brother-in-law to have given me some fantastic parenting. Enough that I know who might murder me, who's good boyfriend material, who might try to take advantage of me in a hotel room."

York jumped when my uncle's hand landed heavily on his shoulder.

"You two weren't planning to stay in the same hotel room on this trip, right?" asked Uncle Joe.

York shook his head in an attempt at calm, collected denial, but the movement was absurdly mechanical. I made my expression wide, in shock, I hope, and not worry. "Wha...? Hey. Come on."

Mom meandered back into the dining room. "What's the discussion about?"

"A trip to California," said Selma. "I think it's a great idea. I've never seen the sun set over the ocean."

"Oh, I've seen it. Been to San Diego twice to visit my friend, Diane. You remember, Olive?"

"Sure."

"Have you ever been?" she asked York.

"They're going," said Selma. "The two of them."

Mom frowned. "Says who?"

"No one," said Uncle Joe. I kicked my sister underneath the table.

"Good," said Mom, "my baby stays here with me." She reached over and wrapped an arm around Selma's shoulder. "Both my babies are staying here. They have to. I don't have anyone left. My husband is dead and—"

"Mom," I said.

"It's true. He knows it, doesn't he?" She turned hard eyes on a stunned York. "Don't you? I suppose you do."

"We can talk about it later," said my uncle. "*Not now.*"

No one spoke for a few moments. My mom took her hand off Selma's shoulder and scooted back into place. She teetered for a second before she picked up her fork and—no lie—pouted.

I hoped she wouldn't speak again.

After dinner, York offered to wash the dishes. I helped him. "How am I doing?" he whispered over the sound of the faucet.

"You don't ever have to wonder about yourself. I should be asking how my family is doing."

"It's fine, really."

"My mom is—"

"This has been a perfectly pleasant experience."

Mom disappeared into her room after we finished dinner, so my remaining family saw us off. I so wanted to be the girl whose mom cheerfully sent her off after a birthday dinner. I wanted the kind of mom who would give my guy friend a kind but no-nonsense final appraisal before she patted him on the shoulder and thanked him for the visit. But I was glad she wasn't around. Sad, but I couldn't deny it.

York always knew the right time to talk my face off. His lips didn't stop moving on the way back to campus. He mostly raved about the superior culinary skills of my uncle, who also scared him a little bit. He went on about how much he used to wish for a sibling and the few apparent perks of not having one.

"I'm very proud of you," I said. "You didn't run screaming. I think you won them over."

"Even Selma?"

"Especially Selma."

## *Twelve*

## WISHES

York and I talked on Monday, but we didn't see one another. I
didn't hear from him Tuesday.

I knew he had a test to study for, and I had my own work to do,
and I knew I could just text him, but my paranoia wouldn't let me. I
worried that after the shock of Saturday had worn off he'd realized
what happened had actually revolted him.

But then, on the morning of my birthday, I got a very early call
from him—so early it roused me from sleep.

"Happy Birthday, I Love," he crooned.

My heart fluttered. "Hi. Thank you."

"Please tell me you aren't busy tonight," he said, "because I have
dedicated literally hours to planning a very special birthday for you."

"I'll be at the library until seven, but after that I don't have plans."

"Good. I'll pick you up after your shift. Oh, and please bring some
dressy clothes."

I had no idea what to wear. All my dressy stuff hung in my closet
at home, so I scooted there right before work.

Selma leaped from her bed when I passed her open bedroom door. "Why are you here?" she demanded.

"I'm not here." I ducked into my room.

As I pushed clothes to the side, I heard her walk up behind me. "Have you been in my closet again?" I asked.

"I keep telling you I've never raided your closet. I hate everything you own. I could never wear your jeans, as they are made by and for hobbits."

"Where's my black skirt, then? My purple shirt with the ruffley stuff on it?"

"You probably lost them. What do you need them for?"

I turned. "I have a date, I guess. For my birthday."

Her eyes widened. "Right. It *is* your birthday today! In that case, hold on." She left, and I continued to dig. I stooped to the floor and dug out a pair of satin peep-toe heels I'd forgotten about.

"Happy birthday," Selma trilled. She'd laid a black skirt and purple shirt on my bed.

"Wow. How do you know my style so well?"

"I pick up on these things."

I put the black shoes on the bed beside the clothes. "I guess this works."

"You don't seem happy about it." She pointed past my shoulder and into the closet. "What about that?"

"What?"

"The yellow thing."

A tea-length dress the color of pale sunshine, strapless with a sheer chiffon halter overlay, hung in the back left corner.

"I don't know. I don't want to draw that much attention to myself."

"What? Afraid you'll look too nice?" She yanked the dress off the hanger. "Listen, I hate that skirt and shirt combo on the bed. It's boring. You're boring too, but everyone in the world doesn't need to know it. You've worn this dress how many times? Twice?"

*Once.* She heard the answer I didn't give. "That's it. I order you to put this dress on."

I eyed it again. I had liked the dress. I'd worn it to a social at my church sophomore year of high school. Dad had urged me to wear it.

Selma insisted I model it for her, shoes and all. "How do I look?" I asked.

"Like an elegant...bumblebee."

My shoulders sagged. "I knew it. It's ridiculous."

"No, no, no. He'll love it. Trust me."

~ * ~

I dressed in the bathroom at work after my shift ended and stepped outside when I saw York pull up. He got out of his car, wearing a white button-down, dark green tie, and black pants. When he saw me, he stopped in his tracks at the passenger side.

"Hi," I said.

"Wow," he said.

"Too much, right?"

He stepped a little closer. "I never knew lemon and chocolate went so beautifully together."

My lungs filled with air.

He opened the door for me and gestured limply. "Please get in before I forget why I came here in the first place."

He took me to a waterfront restaurant at Moncure Beach called Bonfilia's. The place was small and romantically lit, pricier than you would imagine when you first saw it, and everyone dressed up to go there. You could hear the Pasquotank River lapping the shore right outside the building.

The bar had an enormous wine selection, so big it required its own separate menu. The server offered us a sample of the special for the day, a *rosé* wine, without carding us. York declined without hesitation.

When I picked up my menu, he leaned over. "If I can make a suggestion, I think you ought to try the chicken-and-gnocchi soup. Apparently it's excellent. Also endless."

My smile, which I realized hadn't left my face since we sat down, grew wider. How had I become the girl who smiled without realizing it? "York Lively, you are a ridiculously good boyfriend."

The server came back with our drinks and a bowl of crusty bread with olive oil and asked for our orders. I took York's suggestion. He ordered steak fettuccine alfredo, since the restaurant used real butter in the sauce.

My soup had a rich, creamy broth, big gnocchi and hunks of chicken. We ate and stared at one another and didn't care if everyone in the place called us total saps.

"I've got some good news," I said after I ordered my fourth bowl. "I figured out a topic for my final article in Intro to Journalism."

"I'm dying to hear it."

"Organ donation."

"Love it."

"I thought you would. And this week I'm signing myself up to become an organ donor."

He sat back. "I can't believe you aren't one already."

"I opted out when I got my license," I admitted. "I didn't want to think about the risks of getting behind the wheel. Freaked me out, if just for a moment. And then it was done, and I only flashed my license once a month or so, and I forgot all about it."

The server brought me another bowl of soup, her expression amused, and checked on York. He had cleaned his plate, and munched on bread while I dug in.

"Okay, she's making me self-conscious," I said. "What's so funny? The menu says 'Endless Soup.'"

"There are few things I find incredibly sexy," he responded. "Watching you put away four bowls of food with no problem in a dainty yellow dress is now one of them."

"That's weird, York." But I shoveled in a behemothic bite just for him, then said around a full mouth, "I told you my devotion was deep and real."

"*Oomf.* I don't understand what you said, but keep talking."

I smiled and brushed off the comment. "All right. Back to business."

"The business of your article."

"Right. I wanted to write about the benefits of organ donation, and I figured I should get a first-hand experience. I'd also like to interview some folks."

"One of them being me?"

"If you wouldn't mind."

"I'll tell you whatever you want to know."

"Good. Maybe we can raise awareness. There's still such a great need for it. People on the waitlist die every day."

Since York told the restaurant beforehand that it was my birthday, the server brought us a piece of tiramisu after I'd had enough soup. It had one small, lit candle in it.

"Make a wish," he said. His face by candlelight looked like the sun, his smile infectious.

I wished for a lifetime's worth of those smiles.

## FIGURES

At the time I was writing my article, approximately 122,344 people in the United States sat on the organ donor waitlist, 3,400 of which resided in North Carolina. Seven percent of people on lists died every year.

The Internet provided me plenty of facts from accredited sites, but I also utilized my library resources to seek volunteers through Donate Life NC. I tracked down and spoke with a DMV Ambassador, then got the chance to speak with a Friends for Life Ambassador.

Then I launched into York's story, talking first to him, then his mom, who jumped at the opportunity to help me spread awareness. My last paragraph detailed how one could become an organ donor, and then I revealed I had recently done it in my father's honor. After I filled out the online form, York called me his hero.

It was the best article I'd ever written, up until then.

## SNAGS

For the first time since I'd known him, York overestimated the outcome of one of his brilliant, foolproof plans.

"My mom is not keen on letting me go to California," he told me over the phone.

"This is not news to me. This is a prophecy fulfilled."

"No, this is a snag in the plan. Just a snag."

"Parental permission is seventy-five percent of the plan. Three of four quarters. Your mom was supposed to be a sure yes. My family is the wild card."

"Just a snag," he repeated. "She didn't say no, *per se*."

"What did she say?"

"A bunch of stuff."

"Like?"

"Eh." I heard a sigh and some movement, then a door closed. "She brought up the supposed fragility of my condition—" *of course*—"and the fact that I don't have a doctor out there—" *duh*—"and the fact that I plan to go with someone who doesn't understand my needs at all—" *UGH*—"and the fact that it's sometimes not a good idea for people with heart problems to travel on planes or some shit."

"All of which amounts to a big, fat NO."

"Not quite. My mom is swayable. She is a swing state in the country that is York. I'll have to appeal to her sensibility is all."

"Face it: she loves you too much to let you risk your health like that. Let's accept her answer now so we aren't disappointed later."

"I never accept defeat prematurely. It is not in my realm of rationality. It is not in my DNA."

"Your realm of rationality is a little...narrower than others'," I pointed out.

"Which means I make stuff happen." He sounded pleased. "Don't think too much—it puts you in a position to doubt."

I threw my head back. "You think your dad is in any way responsive to this trip?"

"He doesn't seem to care either way." He sniffed.

"That can't be true."

"He seems to think I'll go off and do what I want to do anyway. My mom likes to give me space, but she has her limits. My dad doesn't even try anymore. 'Sure, kid. Have fun. It's what you do best.'"

"You made a mistake or two. Most kids have. Kids do stuff behind their parents' backs all the time," I said. "No one wants to be judged for it forever."

"I think I've already worn out my chances."

"Well, put him out of your mind, then. If he won't hurt your cause, he won't influence it at all. Stick to your mom. If you say you can make her comfortable enough, you can. I'll stop with the what-ifs."

I only said that for him. I what-if-ed all the way to bed that night. What-ifs danced on each deep breath I took as I drifted into sleep. What-ifs picked at the edges of my thoughts every day after that.

This did not look promising, but you couldn't tell York that.

## BRIDGES

We studied together several nights in a row for my four final exams, his five, which meant we had to put talks of the bucket list on hold. On the last day of classes, we hung out with Nick, who I recognized from the graduation party. A year behind York and me in school, he had been accepted to UNC Pembroke, so we all had something to celebrate, and we spent the afternoon at the beach.

Nick was much nicer and chattier this time around, and while I didn't know him well, I thought I knew why. When my mom was drunk in public, I watched her like a hawk. I barely interacted with anyone. I figured Nick must be the type who really cared about his friends.

"I finally figured out where in California we should go," York told me as we strolled Kitty Hawk's coastline. "San Francisco."

"And why there?" I asked.

"I am so glad you asked. Flights from Norfolk into San Francisco are some of the cheapest I've seen. The city is full of stuff to do. And. Are you guys ready for this?"

"Oh, you tease," Nick said.

"Two nights ago, my mom made the mistake of mentioning she has a friend named Barbara who lives there. She even came to visit my family couple of times when I was a kid. If we stay with her, we won't have to pay for a hotel, we'll have access to a car, and we'll be with someone who knows me and my family, someone my mom trusts."

"Your mom definitely made a mistake," I agreed.

"It's brought her number of excuses down from a million to about two."

"Being you'll still be across the country, and she still won't be able to come with us."

"Exactly. I'm wearing her down, though. I told you I would."

"Is your mom's friend seriously going to trust you with her car?" asked Nick.

"I'm a trustworthy guy."

"I'm just saying, I hope Barb is the kind of lady who doesn't mind you getting her car stuck halfway off the Golden Gate Bridge."

"What?" I asked.

"You make me sound like a crap driver," York protested. "I am an excellent driver."

"It's not your driving I'm concerned about, dude. It's your give-a-fuck. It's turned down a little too low. You'd make eyes with some guy at the start of the stretch and end up racing him from one end of the bridge to the other."

"Oh wow, what a rush that would be, huh?" York's face lit up.

"Should I be concerned about getting into a car with you from now on?" I asked.

"Nah," Nick said. "I mean you've already done it. The fates have been tested. I'm sure you'll be fine."

"That's...good to know." I looked at York. "So, San Francisco?"

"Sounds like a good plan?" he asked, wrapping an arm around me.

"An excellent one."

It had sounded like a good plan, in fact, which frustrated me all the more to have to wait for permission.

I took a cue from York and remained optimistic. I saved as much money as I could out of my meager library checks every two weeks. He offered to help me in any way he could financially, but I could not let his mom think I intended to use him. I didn't know if she realized how much I liked him, or maybe she didn't want to realize it. At any rate, my uncle was sure to help me make ends meet.

If he could convince Mom to say yes.

## *Thirteen*

## BARING IT ALL

He called me one night shortly after I moved back home for the summer.

"Hello," I said.

"I have an idea," he said.

"Uh oh."

"It's a fantastic idea, I promise."

"What's it pertain to?"

"Streaking."

"...Uh oh."

"You knew it was coming."

I fiddled with my camera for a moment, wondering how I would feel when the time came for me to take a picture of his naked body. Then I started to wonder about his naked body. "Okay. What did you have in mind?"

"Nick is trying to cook up a massive senior prank."

"Classic."

"As we all know, it's Go Big or Go Home with senior pranks. You either commit one-hundred percent and make it good, or you don't participate. Since I was trapped at home this time last year, I feel completely robbed of the experience, and I figure teaming up with Nick will provide the perfect platform for my next goal."

"Are we about to streak with the Fleet High senior class?"

"Get ready to see a side of me you've only dreamed about."

~ * ~

My small hometown built its only high school to accommodate the entire consolidated city-county's population of fourteen- to eighteen-year-olds. The two-level building stretched over quite a bit of land that it shared with the football field right out back.

The audacious seniors decided to streak on Sports Awards Night, as the school held this event on said football field every year, at night. Students, mostly upperclassmen, and parents gathered in the balmy late spring air on the shiny metal and concrete bleachers.

Meanwhile, I hid at least fifty feet away from the unsuspecting audience and school officials with York and over twenty high school seniors. Anyone in the press box, or even the very top row, could have seen us over the wall.

Luckily, Fleet High's marching band was always allotted the top two rows: fifty-four students dressed in uniforms of blue and silver band t-shirts and black pants. Nick had somehow convinced the entire band to blare their instruments loud and proud during their performance pieces to conceal the presence of our group congregating behind the massive brick wall that ran perpendicular to the bleachers. They held up their part of the deal.

Still, to cover our bases, we'd arrived at the school an hour before people started to show up and kept our voices low and our movements minimal the entire time. By the time Nick finally got everyone's attention, I was so stiff I could hardly twist my neck or flex my arms or legs.

"Remember, guys, this has to be epic. No chickening out," he whispered. "We're doing this to prove our badassery. And we're doing it for York here."

"No, no, no, don't do it for me," York protested. "Do it *with* me."

Everyone began to disrobe. Many stripped with no hesitation. I glanced at York, the only person I really knew, and shimmied out of my jeans. He took off his shirt first, and I saw the thick, shiny, red evidence of his near-death experience spanning the length of his chest right between his pec muscles.

I stared at his surgery scar for longer than I meant to, transfixed, imagining doctors cutting him open and cracking his ribcage in half.

"I know, I know," he said. "I'm breathtaking. Drink it in."

He really was nice to look at, well-defined without being overly muscular, but I still smirked at him, happy he was teasing me instead of calling me out.

I tugged off my shirt. Next came his pants. Then I took off my bra. Off came his underwear. Then mine.

I only saw bits and pieces and brief flashes of him, both wanting and nervous to look. I covered my breasts with one forearm and let the other hand hang half-heartedly across my stomach and over my privates. He cupped his package with both hands.

Everyone around us giggled, tittered, made rude noises, and expressed bravado. York and I just stared at one another.

"I will have to ask you not to judge me at this particular moment," he said. "It's, uh, it's a chilly night. And I'm nervous, you know."

"No, it's totally chilly out here," I said. I regarded my chest. "I want you to know I've lost quite a bit of weight. Like, three-hundred pounds, maybe. And, you know, I tried to get the boobs to stay, but they just...melted off."

"You're perfect, Olive." He said this like we had already gone over it a thousand times.

They made the plan simple and quick: streak down the track in front of the grass, double back in front of the crowd toward the brick wall, grab our clothes, and hop into our cars before we could get caught. They rationalized it would be difficult to catch that many people at once, so we all had a good chance to make a quick getaway. Many of them had driven trucks to pile into as they made their escape, but York's car would have to do for the two of us.

Some people, mainly the girls, brought colorful wigs to obscure their identities. Most of the guys wore ski masks. York and I didn't bother because we wouldn't be readily identified as students, but it meant we had to be much quicker than everyone else.

The basketball coach began to introduce the year's MVP. Suddenly, too late, I felt bad for ruining someone's big moment.

The crowd started to cheer, the band started to play, Nick yelled "Go!", and we started across the field.

All the sounds around me muted as I focused on running straight. The track under my feet felt spongy and warm still from the day's sun. Everyone surged around me. I caught sight of a couple of surprised faces on the field. The audience began to shout, some in disdain, some in enthusiasm.

In a brilliant move, the band played a loud fight song to accompany our sprint. Caught up in the ridiculous hilarity, I took York's hand, and we raised our arms in a victorious fist pump.

From my position close to the front of the group, I became vaguely aware that our prank had turned into a chase. The lot of us dove around one another—cheered on by a large group of students—and back behind the wall, where I grabbed at our pile of clothes.

People leaped into truck beds and driver seats and trunks of SUVs in the parking lot beyond the wall, and York and I hopped into his car, still naked, and sped off. I could still hear people yelling and screaming at the football field and the band continued its lively tune.

"Holy shit!" York screamed and laughed at the same time. "Holy shit, Olive!"

"Are we going to make it?" I asked.

"That SRO was right on us!"

"God, he was so fat!" I guffawed. "Watch out for that car coming up behind us!"

"I don't know what they thought would happen sending *that guy* after twenty teenagers."

"This school never sees any action—hell, this *town* never sees any action. No one expected it!"

One moment we had our heads thrown back in hysterics, blinded by the adrenaline and bliss coursing through us, and the next we were lurching forward, then back, because York had crashed into something.

"Whoa," he said, suddenly serious. "Are you okay?"

"Yeah, yeah, yeah, I'm fine," I assured him, my heart pounding and my knees trembling. I touched my head and shoulders and chest to be sure.

I could still hear the commotion at the football field, which worried me. We were still making a run for it, and one very big roadblock—a midnight blue Audi with a busted headlight and dented in front corner—sat in front of us.

We tugged our clothes back on as the driver stepped out the vehicle, but when the headlights revealed him, York stopped with his pants at his knees.

"What are you doing?" I asked as I pulled my shirt over my head. "What's wrong?"

York rolled down his window. The man leaned in and said, "What in the world were you thinking, kid?" Then he fell silent too. They stared at one another.

"Mr. Kiger," York said finally. "Long time no see."

*Fourteen*

## DAMAGES

Sometimes I think I have an oral fixation.

Whenever I talk to someone, or I'm looking for similar traits between two or more people, or I meet someone for the first time, my eyes automatically go to their mouth.

I immediately disliked Ronald Kiger, because Ronald Kiger chose that precise moment to sneer like a hyena.

"Well," he said. "Got yourself in a bit of trouble?"

"Actually, it's not what you think—" York said. Cars full of whooping, naked kids continued speeding around us. Someone could have called the cops by now, for all we knew. "Can we—can we pull off to the side here so I can explain?"

"You hit my car and expect me to leave the scene?"

"Yes, I do. We kind of have to get out of here." He arched his pelvis to the roof and yanked his pants up the rest of the way. I averted my eyes, suddenly hot, and draped my jeans across my lap.

"I've guessed that," said Kiger, "but when I call my insurance company, they'll need a police report to—"

"No no no no. That's not necessary, really." A small town police department like the one in Fleet might not be able to track down twenty-some semi-anonymous kids for streaking, but if they caught a couple of them at the scene of the crime—

"Where do you expect us to go?" Kiger asked.

"My house, out of the way. We can talk to my dad."

The man took out his phone and made a call. "Hey. Yeah, I'll be a little longer—I got into a car accident. No, no, I'm fine. The car's a little banged up though...it's York Lively."

I winced at the way he said those last three words. Like a punishment.

He ended the call and turned on his heels and slammed his driver side door behind him. He backed out, his Audi still perfectly drivable, and led the way to Collins Court.

"He seems great," I said as I put my pants on.

"He lives two streets over from us. Thinks he's some kind of Lively family police. Every time I get in trouble, he uses me as an example. 'Don't be like that kid, Jacob. You're smart, remember?' You're going places." For the first time, all traces of his trademark humor left his face. I didn't recognize him.

"He's your dad's friend, isn't he?"

"They bonded immediately."

Mr. Kiger drove all the way to the house and backed his car into the driveway. York's mom was already walking out the door when we pulled against the curb.

"Oh no," I said as York jerked his car into park and leaped out. "Oh no, oh no."

"What happened?" she asked.

"I'm sorry I had to call you," said Mr. Kiger, "but I ran into your son here at the high school—actually, he ran into me—"

"At the high school?" Her eyes darted to us. When we left that evening, York told her we were meeting up with some old friends. He hadn't actually told a lie.

"I was there to see my son get his sports award," said Mr. Kiger, an announcement made casually enough, but which visibly put York and his mom on edge, "when all of a sudden, a bunch of naked kids fly out the school parking lot, hooting and hollering and carrying on."

"Are you hurt?" she asked York.

"We're fine." He indicated me as I trudged slowly to his side.

She regarded me the way she usually did: with a mix of pity and circumspection. I suppose my presence and my willingness to subject myself to all the trouble her son could cause me—emotional and otherwise—confused her. She would never really be happy about any girl her son brought home, even if the girl's father had saved her son's life.

"Why were you even at Fleet High School?" she asked.

"We...I—" He looked at me. "My bucket list. Number five. I wanted to streak."

"Oh, damn it, York."

"We pulled a senior prank."

"Last time I checked, you weren't a senior in high school," said Mr. Kiger, putting his hands on his hips. "You were an adult in college, last time I checked." He had all the bravura of a fiercely proud Southern man, and he had thick, dark hair and an even thicker accent.

I saw Mr. Lively emerge from the house, harried, as if he'd been pulled away from some important work. "What's happened now?"

"He pulled some stunt with the seniors at the high school tonight," said Mr. Kiger. "Hit my car and smashed my driver's side headlight."

Mr. Lively looked at the cars, then at York. "What did you do?"

"I was trying to leave, and I didn't pay attention to where I was going."

"What did you do?" Mr. Lively reiterated, leaving the same amount of space between each word.

"We streaked."

"Wow. Breaking all kinds of decency laws. Great way to spend your summer away from college."

"Yeah, it was quite a moronic thing to do. Thanks for noticing."

Mr. Lively let his head fall back a little and blew out a small breath. "All right. How much have you had to drink?"

"I haven't."

He put his hand on York's jaw, squeezed a little, and leaned in to sniff his mouth. I don't think my eyes could have gotten any bigger.

"Stop," said York. The word, while spoken calmly, sliced like a razor blade.

"I don't doubt those kids all got wasted before they tore through that school," said Mr. Kiger, and I'd never in my life wanted so much to tell someone to shut the fuck up. "Peeling out of the school parking lot like bats out of hell. Jake won an award tonight, and I doubt he'll get to have his big moment now."

"I'm sorry. This is about your car, right? How much damage did he cause?"

"See for yourself!"

York's car also had a smashed-in headlight, and the impact had dented the left corner. Both vehicles seemed fine otherwise, cosmetic damage only.

"This is easily fixed," he said. I think even he had grown tired of his friend, if you could call him that—all they really had in common was busting York's balls wide open. "We'll take it in ourselves."

"And what about your son's behavior, Paul? Jenn?" I could feel the air change beside me when the man turned on York's poor mom. "When the police catch kids in stupid situations like this, they slap them with a misdemeanor. A felony, depending on your record. Hasn't this whole heart debacle put you all through enough?"

"I don't have a record," York pointed out.

"You know what?" said Mrs. Lively. The mostly male crowd looked at her, and Mr. Lively actually jumped at her outburst. She breathed in and out for a few moments, then lifted her head and cleared her throat. I imagined a mama lion or something, drawing her claws back in.

"Ronald," she began again. "I'm so sorry about our son's recklessness. I'm sorry he damaged your property. He'll take full responsibility for it. You don't have to call your insurance company. He can pay for the damages to your car, okay? It's a headlight and a dent."

"Money isn't an option. Cars can be replaced." Even as he said this, I could see the smug pleasure in his eyes, hear it in the way he shaped the words. "He's running the show here."

"No, he isn't. I'm sorry he and his friends ruined the night for your son, but I don't have to defend him to you. I do appreciate your... concern, nonetheless."

Mr. Lively shook the man's hand and followed him to his car. I heard them discussing the problem in lowered voices. The three of us that remained stood there. I felt so awkward I wished the world would swallow me up.

"Sorry, Mom," York said. "It's all my fault, my dumb idea. Not Olive's."

I wished he hadn't said my name, because her emotionless eyes shifted over to me. I made my expression scream the apology I knew she didn't want to hear.

The man pulled off, and York's dad made his way back up the driveway. When he approached us, he blew out another breath and shrugged his shoulders. "I hope you had fun tonight."

"Dad..."

"I don't get you. I never really have. You have all these opportunities, family and obviously also friends who love you." He cut a glance my way. "Maybe we love you to a fault. Why else would you have developed this need to throw away your life?"

"I don't—that's not—" York was helpless, and I didn't like that. "Look, I know we had a hard time with my health, and I know I've been given a second chance to be different. And I *am* different. But I won't let what happened stop me from living. I'm still me. It doesn't make me a bad person."

"The problem is you don't seem to care about anyone but yourself. You go out and do crazy and illegal things with your friends. Your mom worries herself sick, literally sick, and you don't even notice. This fender bender nonsense adds another bill on top of the many we're expected to take care of for you. But York always gets the good deal, the 'Get Out of Jail Free' card. York gets to be happy while we're left to pick up the pieces."

He no longer seemed to care that I, not a member of the family, was witnessing such a personal matter. In fact, he jabbed a hand in my direction. "This girl's father died for you. You get that? You took his heart when your old one wasn't strong enough and you got a second chance. And still, *still,* you waste it. You're wasting another human's organ."

York stood stock still, every feature hardened. "Maybe it was a mistake that I got Mr. Grant's heart," he said. "Certainly would have been a lot easier on everyone if I hadn't."

"Maybe so."

Silence. Mrs. Lively looked at me, this time in embarrassment. My eyes turned to Mr. Lively so sharply he actually might have felt the sting.

"Are you fucking kidding me?" York said.

"I can't...I can't have this conversation anymore," said his father. "Not with you, not with you—" he said to his wife, silencing her right as she opened her mouth to speak, "not right now. It's making me say things I don't—"

What? Don't mean? Don't want revealed?

He turned on his heels before anyone could fill in the blanks and disappeared inside the house.

"I'll go," I said. I didn't want anyone to feel like they had to put up a front for me anymore.

"I drove you," York reminded me.

"Come in, you two," said Mrs. Lively. "Come inside. Right now."

We went straight into the living room and plopped on the couch beside the cat, who chirped in alarm.

Mrs. Lively didn't follow us in right away. We waited for what seemed like a long time. He sat with his back nearly on the seat of the couch, his head where his lower back should have been, long legs stretched out in front of him, arms crossed over his chest. He stared straight ahead, and I didn't try to offer a helpful comment because I wouldn't have wanted to hear me speak, either.

His mom came in a little while later. She approached as if she anticipated gunfire and didn't know which direction it would come from. She held both hands clenched in front of her chest, and as soon as she saw her son, her expression melted like a wax sculpture in a fire, morphing from disbelieving to mortified.

"I'm sorry," she said.

He shook his head. "It's okay."

"No, it isn't."

"Yes, it is."

"You know he doesn't mean it," she said. "You know he's just angry. You know we worry."

"Yep."

She sighed. "Still, it's no excuse. Words burn, even when said in the heat of anger."

He stayed silent.

"This whole night has been blown out of proportion," she said. "We have to talk about it after we've calmed down. We have to talk about how we feel about each other, as a family. We have to let it all out or the pressure will build up and we'll explode."

"I think pressure is good," he deadpanned. "Doesn't distort the truth. Makes it come easier."

"No one feels that way."

"If you say so."

She stared at me for a moment.

"I'm not a troublemaker, I promise," I said. "Literally, I'm a do-nothing. I never even went to a party in high school."

Though she regretted what I witnessed, I didn't think she believed me.

"I can't condone this behavior," she said, "because, York, I know you know better, and, Olive, I'm sure your mother would agree. The fact my son could think making such a reckless decision was a good idea makes it worse." She paused a beat and rubbed her hands up and down her face. I noticed how her hands didn't really match her face, the wrinkles and brown spots and veins betraying the age her face kept well hidden. Maybe she held all her stress in her hands.

"That said, you two pulled a prank," she continued. "It was risky and foolish, but we've all done it. That Ronald Kiger is a damned fire-starter, and he pissed me off tonight. So Jake won some stupid award, and Ron will have to drive the older Audi instead of the newer one—so what? It doesn't give him any right to judge my family the way he does. He can go to hell."

I realized for the first time how often she truly went against her compulsion to keep her son in a bubble. She did try to let him live, because he was so alive, and, maybe, because she didn't know how much alive he had left allotted to him. The dread began to pulse, heavy in the pit of my stomach, when I realized I sometimes shared the same anxiety.

"Mom," said York, "you know I'll take whatever punishment you and Dad decide. You know I plan to pay for both cars. I'll take all the responsibility. But... Olive and I—this bucket list is—"

She raised a hand to cut him off. "I know how much this bucket list means to you two, and I admire the lengths you'll go to see it completed. But enough is enough. If this is the kind of stunt you'll pull here, I don't want to think about what you'll get into across the country for the sake of this list."

"But San Francisco—"

"Your father and I talked about your little California idea. He won't allow it."

"Of course he won't. You know Dad." He sat up. "Can't you tell him what you told me? Can't you tell him how you feel about all this?"

"I feel like it's time to be a parent now. I love you too much to let something happen to you."

"Nothing is going to happen."

"I suggest you take the summer to focus on how you'll earn the money to fix the cars you banged up. Less hanging out," she looked at me, "and no list."

"But—"

"No more list. Say your goodbyes to Olive for now. We need to talk as a family. We need each other." She turned to leave the room. "York, I expect you in the kitchen in one hour."

## PROMISES

He didn't speak when we made our way out to the car, nor did he speak on the way to my house.

As we idled in my driveway, I turned as much as I could in the seat. "I'm so glad you're here."

"You don't have to do that. My dad is—"

"Listen to me. I'm so, so incredibly sad my dad is gone. And I'm so, so incredibly grateful you're here."

York stared past me for a moment. "I've often wondered what happened to him. I figure maybe he was once a nice guy? For a while there I thought I was the one who turned him rotten."

"You know that's not true, right?"

"Actually, it could be. People can change because of other people. I'm kind of an impossible human being sometimes."

"If it helps, I don't regret choosing you for a minute, and I never will."

He put his forehead against mine and tangled his hands in my hair. We listened to one another breathe for a moment.

"I Love," he exhaled against my lips.

I smirked, having grown to adore that nickname. "Yes?"

And then he kissed me. He kissed me long and deep, sucking all the air from my body, making me wonder if the drawing in and expelling of air from the lungs in order to extract oxygen and excrete waste gases was overrated.

He pulled away and asked, on a large sigh, "So you don't think I'm doing an awful job at this whole 'second chance at life' thing?"

"You've lived your second chance so far with much more meaning than I'd ever have the courage to."

"It's because of you, you know."

"It's because of *you.*"

He smiled a little, and every cell in my body released in relief. He opened his center console and fished out his bucket list, turned on the light and smoothed it out on the steering wheel.

"So, did we complete this one, successfully?" he asked me.

"I'm not sure," I said. "What do you think?"

"As far as breaking the law, getting into a fender bender, owing someone I hate for his expensive car, and being emotionally wrung out like a wet towel are concerned, I think we came out like champs." I laughed. I couldn't help it.

But then I confessed, "I'm sad about California."

"Me too. My dad feels like he's got to prove to Mr. Kiger that he's got me under control, and my mom's more worried now than she's ever been. They're both too prideful to let him think they let me get away with this."

"It's like one goal cancelled out the other."

He sat back and deflated. "I know. But listen: the moment I can get out from under my parents' thumbs, I mean the second this all blows over, we'll figure out how to chase the sun. No more list, my ass. I didn't almost die to give up at goal five."

"Sure. I'm sure we can come up with an alternative."

"And Olive, one day we won't be teenagers, and you'll be out on your own, and I'll have some amazing job, and I'll take you to California. On my word, I will."

I smiled, grateful for that old, familiar spirit. "I believe you."

## *Fifteen*

## UNDER THE RADAR

I went a little over a week without seeing him, during which time I became desperately aware of how boring my days were without the bucket list. I worked, helped Selma study for her exams, consulted with Uncle Joe on how to get the bills paid for June, and tried not to think about all the pictures of York and me that I would have been taking while I took pictures of other stuff.

He slowly wiggled out from under the weight of his mother's watchful eyes and his father's critical eyes, and after eight days began talking to and seeing me more regularly. I got the impression he'd never been formally punished a day in his life.

I never asked how the conversation went between him and his parents on fender bender night. For once, I kind of didn't want to know.

## A WHIRL

On the last day of May, I got an email from my journalism professor. She asked me about my summer so far and expressed hopes that I didn't have much planned.

Then she wrote this:


*Of course you know you received an 'A' in my class. You should feel very proud. The improvement in your technique impressed me! In fact, your last article about organ donation blew me away. The story behind it employed a lot of empathy, which really grabbed me as a reader, and it also managed to be informative.*

*It impressed me so much that I submitted it to* News Matters – *Pasquotank. The editor is a friend of mine named Curtis Holbrook. I hope you don't mind – I do this every semester for students who have done an exceptional job in my classes.*

*Not only did he love the article and offer to publish it, but he offered you an unpaid internship which, if you accept, begins in June. Curtis' newspaper is majority online, so you must only report to headquarters once a week to gather your assignments and touch bases. This job is very open to freelance articles as well, which gives you a lot of creative opportunities.*

*Please let me know what you think! Curtis said he'd love to have you onboard, and I believe you've earned a spot on his team. This experience will be beneficial to your future career, and, who knows? You might one day get hired with* News Matters.

*I'll be glad to forward you the details.*

*Terri Spaulding*


I died a little. Only because my heart exploded with joy. I raced out of my bedroom and burst into the living room, where Mom and Selma sat on the couch.

"Guess what happened?"

"What?" my sister shot back in a mix of alarm and parody.

"My professor of journalism liked the work I did in her class this semester and sent my final article to the editor-in-chief of a newspaper in Pasquotank called *News Matters*, and he offered me an internship!"

"So that crazy lady finally noticed all your talent? About freaking time."

"An internship this early in the game is a major stepping stone. I could have a set career path before I'm out of undergrad."

We both eyed Mom, who sat in her spot and didn't react for a short while.

"I'm very proud of you," she said finally. "When will you start?"

"Mid-June, I think. The newspaper is majority online, so I'll only have to report downtown every so often, which means it shouldn't interfere with my responsibilities here."

Her smile faded a little. "You don't have to worry so much about me. Focus on your internship. You'll want to do a good job, make a good impression."

"I know, but we still have so much to keep up around here, and I—"

Selma pursed her lips. I was about to make Mom sound like a burden again.

"I mean, the job is very flexible, from what I understand. There's no reason why our routine needs to change."

My mom liked being taken care of. Always had. I didn't miss the expression of relief that blinked across her face.

I sent an email of acceptance back to Professor Spaulding, then hopped on the phone to spread the good news. I called Stefanie first, then York, who answered on the second ring.

"I Love."

"Hello, York."

"You sound like you've been running."

"I know. I got an email from Professor Spaulding." I had to pull the phone away from my car as he congratulated me after I told him.

"This calls for a celebration," he pointed out. "I want to hear all the details."

"Will you come see me?"

"I'm already halfway there."

He wasn't, of course, but York was the King of Hyperbole.

## ONE MORE

Though Mrs. Lively didn't like it, I spent as much time as I could that summer at their house, and I made sure to stay as far under the radar as I could—I didn't so much as sneeze too loudly. The relationship between York and his father became even more strained, but Mr. Lively still spent much of his time away from home.

Selma spent at least three nights out of the week at friends' houses and her days at the beach and the mall. I took majority of the responsibility for her, even though at almost seventeen she didn't feel she needed watching.

I knew we had abandoned my mother, but we had finally begun to adjust to a house without Dad in it. Our mother preferred to wallow in that absence, but my sister and I couldn't take it anymore. If I had to be in Fleet every day for the next three months, I would need an outlet.

York's birthday fell on the first week of June, on a Friday, so that morning I got up and began to bake him peanut butter cookies from scratch. I made sure to use real butter and left out the cornstarch I usually used, even though it always got me the chewy consistency I loved. I went to two organic food shops for a specific peanut butter that guaranteed a tree nut-free processing environment. I even distributed peanut butter morsels in the batch for extra peanut-butterness.

I took him to the Pasquotank River and stuck a candle in a tower I'd made of the soft cookies.

"My God, these are delicious," he said.

"You sure they're not too peanut-buttery?"

"Did you say the words 'too' and 'peanut-buttery' in the same sentence? Has my proficiency for putting words together that don't belong rubbed off on you?"

I tried one. They were very good. I suppose they didn't need the cornstarch.

"Can I pay you to make these for me once a week?" he asked.

"Can I pay you to stop flattering me?"

"I don't flatter anyone, ever. Not even you."

"I guess I have noticed that. But no, I won't accept monetary gifts from you."

"Fine. I'll use my body."

"Hey! Hey now! Prostitution? How low will you sink to get what you want?"

He held up a cookie. "I'm an opportunist, you remember...though I have made some questionable decisions in recent weeks."

"I actually think you have a lot to be proud of. Because of your recent shenanigans, the name York Lively—while commonly attributed to a Spinoza-worshipping, accidental bestselling author from the early twentieth century—is now also quite associated with mischief, mayhem, and a way-turned-down give-a-fuck. I think you've done well for yourself, sir."

"That, I Love, is the best compliment I've gotten in my eighteen years of life."

"Nineteen," I reminded him. "Happy Birthday."

## OCCLUSION

By the time I got home almost every night, Mom had already gone to bed. It was such a weight off my shoulders to spend time with my closest friends, people who helped me carry my own emotional weight and didn't add their own to it.

I spent the night at Stefanie's the Wednesday after York's birthday. When I pulled up to my house with York that next day, I was in higher spirits than I had been in a long time. We were blathering as we sauntered up to my front door. He smiled and joked, and it had been a nice summer day, not too hot.

The smell hit me first, as soon as I entered the foyer: acrid and heavy, so many kinds of body odor, and so strong. I immediately equated it with death.

I didn't call out to Mom. Not yet. She had been fine when I left the day before. Okay, she'd downed a couple beers by 9 a.m., but she had been standing and functioning. Selma had been there. Where was Selma? I thought for two seconds and remembered her telling me about plans to spend the night at a friend's. I had been so caught up in my own fun, I forgot to ask about Mom.

"Mom?" I croaked. We were almost down the hall. I could hear the low murmur of the television in the living room. The smell grew stronger. A line tightened from my throat down to my gut.

And there she sat, on the couch. She stared at the television with a tall can of beer wedged between her thighs.

"Mom?"

Her eyes didn't blink for several seconds after we entered the room. And then she moved her head slightly to her left, toward us.

"You okay?" I asked, scanning her from head to toe. She looked like Mom—thin, frail, tired. Drunk.

She stared. Had she gotten so drunk she couldn't speak?

"Talk to me," I said. "I need you to talk." I was not getting used to the smell, so pungent it made me queasy.

She moved a little in obedience, a kind of shrugging motion.

"What is wrong?" I asked each word firmly.

She mumbled. "What?" I asked. More mumbling. Her mouth wasn't moving right. I noticed a dark stain on the carpet at the entrance to the kitchen. More blood? No, the stain was far too big and blacker than the red black of blood. "What are you saying to me?"

She took a deep breath, wagged her head. *"Fine."*

"Fine, what?"

"Fine." She lifted her left arm. Her right arm stayed limp at her side. The right side of her mouth sagged in a similar fashion.

"You're fine?" She nodded. "Are you sure?"

Her eyes rolled back to the television.

I took a deep breath and wanted to gag. I couldn't imagine how York felt. "Good. I'll be right back."

Outside on my porch, I inhaled and exhaled a good dozen times, my hands on my hips. I studied the sky.

"I'm so confused," I said. "What the hell is wrong with her?"

"I don't know."

"I've never, ever seen her this drunk. How am I supposed to stay here tonight when I have so much to take care of? Who can I call to help me?"

His eyes probed gently until they seized mine. "You should call an ambulance."

I stared at him, taken aback. I don't know if I was in denial, or naïve, or so scared that I couldn't think straight.

"You think? She started drinking yesterday morning. Who knows how many beers she's had since then. I don't—I'm not sure if—"

"Olive. I've been really drunk. I've seen really drunk. I know you have, too. And that, in there, is not really drunk."

His tone was even gentler than before, and for some reason this was what made me start to panic.

We walked back into the house, and the smell hit us anew. "I'm calling an ambulance," I announced.

Her eyes shifted slowly toward me. "What?"

"You're going to the hospital."

"No no no no no no," she inched forward, and the beer tipped over and dribbled onto her shoes. Her right side dragged along.

"Yes," I said as I dialed 9-1-1. I had an operator on the line in seconds who sent an emergency vehicle. I left her slurring *no no no* as I walked into the kitchen, stepping past the dark spot. There, I discovered at least some of the source of the awful smell: a pot of food which had half-burned, then been left to sit and begin to grow mold. Yesterday's breakfast, I imagined.

I stalked back into the living room and took the beer from her lap, then I returned to the kitchen to dump it into the sink. She tried to get up several times and we kept her calm, told her that she had to go no matter how much she resisted or pleaded.

Was this it? Was my mother dying, too? Would Selma and I be orphans?

I met the ambulances and fire truck in our driveway and answered every question the emergency personnel fired at me on the way back inside.

Two EMTs studied my mom's vitals and attempted to ask her questions while one fireman talked to York and me. We told him the situation as best we could and they brought in a gurney. The man and woman EMT lifted Mom's frail body, strapped her down, and covered her up. York stared at her as they wheeled her from the house and down the steps.

"Are you riding along or following behind?" an EMT asked me.

"Um." I looked around, numb. "I'll follow. I have to clean up. Pack a bag for her."

The door closed, and York and I were alone.

He didn't speak except to ask me what he could help me with. He grabbed a trash bag and we dumped empty beer cans into it, one empty fifth of what appeared to have been white liquor—she hadn't had any of that stuff since right after Dad died—and one filthy sock with a mysterious and horrendous-smelling substance on it. We made our way into the kitchen and dumped half-eaten plates of food and the burned stuff in the pot on the stove.

"You might want to come see this," I heard York's voice down the hall as I swept. I joined him at the hallway bathroom, where I discovered the other source of the smell: a mixture of puke and urine and dark, liquid feces that had dripped down the side of the toilet, pooled on the floor, and trailed down the hallway.

I dragged him away.

We entered my mom's room and I grabbed the first duffel bag I could get my hands on: dad's old basketball bag. I began to stuff clean socks and underwear inside. I grabbed two sleep t-shirts and a pair of regular pants and a blouse. I didn't know what to pack in this situation. I rushed into the bathroom and grabbed her toothbrush, her toothpaste, soap, and a comb.

York took the bag for me and we hurried back down the hall. I shut off the television before we left and saw a spot of the same mixture of urine and shit on the couch where Mom had been sitting.

~ * ~

I went into the emergency room's bed area while York waited in the lobby. A team of nurses were catheterizing Mom as I walked in. She lay there, eyes so dead and unseeing I truly worried if they were sticking a tube into a corpse, but the monitor told me we still had her.

The young, kind-faced doctor asked me if I was her daughter, how old she was, how long she'd been like this. *An alcoholic?* I asked, *or in this condition?*

They were positive she'd had a stroke, but they would run some tests and take more stats. She would stay in the hospital to safely, medically detox. At five feet and nearly eleven inches, my mother weighed a mere ninety-nine pounds.

York sat with me for hours while I called every family member I could reach. I told Selma to stay put at her friend's house. Uncle Joe came at ten o'clock that night to relieve us, but I wanted to stay. York didn't leave either.

On the stroke unit floor, he and I slept—kind of—curled up on a hard couch while a television murmured on a nearby wall all night long.

## STABLE

Early the next morning, a doctor told me his team managed to stabilize Mom's condition, but I couldn't see her yet. He told Uncle Joe and me that he'd give us more information later on that day. My uncle bought us all coffee and then went home to change. He promised to make us leave and get some real rest when he returned.

"I need air," I told York hoarsely.

"I know where we can go."

We took an elevator up to a quiet, empty floor. We followed a short corridor with windows on one side, through which I could see a deserted outdoor courtyard. He pushed open the glass door and it made a faint suction sound, and I heard the rattle behind me as the door slid back into place on its hinges. My coffee cup trembled in my hands as I placed it down on one of the bright blue thermoplastic picnic tables.

"My neck hurts," he said, grimacing as he touched each ear to either shoulder. "How are you not as stiff as I am? I'm the one with experience sleeping on awful hospital furniture, not you."

I shook my head. "Don't. Not now."

His eyes became sober. "It'll be okay."

"You sure? Because I'm not so sure." I blew out a heavy, shaky breath. "This is my fault. It seemed like my life might start falling back into place, and I got so distracted with all this stuff and your list and then..." I trailed off, noting the brief, stung expression on his face. "I should have watched her closer. I let my sister stay in that house alone to deal with her. I didn't do what I was supposed to."

He took in my words without any sort of reaction. Then he asked, "Can I push my boundaries a little?"

"Yes."

"It is not your responsibility to take care of your mother. It's not your sister's responsibility, either. For God's sake, who's taking care of *you*?"

I laughed. I always seemed to laugh at the wrong time with him.

"Huh. I guess you are," I said, the thought so ridiculously obvious. "That's what scared me, though, all those months ago when we first started talking. All the times I wanted to tell you about my life but felt like I couldn't, I was afraid of putting you here, where you are right now."

He didn't reply. Whether he couldn't or decided against it, I didn't know. I didn't want to know, so I kept talking.

"Here's what's really important for you to know: This," I indicated the towering brick and mortar of Pasquotank Medical Center, "isn't new to me. My family has been here with Mom before. This is my life, and it's hard, and it's going to keep being hard. So—" the words became more difficult to say the closer I got to saying them, "I wouldn't blame you if you decided this was more trouble than it's worth."

By *this*, I meant *I*. Me.

He stared at me with eyes that were somehow still soft and gooey despite the hard truth I'd just dealt him. "None of this has changed how I feel about you," he said quietly.

I felt my face forming a frown, and he shook his head. "None of it has changed how I feel." He punctuated each word with the most definite period I'd ever heard, willing me to just get it.

"I'm still glad I met you," he said. "I'm still glad I fought for you. I'm still glad we've done all of this crazy stuff together. Because Olive, I—"

He lowered his head and scoffed, then looked at me with a small smile so forbearing I almost took it as an insult. "Olive, I am *so* crazy in love with you."

It felt like getting hit, only with a blow so wonderful you realized too late you had your arms wide open the whole time to receive it. I let my face fall into my hands, and for a moment I couldn't figure out if I was laughing or crying. I felt the tears wetting my fingers, but I also realized the intensity of the joy rampaging through my chest.

I lifted my head to gaze at him, and he still stood there, still patient, that one eyebrow cocked, daring me to feel. He was so exasperating.

I just sighed and said, "You'd have to be."

And he smiled so wide I thought his face would tear in two. I wrapped my arms around him and he wrapped his around me, and we held each other until I knew I could go back downstairs to the stroke unit and face the next hours.

### *Sixteen*

## CLEANING UP

A hemorrhagic stroke. Doctors made one hundred percent certain of it before they told us. They discovered a spot of blunt trauma on the side of her head which suggested a recent fall, but the bleeding had clotted on its own. Mom fell all the time. She could have fallen the morning I left, which meant she spent almost thirty-six hours alone.

My mom didn't know what year it was and could barely remember me or Selma. She didn't know Uncle Joe. She had very little short-term memory, and her long-term memory was all screwed up. When she asked where Dad was, I almost broke down because I didn't know what to tell her.

I called to postpone my first day with my internship, and I spent a lot of time at the hospital. York did, too.

He, my sister, Stefanie, and I cleaned the house the day after I should have started my internship. We deep cleaned the kitchen, washed all the dishes, dumped crusted-over plates, mopped, took out trash, and threw out all the old food in the refrigerator. York took on the sweeping, and I had enough good humor to apologize for us not having a hidden vacuum unit. He made a face at me, and my sister and Stefanie demanded an explanation, their eyes first widening in wonder before they burst out laughing.

We tackled the living room and hallway, then we straightened Mom's room. Selma and I cleaned the bathroom; we wouldn't make the others get involved. We closed the door behind us and stayed solemn and quiet for the first time all day.

We took a break in the living room, and York went out to get us pizza, delivering it like some jolly pizza Santa Claus. He tried to teach my sister how to juggle. She was hopeless, but he was patient. When he showed her a perfect four-ball toss again to help her see her errors, she knocked the balls out of mid-air in defiance.

It was a good day in a sea of chaotic ones. Mom's siblings flooded in to see her those first few days, then trickled in after. Five sisters and three brothers comforted and poured on their love, discussed her right in front of her face, and decided what would be done for her. Uncle Joe and I seethed. They came in and assumed responsibility, as if they had any idea what had happened. My uncle confronted three of them at once on this and a blowout ensued, claims of overreactions and insensitivity and, yes, even glory-hogging.

Everyone pointed out the obvious: that Mom had been helped by nearly every sibling at least once in her life at some point, and each of them had jobs and children and work and lives, and each was busy and frustrated and tired. My uncle pointed out that Selma and I had suffered since my dad died, and what about us? And they hadn't even seen us since the funeral, and my uncle also had a job and two daughters and a life, and was also frustrated and tired.

It didn't go over well, and after they showed their faces for those first few days, I didn't see them again. They'd done their part, and they couldn't bear to watch Mom in that hospital bed, especially since she had become such a shell, such a vegetable of a person, and anyway she had done this to herself.

## WHAT MATTERS

I donned my favorite white, sleeveless polyester shirt with the high, ruffled collar, and tan skinny slacks. I'd tied my thick hair into a bun atop my head. My entire ensemble screamed "Stand tall!"

I decided I should call out again this week, maybe even for the whole summer, with Mom in the hospital for such an indeterminate period of time. Maybe I should forget about the opportunity entirely.

"Nope," said York behind me. He sat on my bed, one foot on the floor and the other planted on the comforter, resting his forearm on his bent knee and rubbing a forefinger and thumb under his chin. "I see that look on your face. You should definitely go in today. No question."

"I knew you'd say that."

"Don't be scared, and don't worry about anyone but you right now. It's a couple hours, and your mom will be fine, and the house will be fine, and it'll all be fine. Do a good job. You want this."

I'd corresponded with Curtis Holbrook several times before I went to Pasquotank County for my first day. A small, nondescript building on one of the busiest streets in the heart of downtown housed the *News Matters* headquarters. The receptionist pointed me toward the elevator and told me to go to the second floor.

The elevator doors opened on a scene right out of a movie. At least fifteen people typed away on computer screens in front of large windows that faced the back of the street. I walked past them, and those who managed to tear their eyes away from their screens smiled at me.

*News Matters* had five total unpaid interns that summer, and all of us met in a small room adjacent to the reporters' area that morning. I noticed one girl from my Intro to Journalism Two class.

"Hi everyone, I'm Curtis Holbrook," said the fortyish man with light brown hair, gray at his temples, and deep crow's feet around his sea green eyes. "Welcome to *News Matters*, where, of course, news matters. Also, we report on news matters that will matter to those here in Pasquotank who value the news. Have I said those two words enough?"

"Not at all," said one guy.

"What's the name of the newspaper again?" I chimed in.

"I'm so glad you asked! It's *News Matters*." The five interns pretended to scribble that bit down in our notebooks.

"This week we welcome Olive—a little late, but better that than never. I hope you'll find this environment fun. Last week we went over what we're all about here: encouraging new ideas, creativity, and honesty. As an online publication, we fight with traditional newspapers for attention all the time. In the same fashion, the traditional newspapers fight for attention in an increasingly digitized world. That is our advantage, but we're a small publication, so all that we report has to make a splash.

"We are not your evening news at five. However, if you know about a significant community event, report on it. If you don't feel there's enough happening in the city, or if you don't live in the city, branch out. Bring people's attention to issues they need to know about."

He pointed me out. "Olive submitted a great article about organ donation, where she highlighted her hometown of Fleet, her own family tragedy, and the inspiring story of a young man who underwent a life-saving operation." He pointed to another girl. "Jill submitted a fantastic article about the local library's summer event theme that highlights homelessness in the city. I expect you'll submit a followup article when Chris Gardner comes into town to talk about *The Pursuit of Happyness* in August?"

"Absolutely."

"The sooner we get these kinds of stories out, the more people will read what we have to say. Journalism is changing, folks. You have to be quicker, more in-your-face, and more creative. I believe you all have the goods, and I'm extremely excited to work with you."

I went home with a small assignment on downtown Pasquotank's upcoming music and culture festival, on which I'd gathered information before I went home. I had two days to get it up on the website, then I had the go-ahead to report on whatever else I wanted before next week. In the journalism world, the more you got your name out there, the better, so I decided I would produce at least two articles a week, more when the school year started up again and I would be back in town. I didn't know if I could handle it all while distracted by Mom, but my competitive spirit kicked in once I started my job at *News Matters*, and I wanted to see how far it would take me.

# EVERYTHING

Mom's condition was improving, but not quickly. People bounced back from strokes at various speeds, and Mom's alcoholism was affecting her ability to recover. The stroke had damaged the nerves on her whole right side, and since she was right-handed, she had to learn how to eat and use her comb and toothbrush all over again with her left hand.

On the Friday of my first week at *News Matters*, York and I visited her in the hospital. He half-watched the daytime show on the television above our heads while I watched her eat banana pudding out of a Styrofoam bowl. She was so frail and dangerously thin for all her height I never inherited. She had always been thin, so I hadn't noticed how bad she had gotten. Or I hadn't wanted to notice.

The pudding had this preposterous amount of whipped topping heaped onto it, so much I doubted there were even any bananas underneath. Some of the topping ended up smeared on the side of her mouth. I felt like a parent watching an infant feed herself for the first time. And then I realized that not eighteen years before that moment, she had done the same for me.

And then I felt hot and my throat tightened in a funny way that unnerved and angered me, and suddenly I hated the heavy-handed lunatic that had put so much topping on the banana pudding, so I told Mom I would be back after I got some fresh air while we waited for Uncle Joe.

York asked if I wanted him to come with me. I let my eyes answer.

Mom's speech wasn't quite back up to par, so she nodded. She leaned over to kiss me goodbye, even though I told her I'd be right back, and some of the whipped topping got on my cheek. York's eyes widened in question as he held the door open for me. Since I didn't want to embarrass her, I left it there and led us out.

I met my uncle coming down the hallway with Selma as we made our way to the parking deck. "I guess you can go now," he said. "We can meet you back at the house."

"I told Mom I'd be back," I said and wiped at my cheek.

"Why don't I go wait in the car," suggested York. "Your mom may not feel comfortable with me there all the time, since she doesn't remember me. You guys can have family time and you can meet me when you're ready to go."

"Sure. I'll just be a few minutes."

When he was out of earshot, my uncle cocked his mouth a bit. "He's a good boy."

"He is a very good boy."

"He knows how to juggle," said Selma. "And he has vacuums in the floor of his kitchen that you sweep dirt and food into. We need one of those. I'd always volunteer to clean up if we had that."

"Really, now?"

"He's pretty cool to hang out with," I said.

Selma shook her head at me. "Are we going upstairs or what?"

"You go ahead. I have to talk to Olive really quick," said Uncle Joe. Selma pressed her phone to her corneas and continued down the hallway before our uncle finished the sentence.

"What's wrong?" I asked.

"Nothing. How do you like your internship so far?"

"It's great. It's work, but it's work I really want to do. It's fun pretending to be a real journalist."

"I'm glad. I'm glad you took the opportunity after all. I know this situation with your mom has thrown you off. You shouldn't have to think about any of this."

"It's my life. I'm used to it."

"You are. Shame."

I smiled. "Did we stay behind just to talk about my internship?"

My uncle turned his head toward the door York left through, then faced me. "Your friend is here with you a lot. Helped you clean up your house, too, didn't he?"

"Yeah."

"You're here so much. Your mom will be in here a while. Maybe through June."

"I know that."

"And then afterwards she'll need lots of care. And therapy. You'll have your hands full for the rest of the summer."

"I know." Most days I tried not to think about it. I became depressed if I did.

"You still doing that bucket list?"

"Oh no. That list is on permanent hiatus."

"Shame," he repeated. "I remember a couple months back you two mentioned a vacation. Seems like you could use one right about now."

"I know I can't leave. Not now."

"Who says?"

Now I blinked several times. "Are you telling me to go to California?"

"I'm not your parent. But, in light of your current parental situation, I feel I have a right to step in and...strongly suggest that you go."

"I can't go on a vacation now. Or anytime soon. My mother had a stroke. My family needs me. What would it look like if I—?"

"You've taken more than your fair share of the responsibility for your mom. You have an opportunity to do this for you, and you won't be happy if you don't take it. Remember how you felt the first day of your internship? You've got to feel that more. You're too young and you've had too much taken away from you."

My chest heaved. "It can't happen."

"Yes, it can."

He didn't know about streaking night, about my strained relationship with York's parents. Of course I hadn't told him any of that. And I didn't know how to tell him now.

"Will Mom be all right?" I asked instead.

"I can take over for a few days while you're gone. Your aunt Linda and I will help Selma and figure out the next steps. We'll take Pam to therapy if she's already back home by the time you leave, and we'll drive her where she needs to go."

I stared beyond my uncle for a moment as if I could see York behind him, beckoning. "I'm scared," I admitted.

"Of what?"

"Everything. Of leaving Mom, of traveling somewhere new without my parents, of enjoying myself. Everything."

"Good. That way you'll be careful."

*Seventeen*

## MUTINY

When you grow up with two parents, it's difficult to get used to a house absent of them. Even with Selma there, my near-empty house seemed too quiet, especially at night, when my thoughts wanted to race out of town. So York stayed a lot.

We listened to music and talked. The night after Uncle Joe gave me his blessing, we were lying on our sides on my bed, our bent knees touching and our foreheads a couple inches apart. We each had an earbud in one ear, connected to each other by a very short cord. His iPod shuffled between songs, and all fell silent for a moment.

I kept my eyes on the ceiling when I whispered, "Let's just go."

"Where?"

"To California."

He shifted his head one inch over. "Really?"

"Is it still possible?"

He seemed to consider his answer. "I know how I planned to fund the trip, if that's what you're asking."

"Did it involve Mom And Dad?"

"A little."

I sat up on my elbows. "I have three-hundred fifty dollars saved. It's not even enough to buy a plane ticket, but it can supplement the holes in your budget."

He looked at the wall for a minute. "I have a savings account I'm not allowed to touch until I graduate and move out. My parents would kill me if I dipped into it now." He smiled. "So. Money's taken care of."

"Are you sure you're okay with that?"

"I'm sure my parents can't threaten my life any more than it already has been." An elated expression—which at this point I'd come to equate with scheming—fell over his face. "We'll have to nix Barb and find a new and very cheap place to stay. San Francisco is expensive, so we'll have to get lucky. I have a good track record with getting lucky."

"York?" I said. "I've just asked you to disobey your parents."

"I know."

"Do you hate me for it?"

His eyes grew serious when they fell on me again. "Are you sure you want to do this?"

I sighed. "I've got to get out of here."

"Then all is well between us."

## GOING...

He picked the longest day of the year, June 22. To him it made perfect sense because it ensured we'd have plenty of time to make it, no matter how many flights we would have to switch or layovers we may experience, and it even left some wiggle room for disasters like the flight losing our luggage. It also meant an eight-day window of time, during which I would have zero chance to save more money.

"I'll have to pay you back somehow," I said.

"It's a birthday gift."

"You already gave me one of those."

"A Christmas gift."

"Too far away to make sense."

"A     thank-you-for-baking-me-peanut-butter-cookies-and-also-saving-my-life gift."

I scrunched my face. "This is too big for cookies, and my dad is the one who saved your life."

"He did. And you did, too."

And those hazel eyes sparkled, and those full lips danced until he could no longer keep a straight face, and I decided those cookies *were* pretty delicious and I *had* searched long and hard for that special peanut butter.

## GOING...

York may not have been so much lucky as he was obstinate. He waded through different stay options in San Francisco for hours before he happened upon an online-based company that connected amateur hosts with adventurous or agreeable or, as in our case, strapped travelers. He communicated with a man named Norman O'Shaughnessy who had listed the ridiculously priced townhome he owned with his husband.

"Apparently, people stay with them all the time, and they've got really good reviews," he told me. "Over fifty of them, in fact."

"What?" I observed the computer screen for myself. The couple had mostly five-star reviews.

"They host one 'family' at a time and run the setup like a bed and breakfast. All payments are taken care of through the website, we provide I.D. so they know our faces, and we can contact them as often as we need to between now and when we get there."

"It sounds great," I said. "What's the catch?"

"Relative uncertainty."

I was learning to accept relative uncertainty as an inevasible constant in life, but the old unwillingness to take risks still proved as deeply tangled up within me as my own circulatory system—the what-ifs would always be that largest vein among a complicated network of emotions.

"If you don't like this option, there are definitely other ways to make the trip work," said York.

"No. I like this. I think we'll have a much more personal experience than if we spent all our money on a hotel."

"Plus," he said, "Norman and his husband don't live far from the Pacific Highway."

"A photographer's dream."

"You'll have to get a lot of documentation for this goal. I've not traveled farther west than Tennessee, so this is probably the biggest adventure I've been on." He frowned. "You'd think I'd have done more by now."

"What does that mean?"

"I don't know. I've got this whole idea about doing life, but really I've stayed very much in one place for a lot of it. Almost dying was, like, the craziest thing I've ever done."

"I think flying across the country on a whim against your parents' wishes to stay with two guys you don't know because your irresponsible girlfriend asked you to, all while having recently survived heart transplant surgery, is definitely the way to start doing life."

## GONE

Never thought I'd see dawn's asscrack, as York had described it, but there it was. And it was quite dark.

On the fourth Friday in June, he woke me in my bedroom at that god-awful hour right before astronomical twilight when the sky is at the line between black and a lighter shade of black.

"York Lively, it is not even four a.m.," I pointed out when I noticed his breathlessness. "How are you so nauseatingly cheerful?"

"Mostly because I'm about to go away with the girl of my dreams. Pragmatically because the sun rises at five fifty-eight today, and if we miss it then Goal Number Six doesn't count, and we've already booked our flight, so we have to go."

"Too many words. Just tell me to get the hell up."

"Get the hell up."

We brewed some coffee, then called to double-check with Uncle Joe before we left. "How many types of identification do you have?" he asked.

"Three, I think."

"Good. Did you two bring at least one pair of pants each? It can get mighty chilly in San Francisco, even this late in the year."

"Sure."

"Don't 'sure' me. Your cousins do that to me. I'm trying to help you out. I'm sure York's parents have covered all the bases, too."

"Sur— Yes, sir."

"Make sure to call when you get there."

"I will. I've got to make sure Mom is all right."

"Mom is fine. I'll want to know you're all right. You."

Me. I would have to remember that.

"'Kay, we've got to go now," I said. "The sun rises only once a day, you know."

"Be careful, please," he said. "I'll be by the airport to pick your car up sometime later on today. Drive safely. Go the speed limit. Make sure you don't get separated in the airport." The fatherly advice swirled around us as we loaded into my car and started off for Nags Head.

We held hands and made small talk while I struggled to wake up on the quiet ride to the Outer Banks. We didn't pass a single car, and once again the time felt loaned to us alone. We got to the beach at 5:30, abandoning my car in a public access parking lot and walking onto the beach. He laid a blanket down for us to sit on.

"You awake now?" he asked.

"Oh yeah, no problem since I've had a few moments with my life's blood here." I held up my travel mug like a trophy.

"You know what my life's blood is?" He pointed at the thin seam of fire that had begun to break over the horizon.

The world cracked open to reveal its red hot core. I took endless pictures on the OneStep, the Nikon, and my phone. The sky burst into a field of red and purple and orange reflected on the puffy clouds. We mostly sat in silence and listened to the water crash all around us and the gulls call to one another.

When the time came, he stood and helped me to my feet. I watched his face come alive, awash in new sun, beautiful with amazement. I almost forgot to keep taking pictures for watching him, but I managed a quick Polaroid of his illuminated profile, of the roaring ocean, and of the red ball peeking over the edge of the horizon.

"Hello there," he whispered, then he turned his head to me. "And... GO!"

We raced to the car as fast as the sand and our sleep-deprived limbs would let us.

We drove an hour-and-a-half to Norfolk International and encountered no traffic until we got close to the airport, but we managed to squeeze through in relatively good time. After we checked in for our flight at the kiosks, checked our bags, and breezed through the metal detectors, we grabbed biscuits for breakfast and waited to board.

York turned his phone over once in his hands. "Here goes," he said and dialed his father's number. Mr. Lively was, of course, already at work and, of course, would be too busy to answer. When York reached voicemail, he cleared his throat.

"Hi, Dad. Sorry I missed you. I wanted to let you know that I'm... I'm sorry. I'm sorry I got in trouble, I'm sorry for everything I said, and I'm sorry for that night. And...I'm on my way to San Francisco. With Olive. We'll be back in three days. So...call me if you need me—"

I snorted.

"—and we'll see you soon. Okay. 'Bye." He managed to hang up before he burst out laughing with me.

"Oh, God," he said between gasps, "do you think all my stuff will be on the lawn when I get back, or do you think he'll just dump it?"

"I'm so sorry." Through the laughter I could feel negative energy spreading through each of my limbs to eat away at the nerves.

"Olive. I'm so ridiculously excited right now," he said. "I feel like...I feel like FancyFace."

"What, your cat? How so?"

"All she does all day is follow the sun. I watched her one day last year when I was stuck at home recovering. From eight in the morning to four in the afternoon, she walked around the house looking for windows that faced the sun. She'd lie down and fall asleep in a warm spot. I thought, 'What a lucky creature.' If humans could do that every once in a while, the world would be a much happier place."

"I agree," I said on a yawn.

"You still think we're being young and ridiculous and reckless?"

"'All great deeds and all great thoughts have a ridiculous beginning'," I said in response.

"An advantageous quote. Yours?"

"I'm flattered. Albert Camus. I started researching wise words I would Photoshop over my senior quote if I knew even one soul on the yearbook staff this year, and that quote reminded me of you."

"I choose to take that as a compliment."

"You should."

We boarded at 8:40, fifteen minutes before departure. York only had a carry-on. I had my purse, which functioned as a carry-on because it held a great deal of my life. We hadn't purchased seats next to each other, but we quickly finagled our way into the same row. He let me have the window seat.

"What do you have in there?" He gestured at my purse.

"The usual: wallet, cell phone, lip balm, this bag of mint-flavored floss stick thingies, hand sanitizer, lotion, 'nother lip balm, umbrella—"

"Umbrella?"

"Doesn't it rain a lot in San Francisco?"

"You're carrying an umbrella in there? Pretty sure it no longer counts as a purse."

"Men and women have conflicting definitions of 'purse'."

"Sure. What else you got in that duffle bag?"

"Uh, gum. Eyeliner. Mascara. Compact. Nikon. Extra film. Pens. Ibuprofen. Trash."

"You are incredible."

"Okay, don't come crying to me when your head hurts and it's raining and you need gum for your morning breath."

"Do I have morning breath?"

"Not really."

My issues with heights notwithstanding, I always got a thrill when I traveled by plane. When we taxied onto the runway and the captain murmured his instructions for takeoff, my eyes stayed glued to the window. We left the ground and soared into the atmosphere, and I exhaled.

I seemed to blink twice and we had already landed in Arlington, a little over an hour after we left Norfolk. We boarded right away for Phoenix.

"I've only ever seen Arizona in pictures," I said. "It's in the same country as North Carolina and somehow it looks so different."

"I never realized how weird traveling across the country would be, all the time zones," he said. "We'll travel for nearly half a day, though technically there's only a three-hour time difference between the East and West coasts."

"It's that wily sun, making us jump through hoops to catch him. We'll spend all day today making up for lost hours. It's like time travel. We'll fly for hours and still be behind."

"What a wondrous thing, time."

For every mile we traveled backward, I began to feel like I needed sleep. After a small lunch, I napped against the window for maybe thirty minutes until he woke me so I could watch our descent into Phoenix. The sprawl of mountains loomed in the distance and made the sky look like a ripped piece of paper.

We had a little more time here, so we moseyed over to the next gate and waited for boarding instructions.

"I promise, body o' mine," York said, "this is the last circadian rhythm disruption I'll subject you to for the next seventy-two hours. Hold out until four o'clock, will you?"

"You would say it like that."

"My brain is trained to think like a biologist."

"And thence you speak like one."

"At least I don't say words like 'thence.' You're practically an English major, you library assistant."

"What does that mean? Thence is a normal word."

"It is. In England. In 1327."

"Thence is a normal word."

"You are incredibly intelligent, I Love. Never forget about those of us whose vocabularies are not as varied as yours." He kissed my forehead and I shooed him away. Thence *is* a normal word.

On the last flight, he powered up his laptop, and we munched airplane peanuts and watched several episodes of some sitcom I didn't much care for. As we descended into San Francisco I dragged his face to the window. "My God, look at that," I said.

The city seemed constructed out of tall, Monopoly-piece-like buildings, and the Golden Gate Bridge stretched a thousand miles long across the blue Golden Gate strait in all its majesty.

We grabbed our bags and checked them for the millionth time that day, and then we wandered around as thousands of people rushed by. Until we caught sight of it, I legitimately feared we wouldn't even be able to find the exit in the airport.

Outside, we took a moment to stretch our legs. The sun from home had begun to head our way, and at home my family had already finished dinner. Here, at minutes before five o'clock, most people hadn't even gotten off work yet.

"We're here," I said on an exhale.

"Awesome, right?"

"I didn't know an experience could be so familiar and so different all at once."

He flagged down a taxi. We planned to ask the owners of our temporary home for ideas for better, less expensive ways to get around.

"Where are you headed?" the driver said.

"Can you take us to the beach in Pacifica? Linda Mar?" I asked. "Um, the most scenic route possible?" York looked at me.

"That's a little way out," he said. He pulled into traffic.

"I know. Thank you."

On the way toward San Bruno, York's phone buzzed and he yanked it from his pocket. "Oh, here we go," he said.

"Dad?"

"Mom."

Here we go, indeed.

"Hey Mom. I—yes, I know. I'm really in San Francisco. I'm fine. I'm fine. She's here, too. I'm *fine*." He put a hand on his forehead, and now my nerve endings really crackled.

"I can't," he continued. "Because I have to do this. I brought the right dosages of my medications, so—yes, I'm taking them when I should. I know you're upset. I'll call you. I'll call every hour. I won't come back until the trip is over. Can we talk then?"

My stomach clenched more the longer I listened. I had helped sever the tie between him and pretty much the only ally he had in his whole family. Why had I insisted on this trip? Why had I coerced him to disobey his parents to make me happy? How could I have been so selfish?

"If he doesn't want to talk to me, that's his problem. Just know that I'm sorry, and I love you, and I'm fine, and I'll call you." He didn't speak anymore, and he hung up shortly after that.

"That was about as awful as I expected it to be," I said.

"She's beside herself," he admitted, "but she's not surprised. This is totally something I would do."

"Not if I hadn't asked you to."

He arched an eyebrow. "Have you met me yet?"

"I didn't want to ruin the relationship between you and your mom."

"It'll be okay." He wrapped his arm around me. "Can we cross that bridge when we get back to North Carolina? I'm on a remarkable journey with you, and I don't want to come down from this high."

Finally, we merged onto Highway 1 toward Pacifica. We spent seven glorious miles on the PCH.

"There's too much magnificence here and not enough eyes in my face to take it in!" York complained.

I snapped photo after photo as we breezed along the highway. When we had almost arrived in Pacifica, we saw more flashes of the ocean that surged on the one side and began to see the rocky cliffs on the other. "This is insane," I agreed.

"North Carolina beaches are so flat!" he said. "The earth dips into the ocean. Meanwhile, the cliffs over here are all tall and dangerous and jagged and resist erosion as much as possible. A big, fat middle finger to the Pacific Ocean, I think."

The taxi dropped us off in the closest parking lot to the beach, and we grabbed our duffel bags and thanked him.

The beach curved to hug the ocean, or pinch it. In the distance on our left a massive cliff jutted outward. The wind had picked up slightly, but we didn't need any extra layers. People strolled all around us, the area alive with squeals and laughter and idle chatter.

"So," I said as we walked, "you never asked me why I chose this beach."

"Olive, why this beach?"

"Excellent question!"

"Thanks. I thought of it myself."

"The tide is relatively low this time of day," I informed him, "and, as with many California beaches, this one is at the top of the list for great tide pools."

I led him south until we came across a collection of tide pools, legitimate pools, not the sad little sandbars we came across at home months ago.

He took my hand and scampered across the rocks. "Olive! *These* are tide pools."

"Show me everything."

He pointed out different organisms as we traveled up and down the rocks.

"Here we're mid-intertidal, I think," he said. "See? There's an abundance of algae here for organisms to feed on. Here are some sea sponges and barnacles. Here are some sea palms, sea stars, anemones."

We tidepooled for at least an hour, until we could hardly see anymore, and the water started to rise, and he had told me all I could comprehend but not all he knew.

We made our way toward the ocean and dipped our feet in the water. The chill reflected the temperate weather. Even in the balmy South, it took the water on the coast until mid-July to warm from winter temperatures. I remembered the icy water from my first trip to Kill Devil Hills, when I hadn't even been sure I should go anywhere with York, and I laughed.

I looked at him and found him staring. "What?"

"You are so beautiful," he almost whispered, the crashing waves taking over most of the sentence. "When you laugh for no reason. It's just really beautiful."

We sat against our bags and kicked off our flip-flops. The sand skittered across my jeans and dusted the hair on his legs. We passed the remainder of the evening watching the coast and comparing it to home. In spite of all we'd broken to get to California, Fleet felt so far away that I couldn't even worry. I didn't regret following my heart, and my life would not get any longer, and I had a sunset to catch.

Beyond the huge cliff, the dying light caused streaks of amber, dark gray, opal, and lavender to mingle in the sky, dragged across the horizon by God's fingers.

"What time's the sun due to set?" I asked.

"Eight thirty-two."

"I'm so glad we're here. I don't want it to end. Not yet."

"We've got time."

We stood up and moved close to one another. I snapped several pictures with the Nikon. Then I switched to my OneStep to get our profiles as we watched the water. The sun continued to sink closer to the same line of fire it had been born from that very morning. And we waited in silence.

It happened the way you'd expect it to. Unremarkable if you think about it for what it is, or if you're used to watching a West coast sunset. Still. I knew the Earth was moving, and the sun was where it had been all day, but the way it disappeared beneath that line where the ocean met the sky made it appear as if the water were sucking it down.

I got a picture of the top of it peeking over the horizon once again, and then it left us and left its colors behind.

"Caught you," mouthed York.

He took out the list, crossed off "Chase the Sun."

"I'm sorry I couldn't hold it there for you," I said. "The sun. I would have held it right there in the sky for as long as you wanted."

We put our foreheads together and listened to the waves crash on the shore. His hands clutched my waist and kept me close to him as the sky's colors succumbed to dark.

## Eighteen


## LIKE HOME

Norman O'Shaughnessy lived southwest of Balboa Park and his townhouse sat at the bottom of a quiet inclined street. The property had driveway enough for one car, and they had parked their other car on the street with all the others from neighboring townhomes.

We had informed our hosts we would arrive after sunset. Norman answered the door—I recognized his coiffed, sandy blond hair—and his brown eyes rounded. "Oh, good, you guys found us! We were beginning to worry."

"We got caught up at the beach," I explained. "I hope we haven't shown up too late."

"Not at all. We've just finished cooking dinner. Come in." We slid in beside him. "I'm Norman—call me Norm. York and Olive?"

The outside hadn't hinted at the largeness of the inside. A number of windows opened up every single wall. The kitchen felt snug, but the floors and cabinets were hardwood. Intricate light fixtures hung from the ceiling; a wood and marble island sat in the middle. Out of the stainless steel refrigerator popped the upper half of Norman's husband, who pulled out several bags of vegetables and a long stick of bread.

"I'm Jeff," he said. He had dark hair and Mediterranean features. He placed the bags on the island beside a bowl and wiped his hands together before he shook ours. "We've prepared a huge meal. Hope you're hungry."

"Starving," York and I said almost in unison. We hadn't eaten since Arizona.

"Please, set your bags down in the living room," Norm said. "We'll get you all settled in after you've eaten."

"Would you like to help me make panzanella salad, Olive?" Jeff asked.

"Sure. Can't say I've ever had it."

"It's super simple and absolutely delicious." I washed my hands and cut the stick of bread into one-inch cubes. Jeff cut up the vegetables. We tossed in our bread, cucumber, tomatoes, bell peppers, onion, basil, and capers, and Jeff drizzled vinaigrette dressing all over it.

"Panzanella," he declared.

The four of us sat down to a dinner of medium-well steak and a wooden bowl full of the salad. Our hosts poured themselves a glass of wine each.

"Thank you guys for all of this," said York. "It's very generous of you."

"It's our pleasure," said Norm, "a little welcome dinner we cook each time we have guests."

"How do you like California so far?" asked Jeff.

"It's beautiful," I said. "We watched the sunset at Linda Mar."

"If you've never seen a West coast sunset, it's a huge treat."

"I thought sunrises in North Carolina were nice," said York around a bite of meat.

"There's so much more to see," said Jeff. "Are you really only here for one full day?"

"Unfortunately, yes. This was sort of an impromptu trip," he looked at me, "and we have to get home on Sunday."

Norm and Jeff shared a look too.

"Well, you'll have to make the most of it," said Norm. "What's first on your itinerary?"

"I hoped you could tell us that," York said. "We could use a good starting point."

"The best way to see this city is on the streetcar. Spells out landmarks very plainly for people who don't live here. It's cheap and the longtime natives will give you directions if you get lost. I know from experience."

"It's how we met, actually," Jeff said. "He's a little, uh, directionally challenged. I showed him the way to Mamma's for breakfast, and then I joined him."

"Mamma's!" Norm enthused. "Maybe we'll take you there before you leave. You'll love us for it."

Jeff and Norm suggested we start at Coit Tower and work our way through Telegraph Hill, a journey which could easily take most of the early afternoon, then said we should see Chinatown if we had any spirit left in us.

After dinner, York and I helped clean up, then grabbed our bags and headed to the stairs, stopping at the base.

We eyed each other. Norm and Jeff's listing had mentioned only one room. York and I said we'd figure it all out when the time came.

After I had fallen asleep beside him in my bedroom on Thursday night, he had gone to a blanket on the floor. I woke up about an hour later and found him there, on his back, one hand on his chest, and watching his chest move up and down at a slow, even pace lulled me back to sleep.

"You two ready to get settled in?" Norm said from behind us.

"Yes," I said. "Thank you."

"Good." His eyes searched us again, but I didn't feel I was being scrutinized. Norm reminded me of an easygoing uncle-by-marriage: won't butt into your business, but knows exactly what you're thinking because he's been around the block a few times, willing to give advice if needed, after which he holds his hands up and says, "It's your life, though" to cushion himself.

I could tell York didn't know what to say; he'd come to rely on my gift for articulation, but the words weren't coming to me so easily either. To be honest, all I could think about was the bedroom. I didn't mind sharing a room with York—in fact, I really, really wanted to.

"You mentioned this was an impromptu trip," said Norm. Then, more slowly, "Are you two celebrating anything?"

"Um." York looked at me. "Life. We're celebrating life."

"Ah," said Norm, clapping once. "Beautiful. Don't need an occasion for that."

"Nope," I said.

"Well, in case you were wondering, Jeff and I prepared the bedroom upstairs, and we also have a couch in the den down here with sheets and a blanket." Norm looked at York. "The sheets are, uh, eighteen-hundred thread count."

"Ooh," said York, nodding. He looked at me again, his eyes all scalpel-like and digging into me again.

"But the guest bathroom is upstairs," Norm added and didn't elaborate further.

I didn't want Norm to think we'd come all the way to California just to use his home as a base for our teenage romping. He would be wondering about our parents and their expectations of us on this trip, and I didn't want to put that type of pressure on the guy. He was too nice.

Maybe York felt the same way. Then again, he had a habit of reading me like the only book he'd ever read voluntarily. Either way, he looked at Norm again, smiled, and said, "Call me a man of expensive taste, but I cannot pass up eighteen-hundred thread count." He shuffled over to Norm and nudged his elbow with his own. "Please show me to this luxury couch."

"Right this way, good sir," said Norm, visibly relieved. "Just holler if you need any help upstairs, okay Olive?" he told me over his shoulder.

"Sure thing. Thanks."

And so York left with our host to settle onto his couch, and I went upstairs. The guest bedroom had a small bay window that lent me a view of the dark street and the city lights twinkling far in the distance on my extreme left. A big, old bed, an armchair, a nightstand with a small lamp, and an antique dresser—which I opted not to use—decorated the room.

The guest bathroom was down the hall from my room. I met him in there after we dressed for bed, and he let me brush my teeth first. I smiled when he caught my eyes in the mirror.

"Uh-uh," I said, shaking my head. "You opted for the luxury couch, remember?"

"I did. Norm and Jeff can see me from their bedroom if their door is open."

I sighed and spit. "Definitely leaves zero room for canoodling."

"Now that's a thought that didn't even cross my mind." He widened his eyes. "What on earth do you take me for?"

"An opportunist," I said, using his words against him. "Anyway, we're only here two nights. I doubt we'll have the time or energy to—" I bent down to fill my mouth with water.

"Canoodle," he said. "Funny word."

I stepped away from the sink. "We have a long, packed day planned tomorrow. I'll see you first thing in the morning."

"See you in the morning."

## LANDMARKS

My body lagged behind in the time difference, and I felt the effects of it. I slept until seven, around which time I started hearing noises in the kitchen.

I laid in bed, watching the pale blue morning turn pale yellow, and every part of me smiled for thinking about York. My dad wouldn't have liked sending me off to California with a boy, but I didn't know how hard he would have tried to stop me. Most girls dread their dads' interference in matters like that, but now I craved it, almost mourned it.

When I called to check in on Mom again, Uncle Joe told me nothing had gone horribly awry during the forty or so hours I'd been gone. He and a few other family members planned to meet later on that day to discuss next steps.

I wandered downstairs fifteen minutes later. Light poured in all over the place, through the windows in the living room and dining room. I found Jeff in the kitchen, popping a K-cup into the Keurig machine.

"You must be an early bird," he said. "I am, too."

"I am if I get some of that stuff," I said.

"A woman after my own heart. This cup's yours. Breakfast Blend."

Actual breakfast came soon after, once Norm emerged from their bedroom in a white undershirt and slacks. Then York appeared from the den, fully dressed as well. I'd checked the weather in bed before I tugged on some shorts, a thin summer sweater with a t-shirt on underneath, and my Keds.

York and I powered through the delicious breakfast of eggs, turkey bacon, toast with avocado, and fried potatoes our hosts had prepared. Before we left, I showed them a few of the Polaroids I had taken at Linda Mar Beach.

"These remind me of the old Polaroids my mom keeps around her house," said Jeff. "The sun makes them look so vintage. I love it." I liked Jeff. A lot.

The weather in San Francisco surprised me: pleasant, even for July, and the high would only hit the mid-seventies. In North Carolina, July—the second-hottest month of the year—could boil your blood if you didn't watch out.

We headed out on foot to Balboa Park, a short and pleasant trek, where we waited mere minutes for the metro due northeast. At Embarcadero, we caught the F-line streetcar. The streets bustled with working folks, tourists, families. After a few stops—I lost count—we arrived at Telegraph Park.

"I'm glad your sense of direction is so good," I told him as we hurried off with everyone else. "I told you already how hopeless I am. I'd have us in Utah by now."

"I would have to be pretty enthralled by you to not notice a journey through the entire state of Nevada."

"Yes, you would."

"Yes, I am."

Coit Tower loomed all phallic and grand a short distance away. We took several touristy pictures of each other outside. Inside, we read about Lillie Hitchcock Coit and her generous posthumous donation that helped bring the tower to life.

"Isn't it crazy how much money some people have?" York asked as we studied the photos of Mrs. Coit. "Like, 'Oh, life is so very droll. Let me offer up a mere third of my estate so you can construct a freaking two hundred-ten foot tall tower.'"

"She loved San Francisco and the firefighters who protected it," I said. "She was born into money, rational as it is, as you recall Mr. Lively-Bingham's philosophy."

"I do believe he said wealth could not be inherently evil if man used it in ways that reflected humankind instead of the human. Which, I suppose, is indeed rational."

"Plus, Lillie Coit was awesome," I insisted. "'Screw social norms,' she said, 'I want to roll with firefighters, gamble with men, and wear pants, because the dresses these days are really long and heavy and hot as hell.'"

"And where would we as a people be if we didn't do what we wanted and follow our passions?"

"Back in Fleet. Internshipless. Powering through a bunch of words on a bunch of pages by a dopplenym even though reading is *boring*."

"And terrible. Don't forget terrible."

We roamed and studied the murals at the base of the tower. The paintings, finished in 1933, depicted life in Depression-era California.

I studied a busy street scene: a mailman somberly retrieved letters from a box; a child with a lollipop stared into the distance; a man robbed another man in a dapper fedora at gunpoint; another man lay in the street, the victim of an apparent car accident. Innocence and depravity side by side, people bustling along even faced with tragedy, people just trying to get by.

I stared at the mural for a long time, hit over the head with the implications of the artist's decisions to include what he had. This was his America then, an entire experience squished into one wall.

"How do you think people decide what details to include when they're asked to describe their point of view?" I asked.

"You pick what comes to mind," York said. "If it hadn't made an impression on you, you wouldn't have recalled it. That's how you know what's important. It doesn't matter if the details flow one into the other in harmony or clash like a child with a lollipop next to a man with a gun. It is, and that's it."

"It's the same with journalism. I'm supposed to use only the most relevant facts to get my point across in an often limited space. That's what I can't get my head around."

"I don't believe it's a handicap. It means you know how to feel."

I nodded. The vivid colors of the illustrations so straddled the line between realistic and delightfully cartoonish that I almost forgot I was looking at depictions of one of the toughest times in U.S. history. Lillie Hitchcock Coit died the year the stock market crashed. How, with all her wealth, would she have fared alongside all that destitution? Would she have survived? Been unaffected? Still as generous?

The murals swirled around us, each scene overwhelmingly matter-of-fact. I got a sense about not only the era represented but the artists who painted them: people picked grapes in fields, factory workers put in long hours, people had their noses stuck in newspapers at a library.

And so the maze of murals went on and on and when we had seen it all, we paid the non-residential fee to climb the winding staircase up to the top of the tower.

The tower opened overhead to reveal a brilliant blue sky and diamond sun. Openings shaped like round top windows lined the concrete around us and provided a glorious three-sixty view of the city. We saw the skyline and the bay and the Golden Gate Bridge. I took photo after photo.

Afterward, we headed through Pioneer Park to tackle the Filbert Steps. In the park I listened for the sounds of feral parrots—red-faced birds native to South America—as Norm and Jeff had instructed us when making our way through this area. I didn't see any.

"They decided to hide today," I said. "I'm afraid we're not the folks they wanted to see."

"Shame. We're fantastic."

"So fantastic. And sexy."

"So sexy. Crazy birds."

I removed my sweater as we approached the stairs and draped it across my bag after taking out my camera. York went ahead, and I got a shot of him from behind and the practically vertical view down.

"Your heart," I said.

"Is fine," he assured me. "Stuffed myself full of drugs, and I'm taking my time."

His dark, curly hair gleamed in the sun. He eyed me over his shoulder when he heard the shutter, and then he grinned for another photo. On the way down, I caught sight of the bay and a large white wall with images etched on the sides (one of the film locations of some big, old Hollywood movie).

There, on those steps, York finally caught sight of a few feral parrots. He pointed to a small green tree dotted with red berries, which camouflaged the birds; if not for their chatter, we wouldn't have even noticed them.

I felt accomplished as we reached the bottom of the stairs, even though we hadn't climbed them. I looped my arms around his neck, and he spun me.

"So, there's an In-N-Out Burger not too far away from here," he said.

"What's In-N-Out Burger?"

"Supposedly the greatest place ever. Doesn't exist on the East coast."

"We must try it, then."

So we hopped back on the F-line, this time traveling north along The Embarcadero. When we found the restaurant, we stepped into a packed building with three long lines.

When it came time for us to order, I smacked my hands on the counter in front of the cashier and leaned forward.

"We're from North Carolina," I informed him, "and we have yet to taste the alleged majesty that is an In-N-Out Burger burger. What do you recommend?"

"All of it!" said the baby-faced blond.

"That sounds awesome," York said, "and we would love to order all of it. But considering my recent heart transplant that limits my sodium intake to a specific amount that dining at this fine establishment will surely get me close to…" he leaned in to read the employee's name tag, "Astor, what is your favorite burger on the menu?"

We ordered two double doubles, Animal style. York got his without cheese. We added a basket of fries to share. Not a bad burger, I had to admit.

"My mom is going to kill me," he said, his mouth full of beef and his expression blissful.

"More than she already wants to?"

"If deader than dead exists, I'm sure I can achieve it."

At the end of the meal, I announced, "It's three o'clock. How much tourist spirit do you have left in you today?"

"Chinatown is an animal all its own. It deserves a full day." He sat back. "Barb's car would have really come in handy. I wanted you to see the art museums and Golden Gate Park and so many other places."

"We came here with a specific goal, and we achieved it. You brought me to California. You've more than kept your promise to me."

"We have to at least see the bridge."

"I'd love to, but I'm not sure how—"

He leapt from his chair and approached Astor at the counter. The guy nodded a lot and his blond hair followed suit. Then he pointed in a couple directions, and York patted his arm.

"Good news," he told me when he came back. "Turns out the main ferry to the Golden Gate Bridge is actually not far from here. We walk back to the F-line and take it all the way." I moved beside him and we checked out the Sausalito schedule. "Next one leaves at three-fifty. Basically we can kind of loop around, walk across the bridge, and end up in the South Tower, which is about fifteen minutes away from here in the opposite direction. Then we can catch the streetcar back to Norm and Jeff's."

"You sure you're up for it?" I asked.

He took my hand and ran me out the restaurant.

At the ferry we waited with a rather large crowd for about fifteen minutes, then we boarded. I'd never been on a ferry, and I stretched my face against the strong, cool wind. York told me about all the times he'd taken the ferry to Ocracoke Island at the Outer Banks.

In Sausalito, we hopped on a bus that took us almost twenty minutes to the Golden Gate Bridge. It wasn't the day for the free walking tours, which Golden Gate tourism provided every Tuesday and Thursday. Next time, we said. We always had next time.

We visited the northern vista point first, where I captured the blue/green water breaking over the rocky shore, the nearly vertical rolling slope down from the one end of the bridge to the water below, and the hazy, silvery city in the distance. I took got so many shots that I had to change my film roll.

Then we walked all the way to the bridge to begin traveling its length on the east sidewalk. Cars whizzed by and bicyclists pedaled around us. Strong winds slammed us here, too, and I had to hold onto York a little for balance. I looked up at the bridge's thick red beams and imagined being part of the construction on such a massive landmark. I angled my Nikon and got several shots.

"This bridge has seen the largest number of suicides in the country," I said. I recalled the factoid from weeks ago, back when we first talked about coming to San Francisco and I'd researched the city for hours. "It's the second-most used suicide site in the world, in fact."

I practically had to scream over all the noise. The sounds of the traffic reverberated on the steel around us, and the whining and thumping and clacking rattled my insides and made it almost impossible to hear.

York peeked over the side of the railing, straining to see the water below. His eyes didn't meet mine again for a long time, and we stopped for a moment while he breathed. Even over the commotion I could hear his breaths, and his shoulders and chest moved up and down. I watched him, reminded of our time on top of the stump in the garden, when he said his heart was beating too fast.

"My God," he said, rubbing his hand over the middle of his chest. "I'm inundated by the death feeling."

I exhaled, laughing at myself for panicking. "How did I know the suicide fact would appall you the most?"

"I do not take life lightly, as you know. And anyway, what is it about this bridge that makes people choose it so often? Is it the location? The fact the water is so cold and the fall is so far? Is it the iconic status? You know, that would be my reason, I think. Even if I wanted to end my own life, a piece of my brain would harp on the Golden Gate Bridge because of the illustrious symbol it is. Like, even though I felt I could not go on a second longer in this life, jumping from one of the most recognized places in the world is very going-out-with-a-bang."

"True, but the real reason so many people end up here is the ninety-eight percent guaranteed fatality rate," I said. "That level of despair is so sad. I'm glad city officials provided preventative resources for people."

"When it all boils down to it, most of us will fight to keep life going."

We completed the nearly two-mile walk, then I pulled him into the History and Engineering Exhibition. He stood around with me in Area Four while I studied each detail of each of the old construction pictures.

Jelly seeped into the bones of my entire lower half by around the time we left the exhibit, but our journey home still required a short walk to catch a bus back to North Point, and a slightly longer walk back to catch the F car. We poked at each other's legs on the bus, then wrapped an arm around one another's shoulders and gritted words of encouragement through our teeth as we made the final long trek for the streetcar. We boarded the trolley for the last time that day back across San Francisco the way we came.

When we got back at close to eight that night, exhausted and starving as we had been the previous night, Norm and Jeff told us they planned to order Chinese takeout and had waited for us. I went upstairs while we waited for the food to arrive, and I took the longest, hottest shower of my entire life. The heat soothed my achy feet and leg muscles, and the vapors' steam cleaned my mind.

"York gave us a rundown of your adventures today," Jeff said as he unpacked my food and placed it in front of me on the island. "Sounds like you got a good taste of the city."

"I can't believe there's more to see," I said on a rush of air.

"They pack so much into one area," Norm said. "I'm not sure it's possible to hit every nook and cranny unless you live here."

"Maybe not even then," Jeff said.

"And I almost thought we wouldn't see the parrots," York said while we looked through my pictures. "They definitely don't show themselves until they're ready to."

"Oh, they run the show in Telegraph Hill," Norm said. "Exotic little divas."

## BREATHING

Our hosts went to bed around 10:30, and I couldn't stay vertical for a second longer. I closed myself in my room and listened to the faint sound of York's shower down the hallway.

I checked my phone and noticed I had a missed call from Mom. I stared at the screen for a moment. Maybe she had dialed me on accident. Maybe Selma had called from her phone.

In the voicemail Mom left, her voice teetered like a newly mobile toddler into my ear for the first time in what felt like ages: "Olive, where are you, sweetie? I cooked dinner. Call me back. I love you, Olive." I saved the message.

I called her, even though I knew I wouldn't reach her, and nearly dropped my phone when she answered.

"Hello?" She sounded weak and slightly disoriented, but more normal than she had in such a long time.

"Oh, God. I'm so sorry I woke you."

"I'm in and out of sleep these days," she said.

"How do you feel?"

"I'm fine."

"That's good." I clenched my fist. "What day is it?"

Silence, and I almost thought she hadn't heard me. "Saturday, barely. Good Lord, you're calling so late."

"And how old am I?"

"Eighteen."

"And how old are you?"

More silence. "Forty... five."

I exhaled, accepting her answer even if she had forgotten my most recent birthday. "Thanks."

"Why did you ask me those questions?"

"You left a message earlier telling me you cooked dinner."

"I said that?"

"Yes. Have you eaten?"

"A little."

"Are you sure? You need to eat." I sounded like Mrs. Lively.

"I'm sure."

I hadn't thought about Mom much in the past twenty-four hours. I texted Uncle Joe as soon as I hung up with her and made sure to let him know what had happened.

The water stopped, and the hallway fell silent for a long time until the bathroom door opened. I heard York padding toward the stairs.

I opened my door and whispered, "Hey."

He looked back. "Yeah?"

"You decent?"

"Pretty much."

"Damn. Want to come in anyway? I'm not tired."

"Neither am I."

He tiptoed in and closed the door behind him. He had thrown on a pair of Fleet High gym shorts and a thin V-neck t-shirt.

"I don't want to go back home tomorrow," I said.

"Me neither. And not even for the obvious reason." He sat on the bed. "Being here has made me want to add more to my list."

"Right? That's what travel does to you. I knew I wouldn't be able to get enough of it once I got started. I might have to actually start my own bucket list."

He studied me. "Are you afraid to make one? Kind of like the organ donor thing, you know?"

"Again, it's one of those decisions you hesitate to make for fear of, I don't know, bringing on some kind of bad juju."

"What would you put on a list? If you didn't have your superstitions?

I shrugged. "I'd like to swing on the edge of the earth in Ecuador and see a Broadway play and snorkel in the Great Barrier Reef. So many of my goals would involve travel. Domestically? I want to milk a cow. I want to be published on a major scale. I want to pet a dolphin."

"You know what I want to add to my list? Us."

"Us?"

"Something about us. It's got to be like the murals in Coit Tower: when whoever gets ahold of my list reads it, they should be able to paint us in a limited space."

I scooted back to the headboard and clenched and unclenched my hands, beckoning. "I want to sit here with you and listen to everything you have to say about love."

He backed in between my legs and rested his head against my shoulder. His hair dried on my t-shirt as we talked in quiet voices for a long time, surrounded by the dim light of the room. The edges of my vision grew fuzzy as I listened to his voice. If being intoxicated felt like this, I saw why people became addicted to it.

"Truly being in love is a dichotomy, I think," he said. "It's quiet and private but also speaks volumes, shouts it from every rooftop it sees. It demands privacy and recognition all at once, because it's special, and because it's so special it would be a crying shame to overlook it. That's being in love, right there in the middle of the two extremes."

I tilted his head back until his eyes met my throat. His lashes brushed my skin. I kissed his chin, and the day-old stubble there pricked my lips. I kissed his mouth, his nose, the space on his forehead between his eyebrows. I could feel his breath accelerate against my hairline.

"York," I said. He flipped over, and I took off my shirt. He traced the scalloped edge of my bra, then he explored the curves of my waist and hips, his hands so unhurried and methodical I was squirming to get out of my clothes by the time he reached my shorts.

He helped me tug up his shirt, less hesitant this time as he was the night we streaked, though I could still see his hesitation, the acknowledgement of what had happened to his body.

I began to touch him, because I could, because I had always let opportunities pass me by, and because I liked the way his breaths got heavier and uneven because of me. His skin flushed everywhere my touch went. I traced the length of that jagged scar between his chest muscles with my index finger.

"It's not pretty," he pointed out.

"It's beautiful," I whispered. "It means you're here and you're alive, and it's beautiful."

I got it now, that thing I hadn't gotten with any other boyfriends or any other boys or any other person. It was scary and intense, and I wondered how he felt when he realized it, and how he hadn't exploded, and how I would keep from exploding. I put my hand over his scar and felt the rapid *pulse pulse* of the heart just to the left.

"I love you," I said, my quiet, private shout from the rooftops.

I thought he might smile, or cry, because his lips started trembling and his eyes looked me over furiously.

"This is me we're talking about," he reminded me. "Are you sure you're mentally and emotionally prepared for that journey?"

And I drew a long, slow breath inward, because I wanted my next words to be as clear as possible: "I will go anywhere with you, York Lively."

And then we weren't talking anymore, just moving. Actually, he was doing most of the moving. I was trying to remember how to breathe.

# *Nineteen*

## TANGLED

The night was a rush—rushing to finish because we were afraid of getting caught, me burying my face in his shoulder and biting his skin to keep quiet.

And a different kind of rush: a totally dumb, self-satisfied, personal rush, exactly the way I felt being so close to him that first time at his house, knowing other girls would have loved to be in my place. By mine and most standards, York hadn't had a bad reputation at Fleet High, but he wasn't known for his innocence. I, on the other hand, had only ever slept with my long-term high school boyfriend, neither an overly passionate nor earth-shattering experience.

Though I'd realized I was in love with York, I figured the fact we weren't free to take our time together that night probably cramped things—no romantic music played in my head, nothing happened in slow motion, or whatever. It wasn't the picture of "making love" I'd had in my Virgin Days.

I did fall into a deep sleep afterward, wrapped in the blanket and the sheet and York's legs and York's arms, and I awoke early the next morning when he accidentally nudged me while grabbing his clothes.

"Please don't leave," I said into his chest.

"If it were up to me we would live in this bed right here in San Francisco, I swear it," he assured me. "But the guys are going to wake up any minute now, and I don't think they'll be happy if they catch me here."

I kissed him. He laughed.

"I should go," he whispered.

"You should stay and stay and stay."

I brought him with me as I rolled onto my back. He pushed himself inside me, letting out this deep gasp when we connected.

Unlike the previous night, he started us on a languorous roll and kept us there, never picking up speed. My sleep-fogged mind wondered if this was that time-slowing-down thing I used to picture, or if he really just didn't care about getting caught anymore. After a while I became nothing but a body rocking with his, the edges blurring where I stopped and he started, and I didn't want to be just me anymore, not when me-him felt like this.

The sky grew lighter, and then he was gone. Not ten minutes passed before I heard Jeff or Norm moving around downstairs, too.

We had a flight to catch at 11:30, so I stood and stretched. I winced, aching all over: my feet, my legs, my inner thighs, my lips. I went to the mirror, naked, and a grinning maniac stared back at me. I touched my mouth, then my neck, then my chest and stomach. I was *glowing*, and it was ridiculous, and it was also pretty beautiful.

Norm and Jeff and York stood talking in the kitchen when I came down. York's eyes met mine, and one of his eyebrows jumped, and all my practiced composure went stupid on my face.

"If you guys are still up for it, we'd love to take you to Mamma's like we promised," said Norm.

"But you've done a lot for us already," I said.

"Eh, we're foodies. It's how we show love," said Jeff. "You were amazing house guests—some of the best we've ever had. Plus, it's so expensive to eat out in this city—"

"And you'll need all your strength for that flight home," Norm finished. "Please. We'd love to."

We arrived at Washington Square right before the restaurant opened. I ordered an omelet, California style, and cinnamon French toast. It's difficult to screw up breakfast, so I rarely worried when trying a new place that specialized in it. Mamma's, however, exceeded expectations.

"This is the kind of place you wish existed all over the place, but you're glad it doesn't," York said. "It wouldn't be as good if it was a big chain, but, like, now I don't want an omelet from anywhere else."

"Have we ruined breakfast for you?" Jeff asked.

"Irrevocably," I said.

## ETERNITY

We said goodbye and thanked the guys for their hospitality. They told us to visit them again any time we happened to make it out that way, and they waited until we had a taxi before they drove off.

The ride to the airport felt shorter this time. We unloaded our bags and got our tickets for home. The trip would not be as many stops on the way back as it had been coming, but we would be on the plane for seven hours straight and fly into Raleigh, where we would meet my uncle for an hour-and-a-half drive back.

"Get ready for another circadian shock," York said.

I didn't want to go home, but we had to go back and face the music. I stood at the wall of glass windows near our boarding gate and stared outside. As a plane left the runway and shot toward the clouds, a large flock of black birds burst out of nowhere and scattered in the sky. I snapped a picture with my Nikon quick as I could and managed to capture the machine among nature.

Then we were off to the machine as well. We settled into our seats, and our travel experience included lunch and dinner with a semi-recent in-flight movie in between.

I tilted my head up from its spot on York's shoulder. Only his eyes seemed to watch the small screen in front of us, not him.

"You have no idea how sorry I am," I said.

He turned and managed a small smile. "Don't be. I'd leave again tomorrow if you wanted."

"Your mom is going to hate me."

"Maybe. Right now. But she'll never fully hate you. You remind her why I'm still here."

"I also seem to be the reason you enjoy risking your health and going against her rules."

"You're not wrong for wanting to leave." He touched my cheek and his dark brows furrowed. "What I hate is I won't be able to be there for you, you know, with your mom. At least not right away."

"I'll be fine. I'll just miss you every day."

His fingers began tracing a slow line across my jaw.

"I'm so glad I stayed this morning," he whispered, and my body reacted like he'd pressed a button. "I'd have regretted it the rest of my life if I hadn't."

"And what would you have done if Norm or Jeff had come out of their bedroom and found you missing?"

"I would simply have had to declare my overwhelming inability to resist you, and they would have had to understand, because there is no other place my bones will lie than with yours."

I let my head fall back onto his shoulder. "I'll pretend we did decide to live there in that bed in San Francisco. That'll help me through the rest of the summer."

"Don't say rest of the summer. It depresses me."

"Then I'll pretend for this very short eternity."

## TIME

In Raleigh I called Uncle Joe, who met us at the bottom of the escalator. "How was the trip?" he asked, hugging me.

"Way too short."

"You guys tired?"

"Exhausted." York was the one lagging behind, though, dragging his bag like it had a dead body in it. "I think I'll lie down in the back seat on the way home," I said. "I've been sitting for far too long."

"This is, of course, after we logged in a total twenty-four hours walking out of about forty-three," York said. "This girl is a machine."

My uncle helped us load our bags into the trunk. "Selma's at the hospital with your mom," he told me. "We'll take York home, and then we can talk about what to do after you see her—" he eyed York, "if that's all right with you."

I wondered what image came to York's mind when he pictured the shit hitting the fan.

We didn't speak much more after that, though we tried to put on the show for Uncle Joe as long as possible. I kept checking on York, and twice, in the flash of light from the streetlights, I caught him staring at the floor. His forehead glistened, clammy, and the guilt wrecked me.

Most people would be asleep at this time of night on a Sunday, and I think York and I secretly hoped for that, even as we edged up to his house and discovered the porch lights still on.

"This is an incredible neighborhood," Uncle Joe complimented.

York didn't have time to comment, because his parents stormed out of the house at that precise moment and made a beeline to the car.

Mrs. Lively yanked open the back door on York's side. "Everyone get out," she barked. "Now."

"I wish you two had stayed away longer," said Mr. Lively. "I haven't had enough time to figure out the words for how furious I am. Do you have any idea what you've put us through?"

"A vague one," said York.

"Is this still funny to you?" asked his mom. "Are you honestly making jokes?"

"I don't... I don't know what to say," he said, sighing. "I'm sorry. I told you that, but I'll tell you again. I'm sorry I left after you told me not to. I'm sorry I worried you."

Mr. Lively laughed. "The more you say 'I'm sorry,' the less it means, York. We don't want apologies. We want you to give us one good reason why we should even have this conversation with you without skipping straight to the consequences."

"What exactly do you think will happen?" York shot back. "I'm nineteen, I called to tell you where I was, and I stole my own money."

For a moment, all was silent except for the crickets, the frogs, the buzz of the streetlights. Mr. Lively's face turned dark red.

"I'm not a bad person," said York. "No matter how you try to spin it."

Mrs. Lively regarded me for probably the first real time in months. "I can't believe you went along with this. I told you this trip could not happen, and you disrespected us in every way you could. Ever since he's met you, he's started acting even crazier than before. That's quite the coincidence, considering you claim to have never gotten in trouble before."

"No," said my uncle. "We're not doing that. I won't let you talk about my niece that way."

"And where were you when they decided to disobey us and run across the country?" asked Mr. Lively. "How can we listen to anything you have to say when you drove the getaway car?"

"Dad," I heard York say, but I was too busy reeling from Mrs. Lively's words.

"Hold on," said my uncle. "Let's clear this all up before we start pointing fingers."

"I'll point the finger at everyone who thought it was a good idea for our children to go three-thousand miles away together, alone, while my son still struggles with the effects of major heart surg—"

Liquid spurted past my shoulder. The smell gave it away, and I saw York retch again and sink to his knees before my mind finished connecting the dots.

"Oh my God," said his mom, and we all just kind of stared, stunned, like crazy people for several moments.

"Have you two been drinking?" asked Mr. Lively. I jerked my head up when I realized he was talking to me.

"What?"

"Have you been drinking?" he practically growled at me.

"No! We—"

"He's gone back to the same bullshit, hasn't he? Hasn't he? And you're following right in his footsteps—"

"MR. LIVELY." I had never heard that kind of voice come out of me before.

York collapsed onto his side, breathing so hard his entire body moved with it. I kneeled beside him, and so did Mrs. Lively.

"Are you okay?" I asked, shaking him. His eyes stayed closed, and he didn't respond. Mrs. Lively's eyes and mine locked, and I saw the look there, and I shook him harder.

"I'm calling nine-one-one," she said and sprang to her feet.

"He's not waking up," I said. "Uncle Joe, he's not waking up he's not waking up HE'S NOT WAKING UP."

My uncle tried to pull me to my feet, but I kept saying it until my voice got so loud I thought I'd burst my own eardrums. I screamed his name once, and then all sounds melded and became garbled and then faded away, a distant and constant ringing replacing them.

The ambulance arrived right around the time I felt like passing out. I stayed with York on the ground until EMTs loaded him up. His mother followed them inside, and the door slammed shut, shutting me out.

I ran to Uncle Joe's car and begged him to hurry, as he stood frozen and confused in the same spot. He fumbled with his keys as he jogged over, and we both sat in shock as he started the engine. We raced time all the way to the hospital.

## FAILING PT. 2

When my uncle and I got to the emergency room, we found Mrs. Lively in the waiting area, slumped in a chair with her head in her hands.

"How is he?" I asked. Her fingers turned into fists. "Please, please tell me," I said.

"Jenny!" I heard a man's voice from the automatic doors. I expected her husband, but a man I didn't recognize ran up to us with a woman following. "What happened?" he asked.

She lifted her head then, and I saw the worst pain I had seen on anyone's face in a long time. "We don't know. They suspect heart failure and...we don't know." Mrs. Lively burst into tears, and the man sat with her.

Heart failure.

My world imploded.

We waited a long time for answers. I sat against the wall, my chest heaving, and I couldn't believe I had ended up in this damned emergency room, this damned hospital, for the second time this year, and for the third time in two years, counting my dad. I couldn't believe I had seen so much of this place throughout my life and had never once been sick enough to be a patient myself.

Numbness wrapped me up tight and shielded me from the sounds and the sights and became my only friend. I didn't speak for a long time, because I feared hearing my own voice would pop my nice, hazy bubble, and I would feel all the crushing agony I knew waited on the other side.

Then the doctor told us that they had to take York into cardiology and were trying to stabilize him there. His condition had worsened, had become too critical for standard treatment. It meant we were racing time even harder than I thought. It meant time was winning.

And I wanted to scream and scream until all my veins burst.

## WAITING

The other man that had shown up was Mrs. Lively's brother, and he had brought his wife, an ER nurse. She knew how to talk to everyone, mitigating the tension by explaining all the good ways she's seen this exact situation turn out. She pointed out we still didn't know the exact prognosis.

I noticed her husband hanging back, his face grim and stony. He had watched her come home after her shifts, and he knew the other side to all this. He'd heard the stories about families she'd spoken with and worked with, heard about possible good outcomes shattered by one unexpected or expected factor. He'd watched her shake her head and sigh, claiming that's life, and death, unfortunately.

So I stayed in my bubble while she talked.

The five of us moved into a different waiting area, and my uncle sat beside me. He didn't say anything for a long time, and the weight of his disappointment crashed against my wall of numbness like the ocean against a cliff.

"I'm sorry I didn't tell you," I said. "You're too noble, and you would have wanted to respect their wishes, and I really wanted to go to California."

"Did you think about York?" he asked me gently. "His relationship with his parents? The kind of toll this trip might take on him?"

I felt a heavy knot form in my throat. "I love him. He loves me. He was thinking about me, too."

"I'm sure." He sighed. "I wish you hadn't lied to me. How can I trust what you tell me? I need your help with your mom. We're supposed to be a team."

"We are. I promise. I won't ever lie to you again. You can still count on me."

"I hope so."

~ * ~

I've heard time flies. You guessed right—this one also strikes out.

Older folks tell me *Enjoy your youth, because a year turns into twenty in the blink of an eye.* To that I want to say: *How much crack have you been smoking?* A year turns into twenty in twenty years, not in a blink. The expression, the exaggeration—whatever—frustrates the hell out of me. Time moves at the same speed, regardless of our perception, no matter how fast we want it to move.

Mr. Lively showed up at the hospital a short time later, and Mrs. Lively filled him in, her eyes wet and distant the whole time. His frown grew deeper as the news got worse. He rubbed his face once, his palm scraping over the stubble on his cheeks and chin. "Did they tell you anything else?"

"Just that it most likely has to do with the transplant, that even though the risk for rejection goes down after a year, there's still a chance when the proper precautions aren't consistently taken."

In a move that surprised me for some reason, Mr. Lively embraced his wife.

"All right now," he coddled. "We've been through this before, remember? He pulled through that, remember?"

"It's happening all over again," she said into his chest. "It's trying so hard to take him out, and this time might be it." She sobbed once, and I wanted to sob, because they were talking about my father's heart, and they kept talking about rejection, and what if my dad's heart hadn't been enough to keep York alive? Why did I have to face losing my dad and York, too?

"That kid is a fighter," said Mr. Lively. "Fought me every step of the way for much of his life. If he's stubborn enough to get himself into this, he's stubborn enough to get himself out."

Mrs. Lively took a step back. "Get himself into this? Paul, his heart is failing."

"And it's failed before. He's been to all the same followup appointments we have. He knew what he had to do, and take, and how to take care of himself."

"They don't know for sure that he wasn't taking care of himself," she said.

"Would you be surprised?"

"Paul!"

"York lives fast and loose, and you know it," he said defensively. "I don't want this to be what happened, but that doesn't take it off the table."

"Why is it always his fault?" she screamed. "Why can't it just be shitty luck?"

She whirled away from him, slumped into a chair, and sobbed more, now comforted by her brother.

I stood up and walked right over to the man, fully awake for the first time all evening.

"You aren't allowed to say York is strong enough to make it through this because you have no idea who he is," I spat. "You're not allowed to encourage us and tell us he's strong. You're definitely not allowed to then turn around and say he brought this on himself. All you deserve is a place standing far away from where the rest of us decent, compassionate human beings are. A place where you can observe and learn how to love someone other than your *dickstastic* self."

"That's very nice, Olive," he said. "By the way, you've known my son for literally a fraction of the time I have, which makes it more likely *you* have no idea who *he* is." He took a step closer to me, a move I found threatening.

"And somehow, in the middle of all the tragedy and insanity that brought our two families together, the blessing got all twisted up," he said. "Suddenly, our son is acting just as reckless—maybe even more so—and we're at the end of our damned rope, and everything bad seems to keep coming back to you."

"Everyone calm down, please," said Mrs. Lively's sister-in-law. "None of this bickering will help the situation."

My uncle and I and York's parents maintained full, challenging, eye contact.

"We need to breathe," she said carefully. "Focus on York. Make sure he's okay. Sort the rest out later."

At some point, we all sulked back to our respective corners, the fight over, but not the match. Would the match ever be over? I wasn't sure I had the strength to roll with the punches anymore.

We waited.

# *Twenty*

## ANTI

Twenty-three hours after we arrived at the hospital, a special ultrasound revealed York was experiencing humoral rejection.

I kept hearing words like "hemodynamic compromise" and "infection" and "aggressive treatment." The one time I caught a glimpse of him, he had tubes coming out of every extremity. Doctors treated him with all sorts of "anti" drugs: antibiotics, antivirals, antifungals. His body was attacking Dad's heart and I couldn't help.

Mrs. Lively stood outside his hospital room and talked to him a lot in his in-between twilight state of consciousness. Sometimes Mr. Lively joined her. Each moment York stayed alive meant we could stave off reality a little while longer.

*Those who choose not to live in the real world may journey wherever they like,* York once quoted York Lively-Bingham, *but each one of us will end up inside solid ground.*

## RESPECTS

In the early afternoon a day later, Mr. Holbrook called me.

"Hope you're doing well today," he said, and I did not for one second desire to put on an act for him.

"I'm doing horribly. Sorry."

"Oh," he stammered. "Would you like me to call you back?"

"No, no. Actually, I was about to call you. I hoped I could get an extension on my articles coming due. I won't be able to focus on work for a good while."

"That's—that's fine. I'm sure we can fill your spots with other stories."

"Thank you so much."

"I did want to mention—" He hesitated.

"Yes?"

"Basically, I called to add a little more work to your already full plate. I want all my interns to write a thousand-word or so blurb for a feature we have coming up. We haven't set a print date yet, so there's no rush."

"I can pull off a thousand words. If you need it."

"If you don't mind, Olive, I'd like for you to write something about your dad."

I seized. "Why?"

"If it isn't too difficult for you."

"*Why?*"

I suppose I stunned him, because he didn't say anything for a while. "In the article Terri submitted to me back in May, you touched on your relationship with him. I sensed there might be something deeper behind it, and I thought you might want to explore it."

"I can't begin to know how to do that."

He paused again, then told me, "I lost my mom shortly after my twenty-second birthday. Someone asked me to write a eulogy for her funeral, and I couldn't. For the longest time, I couldn't write her name in any form. It ate me up inside." I heard him shift around. "I'm not saying that's happening to you, but I do know how writers deal with painful situations: they write about them."

"You want me to eulogize my dad."

"Never too late."

## THINGS I'D RATHER

Selma came with me the day I could finally see York. Her brand of "comforter" was just what I needed; she always knew what to say, knew when her cynical humor was appropriate and when to be serious. I needed someone with me who saw life for the general hot mess it was and didn't let it affect her, someone who wouldn't break down so easily. My sister and I were pretty resilient people overall, but in ways she was much stronger than me. That's why I didn't worry about her.

York's mother rarely left the hospital, and I worried she would keep me from seeing him. When I showed up at his room, she didn't speak to me, but she did leave. She'd made it so easy, apprehension and suspicion picked at the edges of my brain, but relief at seeing York took over and kept out the negativity.

He wasn't awake, and his head resembled a deflating beach ball, and he still had tubes coming out of everywhere, and I couldn't see his smile. But I could see him and touch him. It was the first time I'd seen him in over a week.

"Isn't it crazy how he can be in such bad shape and still look so good?" Selma asked.

"*Shh.*"

"Oh, he's all drugged up. He can't hear me."

"You're so embarrassing," I said, sitting in a chair beside the bed.

"Hey, I've been through enough of this shit. You know this is how I cope."

"Don't cuss. You're too young to cuss."

"Shit, shit, shit. To hell with all this shit. To hell with sickness. You know, you might benefit from a little cussing. Let out your emotions."

I shook my head and watched York's chest rise and fall.

"What are you most scared about?" she asked.

"My God. You got two days and a notebook?"

"I said most, you non-listening twit."

My shoulders drooped. "Failure."

"What? His heart?"

"Dad's heart," I reminded her. She stilled. "If York doesn't pull through, we failed him. Dad will be gone again, and so will he."

Her eyes appeared to follow the movement of his chest too, now. "I've decided I'm never going to fall in love. Too much to lose."

"It sucks," I said. "Not the love part—the other stuff. You become this ball of everything and nothing at once. It feels so complete and it's terrifying because when a piece chips off, you feel totally broken."

"Nope. Won't put myself through that."

"You should, one day, when you can handle it. It's kind of wonderful."

She frowned. "I feel responsible too, now. What you said about Dad's heart... I mean, I actually like York. What if...?"

We fell silent for a long time and watched him sleep his forced sleep. Was he struggling inside, screaming for awake, free, alive?

"Things I'd rather do than sit here while my boyfriend's unconscious body rejects my father's heart inside it," I said. "Go."

"Hmm. Try to split hairs with a razor blade. Go."

"Do the Electric Slide over hot coals. Go."

"Bang your head against a brick wall to the beat of 'We Will Rock You'. Go."

"Let a pirate give me a dental exam. Without gloves. Go."

"Shower with a loofah that's been lightly tossed in dumpster juice. Go."

"Literally rip my own heart out."

My little sister wrapped her arms around my shoulders to stop me tearing in two.


## SHORT TERM

A period of time after York's treatments consisted of waiting and not much else. Doctors needed to assess his condition and stop the downward spiral.

Over the following five days in the stroke unit of the same hospital, my mom regained a great deal of her cognition. Uncle Joe and I walked into her room after I visited York and found her sitting up in bed and watching television. She directed her round eyes at us, eyelids drooping over coffee bean irises tethered by wiry blood vessels.

"Joe," she said, "I called your cell. I need a cigarette. Tell me you brought some."

It took all I had in me not to gawk at the sight of her. For half a second I feared I had walked into the wrong room.

"Mom?" I said. "Mom, do you remember what Dr. Younts said about smoking?"

"What did he say?"

"You can't do it anymore."

She blew out a breath. "I remembered that, but I hoped you had forgotten."

Then my uncle remembered how to speak. "When was your birthday, Pam?"

"Just passed. February."

"And Olive's birthday? What about Selma's?"

"April and November." She blinked at us. "When was my wedding anniversary?"

We stared. I held my breath.

"May." She returned her eyes to the brightly-colored morning talk show on television. "It would have been May eighth."

~ * ~

The hospital discharged Mom two days later. She had permanent memory, liver, kidney, and muscle damage. Her doctor gave my family express instruction to watch out for her around the clock and monitor her mental recuperation in the upcoming weeks—her short-term memory, motor skills, et cetera—for the physical therapist to consider.

She received four different prescriptions: a beta blocker for blood pressure; a diuretic for her urinary troubles (making the situation worse because she had completely lost control of her bowels, and now she ran to the bathroom constantly; we had to buy her adult diapers);

an osmotic for cerebral edema; and an antidepressant...you know, because of the death of her husband, and the devastating alcoholism.

Her medications were expensive, and we'd had enough trouble paying the insurance premiums on the plan that she'd been forced to take up when Dad died. My uncle had applied her for disability benefits, but who knew how long it would take the government to accept, if they even accepted the first time?

She began to attend physical, occupational, and speech therapy sessions every Tuesday, Thursday, and Saturday at the comp rehab center a block away from the hospital. Sessions started at 11 a.m. and Uncle Joe shared the driving duties with me. This meant when school started back I would have to use my breaks between classes on some Tuesdays and Thursdays to take her there.

Dr. Younts said the sessions would be two hours long, and from them he would design a routine based on her personal progress, work on her motor skills, speech therapy, exercise. He would also counsel her on how to up her weight and conquer her alcoholism.

"So you've got to gain some weight," I told her one night. I wondered if she understood the import of the information I'd just given her. "I can't bring you back there weighing less than you did when you left, or they'll...I don't know. Social Services will come and take you away from me."

She laughed. It was the first time I had heard her laugh in so long.

"Okay, sweetie," she said. "Okay."

"That also means no cigarettes or alcohol. One more bad decision and you're done for. Doctor's words, not mine."

"I hear you," she said slowly. "I am finished, I promise. No more."

I wanted to believe her, but I had heard those exact words more than once.

*Maybe this time really is different*, I let myself think. Maybe it took her losing what little independence she had left to realize what she needed. Maybe this was it.

## *Twenty-one*

## DROPPING THE BALL

The next time I saw York, he was awake.

He had a thin blanket pulled over his chest and kept his eyes on the ceiling, only moving them when I crossed his line of vision.

"You're here," he said.

"I've been here."

"I know." His eyes were anguished.

I sat down. "What's wrong?"

"Everything."

"Tell me." He shook his head. "Please."

His face was still round, and the effect made him look like a much younger, more vulnerable version of himself.

"I lied to you," he said.

"About what?"

"When I told you I was taking care of myself. I've been lying to you for months. I'd skip taking my medications if I felt good, or I'd get caught up in my own stuff and...I forgot, I—sometimes I'd just forget." His voice didn't sound good now, as if choked by sob. "I didn't even have them with me when we went to California."

"What? Why?"

"We were only going for a couple days. I couldn't leave with them, or my parents would know something was up. I wanted to feel like myself again; for *five seconds* I wanted to be a normal guy taking a trip alone with his hot girlfriend and not having to think about dosages and heart palpitations and mouth ulcers and fucking heart failure and *failure*.

"And you think my dad is awful and a jerk, but he's right about me. It's always my fault. I'm not saying that to be melodramatic or to get any pity from you. It is literally always my fault."

"York."

"I only thought about myself. Not your dad or my parents or my friends...not about you. I told you I loved you, and I couldn't think enough of you to take my medication." He managed to laugh and look angry at the same time. "This is it. This is what I get. I didn't do what I was supposed to do, and now I'm dying. Again."

"Not necessarily."

"Necessarily. As is the result."

"No. I've researched this. They can adjust your medication. They can...they—"

"I've researched, too. They can adjust, and it won't work. They can adjust, and it will work. And then my body will freak out, and I'll be right back in this boat. Or I won't, maybe. So many maybes. I'm getting tired of them. I'm getting tired of failing everyone, and I am tired."

I couldn't tell him I knew more about his condition than he did, and I couldn't encourage him in any way that wouldn't patronize him.

"I love you, York," I said instead, trying to stop my own voice sounding choked. "I really—I really, really, really, really love you, and I know you're scared, and I know what it's like to be that tired. Trust me."

"Could you say it again?"

"Trust me."

His head fell back and managed a small, frustrated laugh. "Oh my God, you know what I'm talking about."

I leaned in and kissed his cheek. "I love you. And I refuse to believe you're dying. And I love you."

## EXHIBIT

For the mere sake of being reliable, I scraped up what little time and mental fortitude I had to finish the article I had coming due for my internship: a six-page spread on Pasquotank's twenty-seventh annual VerneFest, a folk music festival which would be poignant that year because its founder and top performer, Bertram Froyer, had recently died at the ripe old age of ninety-one.

*News Matters* already had several photographers on staff, but I showed Mr. Holbrook my quasi-portfolio from high school and Photo Media before I left for San Francisco, so he allowed me to use a shot I'd taken of the volunteers as they set up the stage for VerneFest as the background for my article. He told me he could see me fitting in as a member of the photography staff as well, when I'd had a touch more training.

~ * ~

**Olive Grant** - 7/14, 11:27pm
Mr. Holbrook suggested I start a blog to get my words and pictures out there more.

I told Stefanie that night.

**Stefanie Velez** - 7/14, 11:27pm
You gonna do it?

**Olive Grant** - 7/14, 11:28pm
I don't know. I don't know if I'll end up investing the right amount of time. People who blog are passionate about it. Plus, what would I write about? And who would care?

**Stefanie Velez** - 7/14, 11:28pm
I'd care.

**Olive Grant** - 7/14, 11:28pm
You have to say that because you're my best friend.

**Stefanie Velez** - 7/14, 11:29pm
I have to say it because it's true! You're interesting and you're snarky, and I think a lot of people would enjoy your commentary.

**Olive Grant** - 7/14, 11:30pm
On what?

**Stefanie Velez** - 7/14, 11:31pm
Well. The library, for example. That freaking place is full of stories. The huge guy that came in for *Game of Thrones*, but had probably never seen a book in his life. Or that one woman who came in and raged about that highly inappropriate erotica series and asked you when the library started to allow such filth on its shelves. Or that one hot guy who came in for *The Infantry Hero* and rocked your world to its very core.

I bit my lip to stop my face twisting into knot.

**Olive Grant** - 7/14, 11:33pm
You think I should write about my love life?

**Stefanie Velez** - 7/14, 11:33pm
I think you should tell the truth about your life. Update people on the bucket list. Write out your feelings so you're not drowning in sorrow over York. Life itself is complicated and fascinating. Anyone can write about theirs.

**Olive Grant** - 7/14, 11:34pm
But you like me already. You already think I'm interesting. How do I make others feel the same way?

**Stefanie Velez** - 7/14, 11:34pm
That's up to you, fortunately.

## Twenty-two

**ARITMETIC**

York went home on July 17, and I didn't even know. His parents didn't tell me. He sent me this text that afternoon:

*Back home. Feel like hell. Mom says don't come.*

The words stung like the snap of a rubber band.

*When can I see you?*

*I don't know.*

I factored that his mother hated me, and that he needed time to readjust before he had company, and that he might be dying in that very moment. Why, then, after all that factoring, did I still feel so unwanted?

## DIVIDE

Along with the often over-rationality of thinking in black and white, I'm also pretty good at turning off entire portions of my brain. I do this whenever I'm in a situation so bad or stressful I don't want to handle it, or when I want to do something I shouldn't and I need to shut up my conscience first, or when I'm putting off certain responsibilities until later.

Numbness, I suppose, is a conjoined twin of focus, at least in me. I can be so focused on how something should be that I forget how I'm feeling about it; even if I'm hurting, I can actually still feel like life is fine. Maybe I, like Mom, simply mastered the art of denial, probably stemming from a need to make sense of my life with her from a young age, and from the death of my father.

I didn't see York for the rest of that month. I barely spoke to him, except the one time I sent him a text to see how his condition was progressing. I panicked when he didn't text back for hours, but at ten o'clock that night I got a one-word response:

*Forward.*

I didn't know if he kept his distance because of me or because of his mom, and I didn't want to push him. I began to take Mom to her therapy sessions and threw my concentration into her.

One morning while she and I waited for her physical therapy to start, she said suddenly, "You think I don't know what's going on. You think I can't understand because of my stroke, but I do. Joe told me about your friend."

"Don't worry about it."

"I don't. I worry about you."

Out of grief or bottled up anger or pure meanness, I scoffed at her.

"You think I don't worry about you. I worry so much. I've always been a worrier, and I've never known how to handle it. Or anything." She narrowed her eyes straight ahead in intense concentration. "I didn't know how to love your dad, but I loved him as best I could.

When I lost him, it broke me. It broke me. Because of it, I haven't loved you and Selma the way I should, either."

Her words started to slur, and I moved closer to her. "Stop. It's okay."

"You think I don't understand, but I do."

"Yes, you understand."

"Don't let this break you. Leave it alone, or hold onto it until it's forced from your hands, but don't let it break you."

"I won't, Mom."

## DYING STARS

I started my blog, *Chasing the Sun*, at the beginning of August.

I covered my webpage with photos of the Linda Mar sunset and various other shots from my year, including the picture of York's and my feet toeing the edge of the stump in Whittmire Garden. I filled the blog with musings, a few of the shorter clips I'd written for *News Matters*, and photos of San Francisco.

Since school would soon start back, Jill Logan and I decided to write pieces for *News Matters* geared toward the college students in the area. I made my subject about mottos, philosophies for life, and hopes for the future. I decided not only to get college students from my school involved, but kids from the technical college, too. It would be an extension of York's story in the organ donation article, the more personal side of it, meant to show what it meant to achieve your goals as a young person.

It felt wrong somehow, now, to try wringing a positive message out of this article when I still didn't know what was happening with York or if he even believed in the miracle of second chances anymore.

I texted him to ask if I could come over. It took him a while to respond, again, but finally he told me he had managed to convince his mom. He also warned me he looked like death run over twice.

His mom answered the door and made very little eye contact with me as she ushered me into the foyer.

"He can't have company for long periods of time," she told me, sounding irritable. "He needs lots of rest and as little excitement as possible." I walked toward the stairs. "Also."

I turned around.

"I can't tell you which York you're going to talk to up there. From day to day, he—really, from hour to hour—"

I nodded.

Mrs. Lively had cleaned his room spotless. He lay in his big, soft bed with the navy blue comforter tucked around him. His many tubes and IVs had disappeared, replaced by an array of pill bottles on his nightstand.

The room smelled sterile as a hospital, but York smelled like sleep. His curls lay limp all around his head. The moon face had settled down, but had stripped away much of the definition in his features.

"Hi," I said.

"I never wanted you to see me like this."

I tried again. "Hello, love of my life."

He lifted his head. "Long time no see, I Love."

"That's better." I sat down. "How are you?"

"Literally?"

"In the grand scheme."

"I'm home, obviously, so my condition is no longer critical. I'm sequestered in this miserable and self-inflicted state of being until my team can fully reverse the rejection."

"How long does that take?"

"I don't know." Every word he spoke cut me. I felt like I'd accidentally walked into a bramble bush instead of his room. "Months? They caught it early enough, and they cleared up the infection. I'm back to pretty much the same old medicine regimen I got stuck with the first time."

I nodded and looked around. His computer and his wall-sized television and his video game system sat sadly, alarmingly untouched. "Do you know how much effort it has taken me to not end up in an insane asylum?" I asked.

"I've had very little control over who I've seen and who's seen me, and also over my own body, for several weeks now."

"I know."

"I've had all these pretend conversations with you, just because of how much I've missed your voice," he admitted. "I tried to call you, like, a thousand times, but everything hurts, and I don't feel like myself, and I can't seem to stay awake for more than thirty minutes at a time, and I honestly, truthfully did not ever want you to see me like this."

"You know I don't care about that."

"You don't understand."

I didn't want to argue with him, so I changed the subject. "So, efforts to keep myself out of an asylum included staying busy with my mom, who is now also back home."

"Oh, yeah. Is she going to be all right?"

"She's got a lot of challenges to overcome, but she can talk and walk and that's more than most people accomplish so soon after a stroke."

"I'm really glad she's home."

"Also, my internship."

"Thank God you're still doing it."

"How else could I distract myself, especially with you out of commission?" I thought I saw his mouth curve a fraction of a degree. "Another intern and I are writing a feature together about college students. I've sort of got a 'then versus now' theme going on my end, so I'm taking everyone I interview back through the end of high school to where they are now, where they thought they were headed and whether they've changed their views."

"Wonder how you got that idea?"

"I just piggybacked on your quotes goal." I sighed. "Okay, I practically stole the concept."

"Only the essence," he said. "Anyway, what idea is ever really original these days? This article seems pretty necessary—you've given us wanderers a voice, and I'm proud."

"Do you think you could come up with a quote for my article?"

He blinked. "Now?"

"At some point. Whenever you're ready. I've got a couple weeks to write it."

"If this is your subtle way of making me think about my new senior quote, I hear you loud and clear."

"While that would kill two birds with one stone, don't stress over it. We've got forever left to work on your bucket list."

"So optimistic." He smiled, but his expression confused me; I couldn't tell if he had just complimented me or insulted me.

"I learned from the best. You don't think we'll finish?"

"Some days I think I won't ever be able to do anything but pop pills and worry about the effects of not popping pills. It'll be this vicious cycle, and I'll turn into the vicious cycle, and I won't have time for anything or anyone else."

"But that's not true. You've been through this once before—you know how to bounce back, what it feels like, that it's possible."

"I've been through this once before," he echoed. "And how many more times? How else can I screw this up?"

"But you're wiser now."

"I'm on the slipperiest slope of my life, and I'm taking everyone down with me. It's the worst feeling in the world, other than a heart attack, of course. Do you want to know what a heart attack feels like?"

"No."

"It feels like a vise grip in your chest. You can't breathe, so you panic, and then you can't breathe because you're panicking, and so on."

"I get it," I said.

"This might happen again, and everyone—including me—is already so tired of it, and you'll feel that way one day, too. Then what'll become of my stupid bucket list?"

I stared at this wan, pouting shell of the boy I'd met and basically crashed into love with. "You sound like me."

"Then I sound wonderful."

"What did you say to me?" I asked. I wanted him to say it, needed him to, but he was forcing me to. "You said, 'Your situation doesn't change how I feel about you. I'm still glad I met you. I'm still glad you're here.'"

"I might be more trouble than I'm worth," he quoted me.

"Stop that. Stop it. This isn't you. I don't like this York."

"I'm sorry."

"Stop. You're not the cloud. You're the sunbeam. You can't turn into this. I won't let you. I'm going to be selfish for once in my life and demand that you stay, here, and as you are, because you are the sunbeam. Everything about the way you are is magic. It's defiance and it's brilliance and it's warmth and it is the fucking sun. You're the scientist, right? Don't you know we'll all *die* without the sun?"

"This is the cost of living," he said, and it felt like I had heard that from him before, "the cost of my life. This is me, right now, how I am when I'm fighting death. You either get me this way, or not at all. Which one do you want?"

"Which one do *you* want?"

His turn to stare. He sat back and raised swollen hands to his puffy face. He didn't answer me. He didn't even look at me again.

I didn't say goodbye when I left.

***Twenty-three***

**STAGE FIVE**

That week, I finally sat down to write the words for Dad that Mr. Holbrook had requested. The finished product sounded wrong when I first read it over, so I changed some of it around and this time I hated it a little less.

Before my father, I had never been to a funeral for someone whose death had truly devastated me. My father's father died sometime in my tenth year. My mother's father died three days before my sixteenth birthday. I had two aunts and one cousin to die. I was sad when they were gone, but I'd been to enough funerals in my life that they never shook me up.

When I felt semi-satisfied with my article, I requested a special meeting with Professor Spaulding so I could get her advice. She taught one summer school class, and I used the special access on my student I.D. to get into the dark room in the art department while I waited for the class to end. I hadn't developed a single bit of my own film in months, so I decided to practice for the sake of my internship.

I met Professor Spaulding in her classroom as the last student left, and we sat at a row of computers. She stared at me as I told her what had been going on, her small eyes animated, as always, but as if forcibly animated by an electric shock.

"I'll be," she said. "You are quite the storyteller."

I had only told the truth. Then I remembered what she'd said about my article on Mr. Velez. Maybe my strength lay in the truth.

"I know this is a dark subject, and you probably need to be grading articles from people who are actually your students," I said, "but I figured you could help me polish my technique—"

"Do you want to know what my first job at the local newspaper was?" She waited for an answer.

"Sure."

"Obituary writer. The job terrified me, but I would take whatever I could get, for the exposure. I will never forget my time on that column because all I did was read and write about the dearly departed. So, you see? I'm very familiar with this. It's storytelling, just mostly in the past tense."

"Oh. Okay then, good."

She read my article. Shook her head.

"No, no. You haven't captured him here. 'Everett Grant was the type of father who would encourage you to do whatever you were afraid to do'? You make him sound like a regular person, and, from what you told me, he was an extraordinary dad."

I took out my notebook. "Do you have a couple more minutes to help me get started?"

"Of course. All right, flash interview time." She used to do this in her classes to keep us on our toes. Kind of like pop quizzes. "Why was your dad away all the time?"

"My mom didn't work, and he had to make sure our bills got paid. He never considered what he would do, just kind of went out and did it because he needed to. If it took him away from us, well…" I stopped, frowned.

"And how did that make you feel?"

"If he had lived as long as other dads do, it wouldn't have been a big deal. He would have had all the time in the world to spend with us when we were older and able to support ourselves. He would have been able to send me off to college, off to my first job, and then out on my own. And I already knew he loved me. So, if he wasn't around, I missed him, but it didn't hurt. It wasn't absence, like it is now."

"Simplify that answer."

"He knew that the most meaningful way he could love his family was to provide for us, and he loved us so much in that way, and he would love us in the more traditional way when he could."

"Simplify that answer."

"He..." Her expression livened, prodded me. "He loved us so much he didn't hesitate to give all of himself."

"There. That's the Everett Grant you described to me. Straightforward. Profound. As is that sentence."

I jotted it down at the bottom. "How's this for an opener? 'My father lived as any other wise man does: with a deep understanding that our time on the Earth needs to be spent doing the most good. His selflessness was sometimes difficult to deal with, but it made him a role model I'll always be proud to have.'"

"Olive Grant, you are going to be a very successful journalist one day."

## CRAB

Uncle Joe stopped by two days later with a container of food and our mail. We leaned against the counters in the kitchen and talked about bills, hospital payments, the usual.

I examined him for real for the first time in months—maybe even a year. His drooping eyes and long mouth lines and new white hairs sprouting from his beard did not go unnoticed.

"Have I ever told you how grateful I am for you?" I asked him.

"Aw, come on. It's my responsibility."

"No, it isn't. That's it. You do so, so much. You know I'd have cracked a long time ago if it weren't for you?"

"It is my responsibility," he repeated, and his eyes grew hard. "You weren't old enough to handle any of this on your own. You still aren't, really, but you're doing a great job nonetheless. Plus, we're family. I don't need to explain myself beyond that."

"Even family gets tired. We both know that. I worry sometimes you'll get tired, too."

He put an arm around me. "I'd never forgive myself if I abandoned you and Selma. You can count on me. I'm not going anywhere."

I leaned into him. "How did I get so lucky?"

"What's that?"

"York told me the same thing."

He moved back to his side of the kitchen. "That reminds me: there's something in the pile of mail with his name in the top corner."

"Really?" I grabbed the stack on the counter.

"Have you two talked since you went to his house last?"

"No." Every day when I woke up, I texted him good morning. Every night around the same time, he texted me goodnight.

"Huh." He pushed off the counter. "I'll leave you alone, then. Dinner's at six."

I stared at the envelope, stared at his name. The front of the card inside said: "I'm sorry about the things I said while I was on drugs."

I laughed until tears streamed from my eyes, and then I opened it. Out fell a crisp one-hundred-dollar bill, which rocked to my feet.

*Dear Olive,*

*This card is in no way intended to make fun of those struggling with addiction, but, I mean, the opportunity was too perfect to pass up.*

*I hope one day you can find in your big, beautiful heart the desire to give me the time of day again. I realize it make take you weeks, months, or centuries, but I'll wait right here the entire time until you do.*

*Also, if/when this happens, please call me. I have several favors to ask of you, and one to do for you.*

*I love you*

*York*

I called him that night, and his weak, husky voice filled my ears. "That really did feel like centuries."

"I only held out for a few hours. How are you?"

"Better. How are you?"

"Worse maybe than I was before."

"I'm so sorry."

"Don't be," I said, but I sighed in relief. "You've managed to pique my curiosity, which is the direct way to my heart. What favors did you need from me?"

"First, if it's not too much to ask, I would like you to buy a tree. A crabapple, to be specific. You can get a young one in a container at the home improvement store."

"That's random."

"It's a gift from the both of us to Mr. and Mrs. Holt. I had planned to do this myself, before all the mayhem."

"The Holts? That's...really nice of you."

"I owe them. Big time. Anyway, I liked that tree. I know Mrs. Holt wants a little pretty in her yard."

"Consider it done, then."

"I also need a special favor from you." He didn't sound so sure of himself this time. "I'll have to explain it to you later, but I'd like you to gather some things that represent the way you feel about us. Based on the events of the past month or so, I'm a little scared to see what you'll choose. Either way, I'll accept them without question or contest."

"What do you want them to be? How big? Perishable? Non-perishable?"

"Anything you want. Not big. Non-perishable, if you can help it."

"This will be tough indeed."

"You don't have to make it sweet. Just make it honest."

I smiled. "You may not want that."

"Honest."

"I'll see what I can come up with." I sat back against my headboard. "Now what did you plan to do for me?"

"You still writing that college student article? The one about mottos and personal philosophies?"

"I've struggled to make it work. I guess I'm not inspired enough."

"Well, if you're still soliciting quotes, I think I've finally got a good one."

## GOAL TWO

I bought the tree—a funny little stick with some twigs and a few leaves—the next day. The size and fragility made it awkward to handle, so I had the men at the home improvement place help me finagle it into my back seat before I took it by Dennis and Agnes Holt's house.

"Olive!" said Mrs. Holt when she opened her door. "Come in!"

Her husband greeted me in kind. York and I hadn't seen them since we finished patching their backyard in March.

"I can already tell your lawn tips are going to make my yard flourish," he gushed. "Your dad taught you well."

"Thank you. I mean, you're welcome." I knew I sounded weary, and Agnes put a hand on my shoulder.

"It must still be difficult for you to talk about your father," she said.

"Oh, no. Yes, it is, but that's not why I'm—I guess I'm not acting like myself."

I told them about York.

"God," she said. "How is he?"

"I'm not sure. Technically, his condition is stable for now, but it's still touch and go. I get to see him later on today, but he asked me to bring this to you first." I nodded at Mr. Holt. "Could you help me?"

We pulled the tree from my back seat. "It's a crabapple to replace the one that died. Fall is the best time to plant in North Carolina, but container plants take well in the summer if you keep them watered."

"How'd York ever remember?"

"He remembers everything."

Mrs. Holt met us as we lugged it around back. "A crabapple?" she exclaimed.

"I couldn't believe it either," said her husband and set it down in the middle of the yard.

"York insisted," I said.

"It's sweet of him, but..." You could tell it pained her to say the words. "It's a gift I'm afraid we haven't earned."

"You let two perfect strangers, two kids, mutilate your backyard. You aided York in his Very Important Quest. He doesn't take that stuff lightly. I don't see how you haven't earned it."

They didn't respond, looked at one another, at me.

"You'd better take it. He's pretty persistent. I may not have ever gotten to know him otherwise."

Mrs. Holt laughed at her husband with watery eyes. He shook his head. "You hold onto that one, you hear?" he told me.

"I intend to."

~ * ~

He was lying down when I entered his room. "Mission complete," I said.

"You're fast." He tried to sit up, and I tried to discourage him. It took him a couple minutes, but he got into the seated position, and I sat with him.

"You're not as tired or puffy as you were the last time I saw you," I told him.

He smiled his smile, and my body began the physiologically impossible process of spontaneously dissolving into a puddle. "Puffy is the least of my worries, I suppose," he said, "though I still want to crawl into a hole right now."

"York, if I didn't fear you'd crack like spun sugar, I'd be on top of you faster than you could say 'Prednisone'."

I never thought I'd be able to make him blush—or that he could blush—but there he went.

"I brought a picture to show you," I said and reached into my bag. My first semester in Photo Media I had a dodging and burning-in assignment. The two techniques are part of exposure manipulation, where you make a picture develop however you want it to. Burning keeps an area on a photo from being underexposed, or too light, and dodging keeps an area on a photo from being too dark. I chose a much more difficult task for myself than I needed to for my skill level, but I enjoyed the challenge.

"I took this at the airport in San Francisco right before we left," I told him. "I dodged the sky during the main exposure to keep it light;

you hold a piece of cardboard in the wide open area of the photo while it's exposing. Then I burned the plane itself to make it almost as black as the birds around it."

The plane and birds stood out—stark, simple black silhouettes of their kind—against the lightened background. It was a labor of sheer neuroticism. My hands had been shaking by the end.

"I call it The Imitator."

"This is most spectacular picture I've ever seen," he said.

"Thanks."

"Thank God for photojournalism, because if you had to choose between writing and photography, one field would have been sorely bereft of a grand talent."

I lowered my head. "I haven't forced you into feeling like you need to contribute to my article, have I? I'm surprised it's even crossed your mind with everything you've been through. I've got time, and you need to work on recovering. I don't even need a quote if you're not up to it."

"I'm ready."

I set up my pen and notepad, and turned on the tape recorder.

"August thirteenth. College student article for *News Matters*. Subject: York Lively." I sat up straight. "All right. Why don't you share your quote about life, amended from your senior class spot in Fleet High school's yearbook?"

He smiled, charming though no one would see him. "Okay. I never understood why people hold themselves back from what they want to do. You play it safe, and you regret it, but you think: Hey, at least I made it through life unscathed. But I know from experience that sometimes outside forces you can't control will infiltrate 'safe.' We trick ourselves into believing we have all the time in the world to make stuff happen. We're all procrastinators, really, when it comes to that. We say, 'I'll do it tomorrow, or next month, or when I have more money.' Then life happens—if not to us, to someone close to us—violently shifting our perspectives. And, suddenly, mortality is real, and we start frantically trying to do all the stuff we put off before. When we do it that way, it's not the stroll through the park it should be, but some mad sprint to the end.

"But mortality is not the end. I believe that, anyway. Death is just another phase of existence. And while we're here, in this existence, we realize—after tragedy or loss slaps us in the face—that not much of it is allotted to us, and we hate that. We curse it because the other end of it is so unsure, and we want this sureness. The upside to it all is that it wakes us the hell up.

"And so I say to you that my quote for life is this: 'Death ends as soon as living begins.' That's from *The Infantry Hero*, a book a lot of people know of but maybe haven't read." He smiled wide. "We are *alive*, Olive. We are young, and we are in love, and we are stupid, and we are terrified, and we just want to keep on living. And even though it is impossible that we should recollect that we existed before the body, because there are no traces of any such existence in the body, and also because eternity cannot be defined by time, or have any relationship to it, we feel and we know that we are eternal."

He breathed. He had memorized Baruch Spinoza's words from *Ethics*, and his eyes were bright by the time he had finished, as if he'd delivered some impassioned speech to the masses.

"And that," he added, "is the most incredible thing."

But in the end, it was just me and my tape recorder, which clicked on and on long after he'd stopped.

I shut it off. "That's it," I whispered.

## *Twenty-four*

**K.I.S.S.**

I sat at my laptop and opened my mottos article. I only had a fourth of it written, mostly containing references and bulleted Points to Add In. I had begun to wonder if I would ever finish.

Maybe my right frame of mind wasn't ready to tackle a project this long and in-depth. I worried my inexperience would keep it from being the piece of inspiration people needed. Maybe I had no business encouraging anyone about their futures.

I spotted the half-finished corkboard collage of Polaroids I'd begun a few months back. A timeline of sorts, it detailed the completion of each task on York's bucket list and our relationship as it had developed. I dragged it out and noticed the snapshot he took of us on that cold January day at the coffee shop—the day we looked at yearbook photos—sticking out from behind the bed.

His wide eyes and grin that extended from ear to ear made my smile—which I had only managed in the spontaneity of the moment—appear tight.

He had asked me to keep it, look at it from time to time, said I would see how beautiful I was after I'd gotten all the exposure and light I needed.

I didn't see anything beautiful about me in the picture, but that wasn't ever the point. My heart thrummed in my ears. I opened a new Word document and started my article over on a blank page. I channeled the advice of Professor Spaulding and made the words simple and profound.

When we are in high school and about to venture into the Wild West of pre-adulthood, we are asked to come up with a senior quote. This is an intense task, not because we worry about sounding cool or smart, but because we know we're expected to condense our feelings about life and the future into a few lines. Many of us realize, years later, that the words we've quoted don't really match how we feel at all. How could they, when, at that point, we still have so much more living to do?

York Lively-Bingham, author of *An Introduction to Rationality* (1915) and *Nature in Action* (1926), in addition to one work of fiction and several other scholarly writings, spearheaded the idea that man must rearrange his priorities in order to create a more productive and thoughtful society. In Lively-Bingham's world, man saved himself so he could save others.

It's difficult for college-aged kids to see ourselves as heroes, since we are simultaneously told we have no idea how the world works and that it is ours to inherit, our responsibility. We have no idea whether the decisions we make for ourselves are the right ones, whether they will impact the world or be part of its destruction. Youth can feel like a burden, but if we can at least come up with an idea of our own, personal philosophy, one to believe in, one to stick by, we truly can save ourselves. We can do some good with the world we will eventually inherit.

I had all my quotes transcribed except for the one, so I rewound my tape recorder to the end of the short interview I'd conducted before

York's. The tape crackled for a moment as it worked its way through the silence, then I heard my voice. Then his.

I transcribed his words, which were often too fast and ardent for me to catch the first time and caused me to rewind the tape and listen again.

I completed my portion of the article by noon the next day.

## IMPERISHABLE

York's followup appointments were going well so far. Doctors fully treated his infection, and he had two new medications and a new exercise regimen from PT. After an appointment at the hospital, I met him at his house to bring what I had collected for his project. The sun had begun to set, casting the whole neighborhood in pink-orange light.

Though his mom no longer greeted me with any particular degree of warmth, she still spoke to me. She must have forgiven me, or at least resolved I would be around for a considerable amount of time. Maybe she felt obligated to treat me decently because of my dad. I didn't question her motives.

Mr. Lively spoke to me as little as humanly possible whenever he happened to be around. I didn't blame him—I had called out his dicktastic-ness to his face. Though I apologized, he didn't have much patience for me, and I wouldn't have, either. I craved fatherly approval because of the absence in my life, but his would have to elude me.

York wore his regular t-shirt and jeans, and he looked so much like he had back in June. He needed some help out to the back deck and leaned on me more than I expected him to; I buckled a little under his solid frame. The lingering heat from the day made our skin stick together everywhere we made contact.

"I can be a bit of an overachiever when it comes to stuff like this," York said with a smirk after he had plopped down and caught his breath, "so try not to be dazzled."

He showed me a tall, silver cylinder, his smile smug. "Is that a storage container?" I asked after staring at it.

His shoulders dropped. "Please, Olive. 'Storage container' makes it sound so ordinary. 'A container in which to store mementos of our great love affair' is more accurate."

I studied it again. "A time capsule!"

"*Yes.*" He shook his head. "This thing is airtight and watertight with an O-ring seal, one of the best I could find."

"Where on earth did you get it?"

"The same website where I found the card. You'd be surprised what you can express ship from the Internet."

We pulled the coffee table toward us. "All right," I said, "it's your turn to resist dazzlement."

I showed him the small wooden box, four inches wide by four inches long and six inches tall. I had made a trip out to Kill Devil Hills two days before to collect a small pile of soft, dark sand to put inside.

Then I showed him the advert for Paco's Fish Tacos, the Polaroid of us kissing on top of the stump, another of me from his viewpoint as I laid on my back in the sand at Linda Mar.

"I appreciate your selective memory," he said.

"I'm a visual person," I reminded him. "This is what comes up when I think about us: not you sick, not us fighting, not even my dad's heart—this. Sand and ocean and kissing and forgetting about the rest of the world."

He leaned over and kissed me. We kissed so infrequently now, and I was hungry for it.

"Are you sure you want to bury a time capsule with me?" I asked.

"I want," he said, and I'd never get tired of him saying that to me.

We placed my memories inside the tall cylinder and he took out some stationery.

"Before we seal it up, I figured we could each write a letter. It doesn't have to be long or deep. Doesn't even have to make sense to anyone else, really, so long as it means something to you."

"Perfect."

I watched him write. He put so much thought into it, his forehead creasing, his teeth digging into his bottom lip. He would stop to think, and his eyes would shift to me, and he would smile and start writing again.

I wrote:

*My name is Olive Grant, aged nineteen. When I met my other half, taking chances seemed like a foolish way to go about life. Only when I realized how alive I felt after embarking on this journey of love with him was I able—no, determined—to entrust in him all my fears and happily watch him toss them to the wind.*

*I would like for it to be known to all future readers that, just as neither he nor I can be replicated, neither can our love. It belongs to us alone, and it can't be taken away or altered.*

*And I would like for it to be known that I love York Lively more than the amount of times my heart will beat in this lifetime and (if there's a lucky recipient out there) the next, more than all the grains of sand on the beach in Kill Devil Hills, more than all the words ever written and unwritten, more than the amount of waves all the oceans on Earth will ever make.*

*If you know anything about the immeasurability of waves, then you understand York and Olive.*

As he wrote, I noted the items he'd brought to bury: a small jar of honey, a tiny pouch of rice, and an airplane bottle of vodka.

We waited until we were both finished to exchange notes. I was already tearing up by the time I got through his second sentence.

*Depending on how far into the future this is, the couple pictured in the photos inside this capsule may be young, married, older, or dearly departed. I pray for the last one, as I want the someone who reads these letters to have to piece our life back together.*

*My name is York Lively. I don't want to explain the majority of the contents of this capsule—that's for you to figure out, dear reader. I do, however, wish to offer a small chemistry lesson:*

*Honey is made of sugar, which is hygroscopic, meaning it contains very little water. Bacteria cannot thrive in a low-moisture environment, which makes honey keep forever.*

*Dry rice, if kept away from moisture, also cannot develop bacteria, which also allows it to keep forever.*

*If alcohol is kept sealed well enough to keep oxygen out, it doesn't have the opportunity to change taste. Therefore, a sealed bottle of alcohol can keep forever.*

*Honey, rice, and alcohol are pretty much imperishable. I hope that gives an undeniable idea of how I feel about myself and Olive Grant.*

*My Olive is an incredible human being. She accepts me like no one else ever has. She's not afraid to take chances, and even when she is afraid, she trusts me enough to go with it. She sees the best in me. She thinks I'm insane, and she loves me for that. And I love her for her.*

"Damn you," I said, tossing my head back. "You always do this better than I do. Can't I sweep you off your feet *one time*?"

"Olive. You know I've been on the ground since the day I met you."

We buried the capsule in a small corner of his enormous backyard, and I took a Polaroid of him patting dirt over the hole.

*Twenty-five*

## SEMI-PERMANENT

My sophomore year at NECU started at the end of August. I moved into a whole new dorm with two new girls with whom I had a lot more in common. Morgan and Yancy moved into an apartment right off campus, and they promised to invite York and me to their first big party of the year.

York decided to take a semester off and start back in the spring. He came with me and Uncle Joe and Selma and Mom when I moved in. He talked to my mom a lot that day, and at one point they disappeared entirely. I spotted them from my window talking on a bench outside. They looked so small and frail together and almost mirrored one another's weary movements, their faces creasing the same way when they frowned and sighed. Mom dropped her head into her hands, and he hugged her.

I made myself responsible for checking in with my little sister every single day. She had already begun her junior year at Fleet High, and she had so much to focus on, on top of the everyday "life with Mom" stress. I vowed to be the female mentor I didn't have at her age.

Uncle Joe and I came up with a system that wouldn't drain us, and he promised it would all work out. I wondered who chose to bless me with such an amazing family member. I still worried he would one day get too fed up and worn out to deal with our stuff and his stuff, but he was my uncle, so I had to believe that day would never come.

York and I settled on the bed in my room that night after my family left. Precarious piles of clothes and shoes and books and other general disarray littered nearly every surface, but York's bag of medications sat safe and untouched on the edge of my desk.

"We're at the end of your list," I said. "Can you believe it?"

"Considering I never thought I'd do it in the first place, I kind of can't."

"Have you thought about the tattoo you'll get?"

"Extensively."

"And?"

He lay back on my bed, upper back against the wall, fingers crossed over his chest. "There are many reasons why this is the last goal. Like the trouble I had with the quote, I'm having a hard time coming up with the words to encapsulate my entire past, present, and future." He smirked. "Imagine that."

"So you think you were a little too ambitious with some of your bucket list goals? No, you would never, ever do that." When he squinted, I said, "There's no need to panic. No one expects you to get it perfect the second time, or the third time, or maybe ever. This is you now. Think about now."

"But I need to get this right the first time. I'm not willing to risk my mental and physical well-being for a permanent mark I'll have to look at every day and hate."

"Mental and physical well-being?" I exclaimed.

"You're laughing, and I'm so very serious," he said, but he was laughing too. "I'll put myself through all of this, on purpose, and what if I get my tattoo on top of a vein, and the artist stabs too deeply, and my blood spurts everywhere like a geyser, and in the end I realize I've made a stupid choice and it was all for naught?"

"Literally zero percent of that is going to happen."

"Not literally. For a while, I thought I might want to get tattooed here." He indicated the underside of his forearm, right below the inside of his elbow. The muscle there flexed under prominent veins, a very alive place on his arm.

"But now you've changed your mind."

"Mostly because of the risk of bleeding out, yes. Also a little because recent events have given me a fresh perspective, and if I can figure out how to interpret it…"

I scooted closer to him. "Take off your shirt."

"Well, that was an abrupt shift in the conversation."

"Off, off."

When the shirt came off he tried to sit up straight as he could, round his shoulders and appear stronger than he felt, but I went straight for his scar. I touched it again, traced the smooth lines and bumpy edges.

"I'm sure you'll figure it out," I said.

## OK'D

We went a month later, mostly because York had to get the OK from his team of doctors first.

He made a seven o'clock appointment, one of the last time slots of the day. He did it this way, on purpose, because he didn't want as many people laughing at him when he screamed or cried or otherwise embarrassed himself.

The place had top reviews, and the staff, while tough and hairy, was pleasant enough. We got two different guys, and both had patience enough to deal with our general ignorance of proper tattoo parlor speak.

We described to our artists what we wanted, as neither of us had seen our visions in their walls and walls of designs. My artist, Glenn (was not expecting that name for some reason) drew up the perfect stencil for me. York had come up with a more painstakingly specific design than I had, because he really was determined to never half-ass anything ever again.

After much consideration, the idea of "forever" hanging over my head, I'd decided on an infinity symbol on the upper right side of my back. One of the ends curved into itself, per the usual, but the other end burst into five small, black birds in flight, two of which were depicted flying off at errant angles but eventually coming back to complete the curve.

"The buzzing sounds a little like chainsaw, no?" York's voice cracked behind me.

"It's a little soothing to me, like white noise," I said.

"Okay. Didn't realize I was dating a psycho, but that's good to know."

Glenn rubbed some alcohol on my skin, then some petroleum jelly, and then pressed the stencil where I indicated: right above my right shoulder blade. I figured him a trustworthy guy because he had tattoos all over his arms and hands and neck—many of them self-done, he claimed—and he sanitized his stuff thoroughly before he turned the needle on me.

"You still good?" I asked York. He lay on his back with his shirt off, hands fisted and pressed over his eyes, long legs hanging over the end of the table. He flapped his bent arms like he wished he could fly away, and his artist, who hovered over him with the needle, told him he'd have to stop moving or the intricate detail of the small tattoo wouldn't come out accurately.

"Just trying not to go completely insane, that's all," he answered.

"You're looking a little pale there."

"I'm a white guy of English descent. Of course I'm pale."

His artist must have hit a sweet spot on his chest because York gave a short, angry grunt. I turned away so he couldn't see me.

"I'm sorry. I'm so sorry," I told Glenn, wiggling from laughter and trying to shut myself up and, God, we were so bad at this. "We'll be a lot cooler next time," I promised. "Won't we, York?"

"Oh, God," he moaned.

Once Glenn got to my tiny black birds, I stopped making fun of York. It stung and *stung* as Glenn went back and forth over the same area to fill in each one.

To his artist, I think, York said, "I keep reminding myself this won't last forever, and it'll all be okay. This will be okay. I'm a tough guy, and this is fine."

That night, in my dorm, we took our bandages off and studied our finished products outside the parlor, where we didn't have to play it cool. He slid his shirt over his head and I took in every single inch of him.

"It's pretty awesome," I said. At the top of his surgery scar, right above his pecs, was a zipper slider. His artist had drawn it a little larger than a standard slider, making the detail more visible. The veined workings of an anatomically correct heart hung from a string at the end.

"No one's getting in here again," he told me. "Not only is it zipped up, but another surgery means I'm out a hundred bucks."

"Priorities," I said. "You have them."

Next, I took my shirt off, and he slowly moved my bra strap down the length of my arm. He removed my bandage and I felt him trace the spot.

"Which bird am I?" he whispered, his breath against my shoulder.

"The one that finishes the infinity."


## THE ENDLESS KNOT

I've heard time is limited.

I once agreed with this one.

We only get a certain amount on earth, after all. I once believed a person inherently limited his or her own time—again, with the clocks and the calendars. But now I see the bigger picture because of York. I see eternity.

"Eternity" has two definitions:

*An indeterminately long period of time.*

*A concept that exists outside of time entirely.*

The definitions contradict one another, and the latter sounds more appropriate anyway. We shift in and out of time, existing in this realm for however long before advancing to the next phase.

"Complete"—like "perfection"—is subjective. I would tack the rest of our pictures on my corkboard alongside all the others that I took of him and us, and my bucket list collage would appear complete. I would make the collage as pretty as possible, because you want to give a project like that a pretty appearance. I wouldn't hint at all the not-so-pretty stuff that had happened and could happen again. It would be the picture of a linear, uncomplicated road to love. And it would have a happy ending.

But, as unsure about so much as I still am, I have York, and I have our real ending—happy and complicated and scary and gorgeously perfect in its own way—that really isn't an ending at all. I have to figure our story will carry on as long as we keep living.

Since we are indeed eternal, I don't think I'll have to worry about that.

*Two: Change My Quote*
Olive Grant


"And I decided, on that day, that I could still be the hero, because in my short life I had discovered something worth saving, worth saving for, and I would hold onto it until the end of time."

Henry Georges
—*The Infantry Hero,* by York Oliver Lively-Bingham

# Meet Bianca Orellana

Bianca Orellana was born and raised in North Carolina, where she still resides with her husband and young son. *We Are Eternal* is her first novel.

## *Letter to Our Readers*

**Enjoy this book?**

**You can make a difference**

As an independent publisher, Wings ePress, Inc. does not have the financial clout of the large New York Publishers. We can't afford large magazine spreads or subway posters to tell people about our quality books.

But, we do have something much more effective and powerful than ads. We have a large base of loyal readers.

Honest Reviews help bring the attention of new readers to our books.

If you enjoyed this book, we would appreciate it if you would spend a few minutes posting a review on the site where you purchased this book or on the Wings ePress, Inc. webpages at: https://wingsepress.com/

# Visit Our Website

*For The Full Inventory*
*Of Quality Books:*

*Wings ePress.Inc*
*https://wingsepress.com/*

*Quality trade paperbacks and downloads*
*in multiple formats,*
*in genres ranging from light romantic comedy*
*to general fiction and horror.*
*Wings has something for every reader's taste.*
*Visit the website, then bookmark it.*
**We add new titles each month!**

Wings ePress Inc.
3000 N. Rock Road
Newton, KS  67114